Also by Mel Anastasiou

Fiction

Stella Ryman and the Fairmount Manor Mysteries
The Labours of Mrs Stella Ryman
The Hertfordshire Pub Mysteries: *The Seven Swans*
The Extra: A Monument Studios Mystery
Pretty Lies: A Ghost Story
Take My Hand: A Ghost Story

Non-fiction

The Writer's Boon Companion: Thirty Days Towards an Extraordinary Volume
The Writer's Friend and Confidante: A Thirty-Day Workbook

FAIRMOUNT MANOR

Stella Ryman and the Search for Thelma Hu

A Fairmount Manor Mystery

Mel Anastasiou

Pulp Literature Press

Pulp Mystery is an imprint of Pulp Literature Press

Library and Archives Canada Cataloguing in Publication

ISBN: 978-1-988865-79-9 (paperback) ISBN: 978-1-988865-80-5 (ebook)

Material in this novel was originally published serially in *Pulp Literature* magazine © 2019–2024 Pulp Literature Press, as 'Stella Ryman and the Locked Room', Summer 2019, 'Stella Ryman vs the Board', Spring 2023, 'Stella Ryman and the Curse of Youth', Summer 2023, 'Stella Ryman Takes the Wheel', Autumn 2024, and 'Stella Ryman and the Labyrinthian Puzzle', Winter 2024.

Cover by Kate Landels from a drawing by Kris Sayer
Interior design: Amanda Bidnall
Interior illustrations: Mel Anastasiou
Printed and bound internationally by Ingram
International version printed by Ingram/Lightning Source

Published in Canada by Pulp Literature Press

www.pulpliterature.com

To Mark

Lucky for me, back in the day, that you missed Belgium

CONTENTS

Chapter One
The Locked Room

On this first mid-morning in May, Mrs Stella Ryman felt that her amateur sleuthing had been of a disappointingly mundane variety, for she had merely managed to deduce that today was a Wednesday. It might be argued that this wasn't an entirely trivial deduction, for every day at Fairmount Manor Care Home was much like the last, and if her friends Thelma Hu, Theo Longbourne, or indeed any member of the Greek Chorus here in Corridor Park wondered what day of the week it was, Stella could clear up the matter for them without betraying their confusion to care workers or to the Director herself. Stella well knew how it felt to be labelled gaga. What was more, she had repeatedly suffered the restrictions in personal freedom and stigma that came with that label.

Stella hadn't been allowed outside unsupervised since her arrival at Fairmount four months earlier. But she had escaped more than once, and gotten away with it too. Still, past triumphs were stale bread in the absence of anything interesting to sink her teeth into. And, as if she needed any more discomfort beyond boredom and frustration, the May heat was beating her down. It descended through the skylight over her chair in Corridor Park and settled almost visibly around her. There was no air conditioning in Fairmount Manor. A care worker had only this morning explained with exquisite patience that a cooling system would only be needed in this climate a few days a year, and so was not worth the investment in infrastructure. As if Stella hadn't heard that exact argument against air conditioning from every school principal she'd worked under in her career in the school system.

At least, in her discomfort, Stella wasn't alone. To her right, Thelma Hu tapped her cane against the floor in rhythm with her huffing sighs, and to her left the Greek Chorus set down their pillowcase crewel work to fan themselves with their hands. In long lost days, the elementary school where Stella used to teach would overheat like this in May, and her child library helpers would scoot about the bookshelves and media storage areas in search of the long poles with special metal tips that opened the clerestory windows, while the sun entered Stella's library office the way a ticket inspector entered a train car.

Now she was eighty-two, and Stella no longer had an office, just her little bedroom called Room 34, and she didn't have to check to know it was hot in there too. Back when she'd had her own home, she kept fans in every room and an air conditioner that fit into her bedroom window. All gone now, with her move to Fairmount, along with nearly all her possessions. She wondered darkly who now owned everything she had given up in her pre-Fairmount fit of finality. Of course, at the time, she had thought she was dying, and so it had seemed right to proceed to a care home with no more worldly goods than a single suitcase full of brand-new coordinating fleece suits and knit tops, a few pairs of socks and underwear, and one faux painting of a farmhouse with ducks and apple trees in bloom, which she had purchased shortly after her eleventh birthday against her mother's wishes.

But Stella didn't die. And she'd spent February to April envying Theo Longbourne his cashmere cardigans and wishing she had kept her wool, silk, and cashmere school clothing. Now that May was here, she longed for the linen cotton shells she'd purchased in every neutral tone from Lady Chapman's on Granville Street, and which wore like iron and never gaped at the armholes. Stella grimaced and tugged at the short sleeves of the floral-print polo shirt the catalogue phone-woman had talked her into buying only a few short months back. *Something bright near the face takes years off, doesn't it?* Stella gazed down at her floral-print polo and reflected that in her real life she would have donated it unworn to the poor or colour starved. Even if wearing colours did take off years, it hardly seemed worth the sartorial discomfort to appear perhaps eighty instead of eighty-two.

She wiped her brow with one short sleeve.

"Stella Ryman, can't you do something?" Iolanthe demanded.

"Yes, you think you're smarter than God's old auntie," Lucille said. "So, what about handling this situation?"

The Greek Chorus scowled at her over the tops of their improvised fans.

Stella met their frowns with a raised eyebrow. Of course, it was true that she had recently tracked down stolen goods, a missing resident, and the author of a set of very disturbing poison pen letters. Still, were Iolanthe, Lucille, and Sally not presuming too much of her personal powers?

Stella said, "You can't possibly expect me to change the weather for you."

Lucille sniffed and elbowed Iolanthe. "One minute she's cleverer than the fools that run this place, and the next she's gaga again." Sally, who never spoke, and whom Stella was trying very hard not to nickname *the Nodder*, nodded.

"Stella, dear, nobody is asking you to adjust the direction of the sun's rays," Iolanthe said. "We're talking about that room."

Stella asked, "What room do you mean?" All the bedrooms at Fairmount were much the same except for the sponge painting on the corridor walls they opened onto: yellow for Daffodil Corridor, pink for Rose, and so on.

Thelma lifted her cane and poked Stella in the knee. "Everybody knows about the locked bedroom in Fern Corridor."

"But none of the rooms are —"

Iolanthe interrupted. "Who knows what could be inside a locked room?"

"A dead body," Lucille said. "A lurking murderer."

"But none of our rooms lock. Please don't worry yourselves on that account."

Iolanthe took a testy stitch in red thread. "Well, if you're not going to listen to us, Stella Ryman, at least you could have the decency to be deaf."

No matter what the others thought, Stella well knew that none of Fairmount's bedrooms locked, because she had entered them all, overtly or clandestinely, in the course of her amateur sleuthing.

Preceded by the rattle of plastic wheels, Ollie trundled his cleaning trolley into Corridor Park. He tucked his dust cloth into his trousers, set his hands on his hips, and beamed. "Well, my lovelies, I'm here to swab the decks. Lift your feet when I get to you, and I'll try not to tickle anybody's fancy with my mop."

They all stuck out their legs in front of them. Ollie mopped under the chairs and down the centre of Corridor Park, humming to himself as he went. Lucille pointed out spots he'd missed, some of which were glaringly fictitious. As always, Stella admired Ollie's patience and jovial aplomb. Ollie was a care worker, not a janitor, but he kept the place clean, anyway. Stella knew that Fairmount's Director, Mrs Perdita Warren, was lucky to have Ollie in Fairmount's employ, and he was paid extra for this custodial work. But not enough, was Stella's opinion, as he swabbed off around the corner in the direction of the dining room. She had no idea how much Ollie earned, but it would never be enough.

As if summoned by Stella's thoughts, Mrs Perdita Warren—*aka* the Warden—swept into Corridor Park. Her arms were full of paper flowers, and a stapler hung from an outlying thumb. She announced in bracing tones, "Today is May Day, and that's the day boys used to bring girls flowers, when you ladies were young yourselves."

"May Day?" Iolanthe inclined her head and took a stitch in her pillowcase. "I suppose that, in my time, I remember feeling a certain glow of expectation on the first of May."

Lucille said, "You could be sure as taxes that somebody somewhere would get kissed."

Sally nodded.

The Warden held out her stapler. "I've brought you ladies paper flowers to staple on the wall. Won't that be nice?"

An ironic silence answered her.

"Well, who would like to staple the flowers?"

Thelma said, "I'd do it, but I'm blind."

Lucille said, "I'd do it, but I'm sitting down."

Iolanthe said, "I'd do it, but our pensions pay Fairmount good money for somebody to do it for us."

Sally frowned and nodded.

The Warden set her paper flowers down on the floor beneath the bulletin board that faced Stella and Thelma. She tested her stapler by letting a staple fall to the floor for Ollie to clean up next time round, and said, "Well, I'll staple them up for you myself."

The Warden set to stapling paper lilies up on an empty bulletin board, her rear end moving rhythmically with the stapler's thudding click.

Stella reflected that decorating Corridor Park must be a bit of an uphill climb for the Warden. For one thing, the bulletin boards above the Greek Chorus's chairs had been strangely bare of motivational posters for some time now. It was no mystery to Stella, however, because she and Thelma were responsible. They had been driven from apathy to outrage by such printed sentiments as *Hang in there, baby,* and *Talk is cheap, but kind acts are priceless,* which had the nerve to be both smug and true. So, she and Thelma had spent several evenings after lights out, rattling covertly down to Corridor Park together on sorties to rip down the damned posters.

The Greek Chorus set their needles and pillowcases onto their laps and peered up at the growing paper flower garden.

Iolanthe said, "Aren't lilies funeral flowers?"

Staple-staple. The Warden returned firmly, "They are spring blossoms."

Iolanthe said, "No, I'm certain lilies are meant to be laid atop coffins."

Lucille added, "Quick, somebody kiss me on the cheek and tell me I look natural."

Stella covered her smile with her hand; she felt more than heard Thelma's chuckle.

The Warden sent Stella a fierce look. "Do you have a similar complaint about the display, Mrs Ryman?"

"It's a lovely display. I've always liked lilies."

The Warden stapled a leaf to the board as if it had committed a terrible crime. "Don't be sarcastic, please."

"It's hard to be sarcastic about flowers," Stella said. "And anyway, I don't like sarcasm one bit. I was a teacher in real life, you know, and sarcasm in teachers is a terrible —"

"Of course, I'm always open to suggestions," the Warden interrupted. "But please do consider whether my university degree and experience in the field might not make me a little more qualified than you are to run Fairmount Manor Care Home."

Stella sat back in her chair.

Thelma leaned forward and poked the Warden's knee with the end of her cane. "What degree?"

Staple-staple. "Bachelor of Commerce."

"Oh, how lovely for you," Iolanthe said. "Well done. I myself have a master's degree in art history. And Sally here is a bachelor of Home Economics, aren't you, dear?"

Sally nodded.

"I have a degree in refusing to tolerate fools." Lucille named a large bank. "I was a loans officer at the downtown branch. Turned down borrowers' applications for a golden thirty-three years."

Stella laughed. She couldn't help it.

The Warden slammed up an orange poppy so that its petals

hung down on either side of the staple like a pinup centrefold. She sent Stella another freezing look. "I suppose you have a PhD in international law?"

Stella had earned her bachelor's in education and a master's in teacher-librarianship, which information she decided it would be unkind to reveal just then.

Thelma said, "*I* have something."

Stella half-expected Thelma to disclose that she was a consultant to NASA.

But Thelma said, "I have a question. I want to know what's inside the locked bedroom in Fern Corridor."

The Warden replied, "Residents may not lock their rooms. There is no locked bedroom in Fern Corridor."

Stella might have forgiven the patronizing look the Warden sent Thelma's way if Thelma hadn't been blind.

The Warden said, "Now if you'll excuse me, we have a new care worker on staff this morning, and I'm going to take him around Fairmount for orientation." She stapled up a final poppy and hurried away.

A new care worker? Stella couldn't see how Fairmount could afford more staff. Not without replacing present employees.

Stella counted up the staff she and Thelma really couldn't do without: Ollie, Cheryl, and Reliza. Were they all present this morning? Had any of the Vital Three not shown up for work?

"I wish you were the Director, Stella Ryman," Thelma said. "You'd do a better job."

"I'm sure I wouldn't," Stella said firmly, although it was just possible that she would. Certainly, Ollie would do a much better job as Director than the present Warden. Stella tried to imagine Ollie sitting in the Director's office, behind Mrs

Warren's big desk, but she couldn't help picturing herself in that position of power instead, ordering better food for all the Fairmount residents, and telling off the Board of Directors for taking too much pay when care workers such as Ollie, Cheryl, and Reliza worked so much harder than anybody else. Well, she couldn't do much about the food situation nor the underpaid, overworked care workers at Fairmount, but there was one thing she could do.

She would do it now. She slapped her hands on her knit-trousered thighs and got to her feet. "I'm going to find that locked bedroom in Fern Corridor and investigate it. Who's coming with me?"

The Greek Chorus blew out breaths. Lucille said, "That's hot work on a day like this one, Stella. You come back and tell us what you find."

Iolanthe and Sally nodded as one.

Stella turned to Thelma. "You'll come, won't you?"

"No."

"Why in the name of little green apples not?"

Thelma scowled up at her. "Because if I show the locked room to you, then exactly what are you investigating?"

Thelma was right. Like tasty food at Fairmount, mysteries weren't an everyday event. They were to be savoured.

Stella nodded. "I will investigate the case of the locked room and report back, then."

Iolanthe picked up her needle and pillowcase. "Take your time, dear. And then tell us everything."

Lucille added, "Don't leave out a single door handle."

Sally snipped off Lucille's thread.

Stella wandered with intent, if not with direction, throughout Fairmount's untrackable corridors, past the front office, the back garden outside the dining room window, Rose Corridor, and along her own Daffodil Corridor. She turned a corner at last that placed her in Fern Corridor. The green-sponged walls were quite restful, especially on Wednesdays, for (as earlier that morning she had detected) most of Fern's residents were off on a mall walk or watching television in the activities hall. She walked slowly, studying the slots on the doors, looking for one without a resident's name. If a room was locked despite Fairmount rules, she theorized that it was most likely unoccupied.

Sure enough, halfway along the corridor she discovered a door with an empty name slot.

She looked left and right and tried the door. It opened.

She stepped inside.

The room was empty of everything but the basic Fairmount furnishings: a bed, a visitor's chair, and a bedside table. The bed had been pulled away from the wall but was unmade, with sheets and a pillow laid out across the centre of the mattress. Stella checked the cupboard and the washroom, but both were empty and ready for a new occupant.

She left the empty room and returned to the head of Fern Corridor. She tried each door lever in turn, only to have every one of them click open to her hand.

She said, "Hmph," and returned circuitously to Corridor Park. There she halted in the middle of the corridor, where she could easily speak to the Greek Chorus on her left and Thelma on her right.

She said, "I have investigated thoroughly …" and paused, knowing her investigative report would likely be the highlight of everybody's day and feeling unsure how best to communicate a negative result.

Iolanthe spoke into the pause. "You can see we're all agog. Please do tell us what was inside the locked room, Stella Ryman."

"I'm sorry," Stella said, "but I must report that there was no locked room in Fern Corridor."

The Greek Chorus stared. "Are you sure?" Iolanthe asked. "You didn't lose count and miss one door and count another twice?"

"Sounds like our Stella on an off day," Lucille agreed.

"I was very careful. There was no locked bedroom door in Fern Corridor."

Thelma said, "Baloney."

"With mustard," Lucille added. "On a soft bun."

Stella was about to make a very courteous offer to lead them to Fern Corridor and show them how wrong they were, when Mrs Perdita Warren gusted back into Corridor Park. This time the Director carried no paper flowers but brought with her a rather decorative man in a navy-blue care worker coverall. Stella thought he looked familiar, but she was aware that some people, even good-looking ones, had familiar sorts of faces.

Mrs Warren led the new care worker along Corridor Park.

The Director named each resident for the new care worker, who greeted them politely.

Finally, the Director said, "And this is Mrs Thelma Hu. She is blind and needs extra care, naturally."

Thelma said, "I'm not blind. I have macular degeneration."

"Of course, dear." The Warden led the handsome new care worker away towards the dining room.

Stella turned to the Greek Chorus. "Did that new care worker look familiar to any of you?"

"Yes," Iolanthe said. "I thought he looked a lot like a young Clint Eastwood."

"No, I—"

Lucille interrupted. "Robert Redford, *Barefoot in the Park*, 1 9 6 6. But with shoes on."

"I mean in real life."

The Greek Chorus shrugged.

Stella stood up and turned to Thelma. "Please show me the locked room."

Thelma got to her feet.

The tone for lunch sounded.

Iolanthe tucked her embroidery under her chair. "Did anybody catch that young man's name?"

"Mrs Warren didn't drop it," Lucille said.

"It seemed rather rude not to introduce us properly, I thought," Iolanthe said.

Sally nodded.

"Now that you say it, I agree," Lucille said. "The Director named each of us, but she didn't introduce the new staff member to us in return. Strange."

"Not strange," Thelma said.

"Why not strange?" Stella asked.

"You're an amateur sleuth, see if you can put your finger on why."

Accordingly, Stella thought over the Warden's quick tour of Corridor Park. The woman had been polite. She'd remembered every resident's name. Why, then, had the introductions grated so?

Thelma explained, "When you take somebody through a museum, you identify the antiques by name, but you don't introduce the people to the antiques."

"We're the antiques, then?"

Sally narrowed her eyes and nodded.

Iolanthe broke the silence with a sigh. "Yes, well … lunch, I think. It's a better use of our time than murdering care home directors, isn't it, ladies?"

"Is it?" Lucille asked.

Stella said, "I could murder a sandwich, anyway." This wasn't quite true, because Stella would gladly have foregone the usual Fairmount luncheon to investigate more corridors with Thelma and see if they could find that locked room.

But Thelma was as thin as a couple of sticks held together with string. She desperately needed every bite of food on offer, so when Theo Longbourne, with his blessedly excellent hair and gentleman's demeanour, arrived and offered the two of them his elbows for his regular Wednesday escorting to lunch, Stella accepted his left arm so that Thelma could take his right.

"How's your tinnitus? Any better?" Stella asked Theo. He had been a professor of music at the university, and she knew how he suffered with it.

Theo said, "Sorry, what was that?"

She nodded appreciatively at the joke. She explained to Theo the Warden's rudeness in treating them like museum pieces.

From Theo's far side, Stella heard Thelma making small but piercing creaking noises. It was no use asking what the noises were about; Stella knew perfectly well that Thelma was pretending to be an un-oiled antique.

After lunch—egg salad sandwiches with low-sodium potato chips, a favourite meal among the residents—Stella and Thelma set out along Fairmount Manor's twists and turns towards Fern

Corridor. Their journey was a protracted affair, for Stella had no sense of direction and Thelma had only a thumbnail clipping of peripheral vision. They passed the activities hall twice, along with the stairway to Palliative Care, where she'd once discovered a friend in the middle of dying.[1]

They skirted the front foyer three times. Once, Stella caught sight of a shadow in the doorway of one of Fairmount's many storage cupboards. The shadow looked very much like Mad Cassandra Browning, who was, for want of a better word, Stella's friend, even though Stella was fairly certain Cassie had died quite a few years before Stella had arrived at Fairmount. But when she dared to look deeply into the cupboard, she saw not Mad Cassandra but Dr Terry in the storage closet he had commandeered for his work here. The doctor had parked his narrow behind on his swivel chair and laid his head upon a papering of files on his desk. He appeared to be deep in slumber.

Stella knew that he was working through a time of heartbreak, for Stella herself had counselled the lovely care worker Reliza to break up with him. It had seemed good advice at the time. Stella wasn't so sure anymore. Still, there was hope yet for Dr Terry and the lovely Reliza. Especially so, if Stella tried again to bring them back together. So long as Reliza worked at Fairmount Manor, everything was possible. But what if the Warden, having overspent on staffing, must again cut personnel?

Stella dashed this worry from her mind. She would instead think about the mystery of the locked bedroom in Fern Corridor.

Stella and Thelma rounded another corner, and Stella braced herself for a third passage of the activities hall. To her delight,

---

[1] *The Labours of Mrs Stella Ryman*, Pulp Literature Press, 2017.

she saw that they had reached Fern Corridor, their destination. But they weren't alone.

Not ten feet away from Stella and Thelma, two men stood face-to-face. One was Ollie, Stella's care worker friend, and the other was the handsome new care worker. Both men wore their shoulders at a defensive angle, and each was talking over the other; it was all Stella could do to make out what they were saying.

Ollie: "Mrs Warren hasn't told me anything about giving you my keys, and I can't see why she would."

The new care worker: "Well, how should I know what Perdita told you, because I wasn't there when she talked to you, was I?"

Ollie, his hands deep inside his pockets: "If you've lost them, then get off your butt and look for your own" — Stella missed a word here — "keys."

Stella, a career educator, was well-equipped to sense impending escalation in corridor disputes. She and Thelma approached Ollie and the new man.

Stella said cheerfully, "Well, well, look at this traffic jam right here in Fern Corridor."

Stella could see Ollie was making a heroic effort to smile.

"Stella *best sella*. And Thelma Hu! You're in Fern Corridor, ladies. Can I help you get home to your own rooms?"

The new care worker shifted his weight impatiently. Stella supposed that he was determined to take Ollie's keys from him. Well, Stella knew a little bit about determination as well.

She said, "I wonder if you two gentlemen would settle a bet."

Ollie said, "What's the bet?"

"Thelma says there's a locked room here in Fern Corridor. And I say there's never been a locked resident's room. Which is it?"

The new care worker shot his polyester cuffs. "What's at stake in this bet, lovely ladies? Then I'll know what side to take, because how else could I possibly choose between you?"

Thelma scowled in his direction. "You're new."

"I am."

"Already I don't like you."

Stella nudged Thelma. Thelma nudged back.

"That's all right." The new care worker laughed. "I'll make you like me. I have my ways."

I'll bet you do, Stella thought. *You're the kind who has ways, all right.*

Again, she thought she heard Mad Cassandra's ghostly cackle and the sound of her bare feet on Ollie's clean floor, just round the corner out of sight. But it was Reliza who appeared instead, moving in her youth and beauty towards Stella, Thelma, Ollie, and the handsome new employee.

Stella observed the new care worker's eyes warm with interest as Reliza approached them. She thought of Dr Terry collapsed in his nook of an office, wan with lack of sleep and love. And she remembered from her long-ago youth a fellow who looked very much like this one. He had appeared in the dance club Stella and her friends frequented, spiffy in a blue suit and shiny shoes. All the girls had turned bright eyes in his direction as he approached their table. He asked Stella to dance. She turned him down. When the others leaned across the white tablecloth and party-coloured drinks to ask her why, she had answered, "Trouble."

When she got to know him better, she discovered that her first impression had been correct.

She certainly wished she'd never married the fellow.

Reliza carried a tray laden with lunch dishes she must have collected from a bedridden resident. The young care worker clearly intended to pass by Stella and the others gathered in Fern Corridor, for she nodded to the little group in a not-unfriendly manner and increased her speed. But the new fellow grinned and tapped her arm. "Don't walk too quickly. You'll make me look bad."

Reliza stopped. She adjusted the tray she held to prevent a melamine mug from toppling to the floor. "Do you need some help?"

"No, but you do," the new care worker answered. With gentle hands, he took the tray from her. "That's better. What's your name?"

"I'm Reliza." She reached out for the tray, but he pulled it away, and she put her hands in the pockets of her white smock.

"Come with me, then," she told him. "I'll show you around the kitchen."

As the two moved away from them, the new care worker said his name to Reliza. *Riley.*

Stella had heard the name *Riley* somewhere, and fairly recently at that. The name resonated with the same sort of negative familiarity that his appearance did.

"Do I know that man?" she asked Ollie and Thelma. "Where have I seen him before?"

Thelma said, "You're wasting a perfectly good mystery. Why don't you investigate and find out?"

But Ollie scowled after the new care worker. "You don't know him. But you might have seen Riley when he dropped Cheryl off in his new car, before it was repossessed."

"So, he's a friend of Cheryl's?" As soon as she'd spoken, Stella saw her error.

Ollie confirmed it. "Riley is Cheryl's ex-husband."

Of course. Cheryl's ex-husband. More precisely, the ex-husband who had sold Cheryl's old beater and leased a luxury SUV for the family when Cheryl was wrestling with creditors, and who passed said lease off as a shrewd financial move. The husband whose SUV had then been taken back, and whose shrewdness meant Cheryl now had to take several buses to reach Fairmount. The husband Cheryl had left. When Stella had heard that happy news, she had only just managed not to cheer out loud.

Now why would a wastrel such as Riley take employment at his ex's place of work for a care worker's small salary? What was more important to a spendthrift than money?

It was a disturbing question, for when money didn't solve a problem, there were bound to be deeper, more dangerous issues in play.

Reliza, and Cheryl of the Giaconda smile and dodgy ex-husband, excelled at settling residents in for supper in the dining room. Stella thought of them as the A Team. Of course, anybody could shoehorn an elderly woman into a chair, but these two talented care workers had the knack of making a person feel welcome and even valued. Almost as if this were a restaurant and they had actually chosen to eat here.

Stella said as much to the table. She asked Thelma, "If you could order anything, what would it be?"

"Moo shu pork," Thelma snapped back.

"Mushroom vol-au-vents," Iolanthe mused.

"Tomato aspic salad with pimento and black olives, created in a jelly mould shaped like a wreath, with mayonnaise filling the centre hollow," Lucille added.

Stella stared at Lucille. "That's one of my all-time favourites." Sally nodded.

A companionable silent contemplation of dishes *d'antan* ensued, cut all too short by a fracas over at one of the Rose Corridor tables. A Nameless Dear care worker scolded two of the Rose ladies, who had apparently lost their medication. The former said, "This nonsense has happened too often. Where have you put your meds?" The latter protested that their meds were served to them with their meals.

The care worker huffed away from the Rose Corridor table, presumably to contact doctors for replacement prescriptions. Stella followed her progress out the door with an unfriendly eye.

Iolanthe waved her spoon at Stella. "Did you find the locked room after all?"

Stella shook her head.

"Have you given up?" Lucille demanded.

"Never." Stella picked up one of Thelma's thin hands and placed it upon her spoon, in case there was soup.

Thelma ran her fingers over the brightly coloured plastic tablecloth. She found her knife and fork and moved them closer to her plate. She said, "Well, maybe I was wrong about the locked door."

"You're never wrong."

Thelma cackled. "You're always telling me I'm wrong, Stella Ryman."

"Not wrong," Stella corrected her. "Just cranky."

"Then if being cranky isn't wrong, I can be cranky all day long."

These were deep waters. Stella changed the subject. "Are these table covers new?"

Iolanthe said, "I asked a woman in Rose Corridor about these horrible plastic tablecloths. She said one of the care workers picked them up three for a dollar during the mall walk this morning."

Thelma tapped her cane against the aluminium table leg.

"I still want to know what happened to our good mahogany tables. And chairs. And all the linens we used to have to go on them. Why are we eating bad food off plastic when we could be eating bad food off linen?"

Stella cheered up a little at the challenge of the problem. "Either the tablecloths were stolen, or they were put away. Were they worth stealing?"

"Only for ghost costumes," Thelma said. "Second-hand linens aren't worth anything."

"I know why used linens are so cheap," Lucille said. "They are too much work to clean and launder. No offence, Thelma."

Stella rolled her eyes. "Thelma was born in China, but that doesn't mean she ran a laundry, Lucille."

"I said no offence, didn't I?" Lucille shifted in her folding chair. "How am I supposed to keep up with race matters in a place like Fairmount?"

Privately Stella thought that Lucille might have kept up somewhat better than this in her eight decades or so before coming to Fairmount.

The swinging door to the kitchen opened. Fairmount's cooks, Annie and Enid, placed bowls of steaming tomato-coloured soup on the steel serving shelves just inside the dining room, along with little bowls of soup crackers in cellophane wrapping.

Stella turned to Thelma. "I think you were quite right that there was a locked room. Therefore, what is the first question we must ask ourselves in the investigation?"

Thelma said, "The first question is, what's for lunch?"

"The cooks are giving us something red in a bowl," Stella answered patiently. "Now you answer my question. Why did you find a room locked one day and I found it unlocked the next?"

"Because I'm a crazy old lady," Thelma said promptly.

Stella frowned. "No, you're certainly not."

"I know, I just wanted to say it before they could." Thelma nodded at the Greek Chorus.

Iolanthe had the grace to appear embarrassed. "None of us think that, dear."

"What do you all think about the locked room in Fairmount's corridors?" Thelma allowed Reliza to put a bowl of soup in front of her. "Why would the door be locked?"

"Well, what goes on behind locked doors?" The corner of Lucille's mouth crooked up. "Romance, that's what."

Stella regarded Lucille with new respect. She felt a little foolish not to have thought of romance. After all, the door led to an empty bedroom. Reliza and Terry? But they weren't speaking to one another.

Cheryl and Riley, her estranged husband? This was more likely, unless you remembered that every second of a care worker's day was spent working very hard indeed under the gazes of a lot of bored elderly people. Stella said, "I think that if a couple of care workers were meeting up for hanky-panky, somebody would already be talking about it."

"I just did," Lucille said.

"But you made it up. That's not the same. That's like television— it isn't a real mystery, it's just a story you invented."

"I want a real mystery," Thelma complained. "One where somebody commits a crime."

Stella nodded. "What crime?"

Care workers left bowls of soup and packets of crackers in front of each of them. Stella helped Thelma open the cracker package, feeling rather excited. She remembered earlier thefts from Mrs MacAndrew's treasure trove. But Alice MacAndrew was dead, and her granddaughter had inherited her valuables now. And the bits and pieces that had gone missing in April had not been taken for their resale value.

She came down to earth with a thump. At Fairmount, what was worth stealing?

Option one: *nothing.* Everything at Fairmount was pretty much tat, veneer, and pilled fleece.

Option two: *something Stella couldn't see,* like money in bank accounts used to buy food like this red soup.

She wiped her mouth with a paper napkin.

A third option: *something that seemed like nothing but actually was worth something to somebody.* Her mind buzzing with assonances, Stella dipped her spoon quickly into her red-flavoured soup so as to finish up and get back to detecting the locked room as soon as she possibly could.

Stella ran her fingers over the sponge-painted wall as she walked along one side of Chrysanthemum Corridor. Touching walls with fingertips was something she had done as a child, getting a feel for the properties of her world. Today the action served to keep track of the door levers she was trying, while her mind flitted restlessly around the question of extreme youth and age.

Her world was indeed small, like a child's world. And the perceived dangers, she saw, were much the same as they had been when she was little. Bathtubs, stairways, busy streets to cross … She had rebelled against them when she was little, and she rebelled against them now. Coming full circle was meant to be satisfying, but actually it was no fun at all.

Full circle. She could see it all around her, a big grey circle, like a great tormenting wind, tugging at her. Pushing her down.

Stella put her hand on the wall to keep herself from falling. A fog of light filled the dizzying circle. It brightened the orange-sponged patterns on the walls to either side of her. She felt a knife-like jab of fear and self-doubt, as if she'd driven a car off the verge in a storm, and she wondered how such a thing could happen to a good driver like herself, and furthermore what was likely to come of her bad choices.

With the shiver that comes with a hard awakening, Stella decided that she couldn't stay one more minute in this place, with a ridiculous number of doors and bedrooms. She must return to her own home and her own life. She wished to see her things around her, to cut May flowers in her own garden, and to walk to the corner store for milk, bread, and eggs. And why should she not? She knew her own address, of course, and even though she had come out today without her handbag, she kept a key under the terracotta moon face she had purchased in Mexico one spring break.

Spring break. School vacation must nearly be over. Time for her to get ready to go back to teach. It would soon be a new term, and she had her wardrobe to go through and organize for the next three months, when the weather turned so warm you almost had to go sleeveless. Thank goodness Jackie Kennedy had made shell tops respectable. Stella sometimes drew charts of her clothing so as not to wear her favourite ecru linen shell more than once a week.

She must get home at once.

Stella took a step into the sponged-on swirls of orange and cream around her, but when she tried to take a second step, the floor wasn't there. She reached for the wall and couldn't find it. She toppled.

And somebody caught her. Long arms held her tightly. She found that she was leaning equally against the corridor wall and the tall form of Theo Longbourne.

Theo looked down upon her, concern in his blue eyes.

Stella said, "Thank you."

"What happened? You look upset." He blinked, and she knew he was too kind to say, *Stella, you are crying.*

Stella wiped her face dry. As sternly as her mother Tanis Marie Seton would have said it, she reminded herself that she had sold everything she owned to come to Fairmount Manor. She had made her bed and must sleep in it.

"Stella, are you all right now? I was out for my walk …"

"Yes, perfectly." She made herself stand up straight. "Theo, what is there to steal at Fairmount?"

"In my experience …" He frowned. "Well, things do disappear out of my wash bag."

"Ah," Stella said. She closed her eyes, picturing the inside of a wash bag. "I didn't really mean toothbrushes …"

Theo didn't answer. She opened her eyes, and sure enough, he was gone, off on his walk around Fairmount's corridors again.

She tried the last door in Chrysanthemum Corridor. It was locked. *Bedroom doors,* she repeated to herself, *are always unlocked at Fairmount Manor, for the safety of residents.* She tried it again, in case she hadn't pushed hard enough. It was definitely locked.

It could mean nothing.

It could mean something.

Nothings and somethings, the building blocks of life's experience. A thrill washed over her. She noted the door number: 42.

But how to remember it? At one time she would have pulled a pen out of her handbag and written the number on her wrist. But of course, now that she was herself again, she knew only too well that she no longer carried a purse. No one did at Fairmount. There was nothing to buy, and just as the backside of one's fleece trousers stretched to contain as much rear end as the wearer might be equipped with, one's pockets held any number of tissues and cough drops.

Stella took a tissue from her pocket and blew her nose. She tried the handle of Room 42 again and considered memory mnemonics. Six times seven was forty-two. Room 42, at sixes and sevens. Her mother Tanis Marie Seton now and then called out that phrase to Stella when she couldn't find her schoolbooks, or she was late for the bus. *You're all at sixes and sevens today, Stella. Try a little harder.* Stella smiled. *For once, you're wrong, Mother. Sixes and sevens are just what I need.*

All through the night, Stella tossed and turned under her slippery duvet. She tried her favourite sleep-inducing games and went through the alphabet twice (one list featured TV series from the nineties: *Anything but Love, Blossom, Caroline in the City,* and so on), but she didn't fall asleep. And when darkness began to look less like a few sleepless hours before dawn and more like the far reaches of the eternal rest that must come to all, Stella acknowledged at last that she needed to address what had happened to her in the corridor just before Theo had caught her and brought her back from memory to the reality of her new life at Fairmount Manor Care Home.

Had she suffered a stroke?

She pictured her mother as she remembered her in her eighties, tucked up in bed like Stella was now. Tanis Marie Seton's right eye and the right side of her mouth had pulled dramatically downward. Stella touched both corners of her own mouth and articulated the small muscles there experimentally. She could feel no difference, but maybe a stroke was like insanity, and if you had it you couldn't tell. If she had experienced a stroke, it must have been a small one; and, big or small, a stroke meant permanent damage. Yet her lips and eyes felt the same to her touch as they ever did.

She turned over in bed and waited for sleep to come. When it did not, she listed TV series from the seventies (*All in the Family*, *The Brady Bunch*, *The Carol Burnett Show*), but memories of entertainment and diversion didn't soothe her worries one bit. Because even in the dark of night, logic wouldn't be denied: if she had indeed experienced a small stroke, she must face the fact that today wasn't the first time she had lost her place in the chronology of life. So, several questions presented themselves.

First, how many strokes might she have had?

Second, how long would it be before a final great stroke carried her off?

And last, what if it carried her off before she solved the mystery of the locked room?

Stella sat up. Her duvet slipped off the bed. Her neck was damp above the collar of her second-best nightgown, for it was a warm night, and these were hot thoughts.

She set her glasses on her nose, went into her little washroom, and with a washcloth wiped her neck, face, and the inside of her wrists. She gazed into her mirror and decided that her features were indeed no less symmetrical than usual. Feeling a little less shaky, she bundled her slippery duvet up off the floor and made her bed again. She looked from the bed, with its excellent mattress, to the door.

She pulled open her door and walked barefoot out into the corridor.

Despite the grit on the floors against the soles of her feet, and despite the care home-specific smells of pine cleaner and (faintly) urine, Stella felt happy. The truth was that there was something magical about stepping noiselessly in grey half-light through places one wasn't allowed to be after bedtime. Again, like a child! In a tribute to extreme youth, she stuck out her tongue as she approached the open staff room door. Nobody saw her, for the room was empty but for several coats forgotten on their hooks, a testimony to the warm weather.

Cheryl's threadbare jacket hung beside an expensive bit of rain gear that Stella thought must belong to the spendthrift Riley.

Stella stuck out her tongue at Riley's coat as well. So much for youth and silliness. There was grown-up work to be done.

Soldier on, Stella. There were doors to be investigated.

She moved along the dimly lit corridors, peered at room numbers, and turned corners, right and left in turn, until she found herself before Room 42, which had been locked that afternoon.

Would the door open? She held her breath and pushed down on the lever. It opened.

She stepped inside.

In the unlit bedroom, she could just make out the bits of care home furnishings, the visitor's chair and bedside table turned slightly out of place for cleaning. The clothes cupboard, faintly lit by the tree-shaded window nearby, showed vacant but for the shapes of empty hangers. The bed itself was like a black hole, with a slightly paler shape stretched down the middle. Stella stared hard, for her night vision was poorer than it had once been.

But she was almost certain that somebody was lying on the bed in this apparently unused bedroom.

The body on the bed let out a wordless groan that echoed faintly in the barren Room 42.

Of course, groaning at night wasn't unknown at Fairmount, which was after all a building full of aged people who longed to go home. Nevertheless, the sound was so chilling that Stella clutched the neck of her nightgown.

Silence followed, unbroken by any word or movement from the person lying in the darkness, or by Stella herself.

She wondered, had this been the groan of a man or a woman?

As if to help her decide, the person on the bed groaned again. Stella was certain now that this was a woman. And the sound she made was perhaps not so much a groan as a moan. What was more, the rasp in the voice was a familiar one.

The moaner intoned, "*Stella Ryman …*"

Stella was certain of it now: the figure on the bed was Mad Cassandra Browning.

Stella switched on the overhead light. She blinked in the sudden brightness. "It's a bit much, you playing ghost, Cassie."

Cassandra Browning broke her corpse-like stillness. She cackled, wiggling her horny bare toes below the trouser hems of her purple velour tracksuit. Slowly she raised one hand aloft. Something hung from her fingers, chiming and twinkling in the light.

A set of keys on a silver loop.

"*There is danger, Stella Ryman.*" Cassie jingled the keys again.

"Oh, Cassie, Fairmount Manor isn't dangerous," Stella said. "It's just bloody boring."

"Are you bored right now?"

Stella was not.

Cassie went on, "There is too danger. Wherever people are living, there is always a danger that they will die."

"Ha," Stella said. "Danger without adventure? I will grant you that."

"Adventure comes from inside you, Stella Ryman."

As if it were yesterday, Stella remembered comforting a third-grade child who was sobbing as if life were ending over the lost pencil her teacher had sent her to find. Cassandra Browning was mad, but she was right, because whether your world was galaxy huge, elementary school small, or contained entirely within a mid-size care home, something heart-wrenching was always at stake.

"Have you been locking Fairmount's bedroom doors, Cassie?"

Mad Cassandra Browning sat up. "Certainly not. I have better things to do with my time. Are you going to insult my intelligence, or are you going to solve a mystery?"

Stella asked, "Cassandra Browning, whose keys are those?"

Cassandra swung her legs over the side of the bed and dangled her feet above the floor. "The keys represent a clue, Stella. You like clues. I'll bet you have already figured out whose keys these are."

"I have not." But Stella realized that she had figured it out. She knew exactly who had recently lost a set of Fairmount keys. And if they were lost in this room, they certainly were an important clue—the first important clue, in fact, in the whole case of the locked room. Room 42, first locked and then unlocked, was as important to the present mystery as she had hoped it would be. She must and would investigate.

Stella peered inside the wardrobe and washroom, but found nothing. A few empty prescription bottles lay in the bottom of the little garbage can by the toilet, but that was all to show that anybody had been here. Stella turned on the washroom light to take a closer look.

"Cassie, at least tell me where you found the keys."

But the older woman didn't answer. Stella heard the slap of bare feet against the floor and then footsteps exiting the bedroom and hurrying along the corridor.

Stella left the washroom and followed Mad Cassandra Browning into the corridor. Cassie was spry for eighty-eight, indeed for most ages, and Stella herself moved more quickly than she would have believed possible. Her breath caught in her chest and her left knee hurt like blazes, but damned if she'd let Cassie get away from her. She sped up again and rounded the corner to her own Daffodil Corridor by the staff room, the door to which still stood open.

Stella stopped. She peered inside the staff room. Mad Cassandra Browning was nowhere to be seen.

But one of the coats was swinging slightly, all by itself. She had previously determined that this was Riley's coat, the expensive bit of kit he must have left behind tonight because of the hot weather.

Stella glanced along the corridor, to one side and the other. She entered the staff room and moved quickly across it to the coat hooks.

She fumbled inside Riley's coat pockets.

In one was a plastic prescription bottle. In the darkness, she couldn't make out the printed label on the side of the bottle. What drug was Riley taking, and for what ailment?

In the other pocket she found his keys. What if she somehow managed to make copies of them? What a talisman they would be to a sleuth.

Outside the staff room she heard footsteps, distant but approaching. Stella replaced the keys and the bottle inside Riley's pockets. She was halfway out the staff room door, and the footsteps were ever nearer, when she saw her double error.

First, detectives didn't leave clues such as prescription bottles in the pockets of coats belonging to dodgy customers like Riley. And secondly, anybody trapped in a down-at-heel care home, hoping to solve mysteries and help out fellow residents, ought to take gifts from the gods—or ghosts, such as Mad Cassandra—whenever they were offered.

Stella returned to the staff room and took back the prescription bottle and Riley's keys. Seconds before the footsteps turned the corner into Daffodil Corridor, she scooted back out and through the door to her own Room 34.

Stella sat on the edge of her bed in the dark, eyes closed, working to calm the frilly edges of panic that had accompanied her back here. It occurred to her that she had two objects clutched in her hands that mustn't be discovered on her person. She turned on her bedside reading lamp and considered where to hide them.

How convenient, from a detective, as from a thieving point of view, that Riley's keys and empty prescription bottle were compact in size. Even in a room such as Stella's, where everything she owned in the world was either out on display for the casual viewer or inside her single chest of drawers, there were places to conceal small objects. Unfortunately, she couldn't just bury them in clothing, for Reliza in her loveliness was apt to tidy residents' drawers for them, rolling socks and underwear into neat little ovoids that reminded Stella of owl pellets. But perhaps sock and underwear pellets were more useful than a simple mound of clothing.

Stella opened the top drawer of her bureau and surveyed its depressing interior. She, once the possessor of a large wardrobe of good quality clothing, including high denier stockings, now owned seven pairs of vari-coloured socks purchased at the same time as her pastel knit tops.

Stella paused, for the memory cut her like a knife. She remembered how her legs looked in good stockings, and the way high heels helped her stride. But nobody could really miss garter belts, with their fiddly ways, and good quality pantyhose ran all too easily. She told herself with the firmness of a lifelong schoolteacher that she was well rid of formal hosiery.

Soldier on, Stella.

Two of her pairs of socks had gone to the laundry this evening, leaving five tightly rolled pairs inside her bureau drawer. She tucked Riley's keys inside a floral pair. Of course, the rolled-up socks felt a bit on the hefty side, but there was no telltale jangling. Stella picked up a second pair of socks, these patterned with watermelons, inside which she decided she would hide the prescription bottle.

But first she decided to satisfy her curiosity. What medication was Riley on, anyway? She grimaced at the nosiness required of a detective. Back in the real world, snoops were widely viewed to be among the lowest of the low. But just as rock 'n' roll musicians must bend now and then to accept the use of soft or hard drugs among colleagues, sleuths—even amateur ones—must remain open to investigating subjects that were arguably none of their business.

She peered through her glasses at the prescription bottle.

The small print sent her over to her bedside lamp, where she squinted up closely to read the label. Nowhere did she see Riley's name. The prescription was for a well-known medication for anxiety. Of course, even a handsome man in his thirties might be anxious, especially one whose wife had recently kicked him to the curb, so to speak. However, he wasn't likely to get such a prescription under the name *Wanda Gretcher*.

Stella read the name on the bottle again. Surely one of the women in Rose Corridor was named Wanda.

Stella thought hard and became certain of it. And she was also sure that Rose Corridor had been mentioned at lunch in connection with prescription medications. For, hadn't she, the Greek Chorus, and Thelma Hu overheard a Nameless Dear care worker remonstrating with two of the women for losing their medication? With slow and careful hands, Stella hid the prescription bottle inside her pair of watermelon-patterned socks.

She dusted off the bottoms of her feet as best she could, climbed back into bed, and lay awake in the darkness.

When trolley wheels and whispering water pipes heralded another Fairmount Manor morning, Stella arose and checked that the keys and the prescription bottle made out to Wanda in Rose Corridor were still in their cotton-polyester sock cocoons. Reassured, she dressed, washed her eyes, stashed the socks with Riley's keys in them in her pocket, and swung open the door.

She wasn't at all pleased to find Riley himself at standing before her, smiling, one hand raised to knock. He held his other hand behind his back.

Had he missed his keys? Did he somehow suspect her? Stella couldn't see how.

"Good morning," she said coolly. "And how can I help you?"

"I'm here to help you," he replied. He had those raised wing-like eyebrows suggestive of depths of charm. Stella's husband had had those eyebrows too. "Or rather to give you something."

From behind his back, he produced a bouquet of flowers.

Stella eyed the flowers; there were roses among the carnations, so they weren't the cheapest a supermarket could offer.

"Why are you bringing me flowers?"

"So that you will like me." The eyebrows rose to new heights.

Stella felt her heart melt slightly. *Darn it.* "Well, thank you."

He pulled back the flowers. "You're welcome. Do you have a vase? Shall I find one for you?"

She used to own at least a dozen vases of good quality, including a tall cut-glass one that would have been perfect for this particular bouquet. "Thank you. Very kind."

He winked and walked off with the flowers.

Stella spent breakfast feeling guilty because of Riley's gift. Perhaps she ought to give Riley back his keys. After breakfast, she returned to her room to consider this question further. When she looked about her little bedroom and washroom, she didn't see a vase of flowers anywhere. She tried to give him the benefit of doubt and headed to her spot in Corridor Park. There she greeted the needleworking Greek Chorus trio and settled into her chair under the skylight.

At Stella's side, Thelma cleared her throat with a wet rattle.

"What have you found out, Stella Ryman? Is there a locked room?"

The Greek Chorus set their sewing projects onto their laps and offered Stella their full attention.

Stella said, "There was a locked room. And then it was unlocked."

Thelma asked, "Did you go inside?"

"I did."

Lucille waggled her hands over her head. "Well, don't sit there like a chicken on her eggs, Stella Ryman. Tell us."

"There were three empty prescription bottles in the washroom garbage bin."

"Is that all?" Iolanthe asked. "I'll bet there are empty prescription bottles in everybody's room."

"That's all." Stella decided not to mention Mad Cassandra Browning, since she wasn't completely certain whether Cassie was a living woman or a ghost. Further, she decided not to mention the keys she had stolen. She might tell Thelma, because Thelma could be discreet. But not the Greek Chorus, who might conceivably embroider the secret in red silk thread on pillowcases and wave them under the Warden's nose.

"Nothing else inside the locked room? Well, that's a disappointment," Iolanthe sighed. "No mystery at all."

"Don't give up hope entirely, because there may still be one," Stella said. "In the meantime, I want to ask all of you something. In your experience, if a fellow gives you flowers, and offers to put them into water, and then doesn't put them into your room, does that mean that he couldn't find a vase?"

Iolanthe, Lucille, and Sally exchanged knowing glances.

Before any of them could reply, Reliza rounded the corner into Corridor Park. She held in both hands a vase of flowers. Water sloshed around carnation and rose stems as she walked.

Stella said cautiously, "Those are pretty flowers, Reliza."

Reliza stopped. She looked down at the flowers with an unfriendly expression. "I don't think a man should give a woman flowers if he doesn't know her well."

Iolanthe said, "Oh dear, certainly not."

Reliza said, "Riley should not have given these flowers to me. If he gave them to anybody, it should have been to his ex-wife Cheryl. I'm going to put them in the staff room so that all the care workers can enjoy them. It will send a message, I think?"

The young care worker moved away swiftly in the direction of the staff room.

It will send a message. What message had Riley sent Stella? Stella thought she knew.

She would bet her watermelon socks that Riley had learned from the Warden that Stella was the sort of Fairmount Manor resident that he could give flowers to with the knowledge that Stella would then forget about the flowers, and he could give the same flowers to somebody else, viz. Reliza. Thus, killing two birds with one bouquet. Poor old brainless Stella, whose incautious heart might be won for a very satisfying moment with a phony bunch of supermarket flowers.

Stella heard herself growl aloud.

Thelma complained, "Was that a cat? I hate cats."

Stella raised herself up out of her chair. She made her way to Chrysanthemum Corridor, checked that she was alone at the door to Room 42. The door was still unlocked since the night before, so she entered and snatched the three prescription bottles from the wastepaper basket. Out in the corridor again, she compared the prescription labels. Each of the three was written out to a different female resident of Fairmount Manor.

And each was for a well-known medication for strong pain relief. The discovery proved nothing.

But it sent Stella … another message.

These bottles meant that something was going on at Fairmount. Something to do with prescription drugs. She instinctively suspected Riley, but she disliked him, and that invalidated her instinctive suspicion. Although he'd had a bottle in his pocket.

She would have to investigate everybody. Well, she had all the time in the world to bring to a new investigation. And she would begin today.

Two Nameless Dear care workers came around the corner, bearing between them bedding and rolls of toilet paper. One of them said, "Excuse us, dear, won't you?"

Stella stepped aside. She looked down at her lightweight fleece suit and her lace-up shoes with their silent soles. Nobody could tell that she was hiding anything in the trousers' capacious pockets. She had to admit that, for investigative purposes, these unattractive clothes were actually better than silk and linens, stockings and heels.

She could never have hidden balled-up socks in a school skirt, nor moved in secret if she had to tap about the care home in three-inch heels. She felt like Sherlock Holmes, disguised as a beggar in rags and tags. She felt like a human Purloined Letter, in full view but disregarded. She felt, in fact, ready.

She remembered Mad Cassandra Browning's words: *"There is danger, Stella Ryman."*

She shoved a hand deep into her pocket and wrapped her fingers around the keys to every door in Fairmount Manor Care Home.

What had Thelma asked for?

A real crime. This morning, Stella could smell crime, as clearly as the aromas of breakfast that wafted along the twisting Fairmount Manor corridors.

Chapter Two
Stella vs the Board

Once a school librarian, always a school librarian. And a person who had for decades adjusted and inked her date stamp did not lightly suffer chronological uncertainty. Stella had deduced from the previous day's (Wednesday's) tuna fish sandwiches that today was Thursday, but now she was dead-set on learning the day of the month as well. She had grown tired of asking the Nameless Dear care workers what the date was, for even they often didn't know, and then they made a meal out of finding out.

Therefore, in order to uncover the chronological truth, she lay in wait behind her bedroom door for Ollie to step out of the emergency exit into the garden for his first smoke break of the day. When she heard the door lever clack shut behind him, she crept out and checked the date on his task clipboard, which hung on the handle of his yellow cleaning trolley. In this way she discovered that today was the sixth of May. Further, she read on his clipboard that Fairmount's Board of Directors was visiting this morning. The inside knowledge was a balm to her sleuthing heart, but the irony of this particular discovery wasn't lost on

Stella. Imagine people wishing to visit Fairmount, when all she wished for was to … *unvisit* it. How she longed to experience May's spring sunshine directly by stepping outside the door of Fairmount Manor Care Home, if only she were allowed.

She shook herself. The morning was wearing on, and this was no time to long for direct sunshine or to launch an investigation into the reason for the visit from the Board of Directors. For today, like every day, Stella had her duties to perform: a series of before-breakfast missions that were both useful and pleasingly clandestine.

As usual, she began her rounds in Fern Corridor, where she knocked on Ruby's door. Ruby was unlikely to answer, as she was very hard of hearing, but civilized beings knocked, even in Fairmount Manor. Stella believed this simple courtesy mattered even more here at Fairmount, where doors were not to be locked, or at least not locked by inmates. Inmates? No, residents. Fairmount Manor was not a prison. Not at all. Although, she noted, with more bitterness than she usually permitted herself, Fairmount did have a warden, viz. Mrs Perdita Warren, Director. The well-supervised children at the elementary school where Stella used to teach had enjoyed more freedom of movement than the Warden permitted her.

Soldier on, Stella.

She knocked again on Ruby's door and then let herself into the room. There, as most mornings, she got Ruby out of bed and dressed.

Not long before, Stella had found Ruby naked and shivering in her chair, waiting for a care worker to dress her for breakfast. For some reason, whether random, geographical, or alphabetical, Ruby was always the last resident to receive care worker help before breakfast, and no amount of pleading by Stella had served to move Ruby up the list. This apparent unfairness infuriated her, but she knew in her heart that every resident on the care workers' morning assistance list was in serious need of help. So, Stella took it upon herself each morning to help Ruby rise from bed and get dressed for the day.

Stella always found it a little unsettling that Ruby believed her to be one of Fairmount's employees. But what harm? None. Except that Stella, as a career teacher and school librarian, was a union woman and worried sometimes that she was violating care workers' rights.

Stella tied Ruby's favourite red scarf in an ascot knot around her fragile neck. "Now you're all set for royalty this morning, Ruby."

"Stella, what is it like to be young like you?" Ruby marvelled. "Think of it. I used to be young myself."

"Now, Ruby, remember I'm older than you," Stella said. It wasn't true but saying so always cheered Ruby. Stella wished her a good breakfast and darted out along the corridor before the real care worker assigned to Fern Corridor caught her dressing one of the residents. With breakfast time still some minutes off, Stella slinked from door to door towards her next stop, Dottie's room. *En route* she passed the Director's office and noted that the empty secretary's desk was missing from its spot outside the office. The Warden hadn't had a secretary for months, which was odd enough in itself; but now another piece of excellent mahogany furniture had vanished.

This disappearance, of the care home's furnishings, was an ongoing mystery, but all she'd discovered so far was that, if Thelma was correct in her valuation, the missing pieces were worth quite a lot of money in the mid-century antiques trade.

Also of interest this morning was the mysteriously well-dressed elderly man slouched in a folding wheelchair next to where the secretary's desk used to be. The man was asleep, and his chair sat parked at an ill-considered angle with one front wheel jammed against the wall of the Warden's office.

Might this be a new resident, then? Careful not to disturb him, Stella turned his chair to face the corridor, so that he could at least look about when he woke up. When she set the wheelchair's brake, he opened his eyes, snorted thrice, and blinked up at her.

Stella said, "You'll be fine. It takes a few days to get used to things at Fairmount."

He didn't answer, and his stare was so uncertain that she wondered whether he was aware of his surroundings at all.

She added, "There's toast and marmalade for breakfast." He looked to her like a marmalade man.

She straightened the lapel of his top-notch linen jacket and hurried onward.

When Stella reached Dottie's room in Fern Corridor, she found her, as usual, standing outside her closed door with her back pressed up against it.

Dottie said, "Hello, Stella. I don't have a cat. It's not allowed."

Stella said cheerfully, "I'll bet you wish you had a cat, though."

"I do wish it." Dottie peered past Stella along the empty corridor. "Cats are lovely. So loyal if you only understand them properly."

"Sure. I'd do anything for a cat myself." Stella fumbled in her pocket and pulled out a paper napkin with tuna fish in it. The fishy aroma arose from the napkin and filled this little area of Fairmount. It so happened that Stella had been saving this napkin full of tuna fish since lunchtime the day before, under the waste bin in her washroom, and she would be happy to be rid of it.

She held out the napkin to Dottie. "Be careful, and wash your hands afterwards. It's starting to turn."

Dottie took the napkin and peered inside it. "Thank you, Stella. I like it best when it goes a little off." She narrowed her eyes like the cat she professed not to keep, backed into her room, and pulled the door shut.

Stella pressed her ear against the door. She heard the tiny mew of feline appreciation from Dottie's cat Percy. She nodded sharply to herself. Fairmount Manor rooms were small, and pets were not allowed; furthermore, Ollie the care worker was a demon with institutional mops and dusters in every resident's bedroom. But there was only one of him, and many bedrooms, so thus far the secret of Percy endured. How did Dottie keep Ollie from barging in and smelling cat? Stella didn't know. She was longing to find out, and she would find out. But not today. Mysteries were to be savoured, not wolfed down.

Stella moved along the corridor towards the activities hall and past its gaping maw of a door. Her personal hell lay within: the hell of bridge tourneys and healthy movement classes. This morning, Stella wasn't looking for hell. She was looking for Theo Longbourne, in order to complete her morning's schedule of good deeds.

Her friend Theo walked Fairmount's corridors all day long, only pausing to escort Stella and Sally from the Greek Chorus to meals and alternating his attention between each of them. Reciprocally, Stella had lately shouldered a secret duty of her own towards Theo, for, even though he had the best head of hair of all Fairmount's male residents, including the expensively jacketed new resident she had this morning discovered in his wheelchair by the front office, Stella had noticed that Theo seemed sad these days. His unhappiness was enough to break her heart, rather like the way Theo's much younger wife had broken Theo's heart by carrying on with her life in the great world outside, without him. It had become Stella's daily goal to make Theo smile before breakfast.

In her search for Theo, she passed Thelma, who was making her way towards the dining room at a pace even slower than usual, pretending that her hip wasn't paining her.

"Let me help," Stella begged Thelma, as she had done every day this week.

"No help. Just tell me if I'm aimed right for breakfast."

"I think so. You know I get confused in the corridors." She joked, "The directionless leading the blind …"

"I'm not blind," Thelma said. "I have macular degeneration."

Thelma did indeed retain a wisp of peripheral vision, so Stella was careful to keep out of her view as she tailed Thelma safely to the dining room door, from whence she returned to questing for Theo. She rounded corner after corner without result until she found herself, Alice-like, back outside the Warden's office.

The wheelchair fellow with the linen jacket was no longer there. No doubt a care worker had wheeled him off to settle him into his new room.

And here came Theo at last, striding around the next of Fairmount's many turnings. She walked up to meet him, and he stopped. He looked at her with such gravity and kindness that she wanted to hold on to him and never let go. She hid her feelings and instead drew upon her teaching experience, which included thirty years of children telling her jokes.

She said, "Knock, knock."

Theo nodded but didn't answer; along with a broken heart, Theo had tinnitus, and Stella tried never to take his silence as a personal affront. He inclined his head to her and hiked off at speed along the corridors, while Stella followed hard in his traces.

She caught up with him in Corridor Park, where he stopped, and Stella worked to catch her breath.

The Greek Chorus scowled at them both, for Iolanthe and Lucille were grumpy before their morning coffee, and Sally was downright green-pea jealous of Theo's friendship with Stella.

Stella said, "Now then, everybody. You know the drill. Knock, knock."

Theo tipped his head towards her. "Sorry?" His tinnitus must have been exceptionally bad today.

"Knock, knock."

"No jokes, curse you," Lucille said. "I can't laugh on an empty stomach. When in the name of Julia Child is breakfast?"

Against the odds, Iolanthe came to Stella's rescue. "I will answer *Knock, knock* with *Who's there?* only if your joke has anything to do with breakfast."

Stella said, "Ha! This joke will suit you perfectly."

Theo took a step towards a bend in the corridor, and she took hold of his arm. She would not allow him to walk off without having smiled.

Iolanthe and Stella chorused, "Knock, knock." Sally glowered.

Theo asked, "Pardon?"

"Saints defend us and send food," Lucille muttered. "Knock, *knock.*"

Theo said, "Who's there?"

Stella answered, "Dozen."

"Er, Dozen who?"

Stella pictured the kindergarten student who had first told her his version of this joke. He'd run away, laughing, down the front steps of the school, kicking through the red and yellow maple leaves to the jungle gym where his friends hung upside down and chattered like monkeys. God in heaven, how she missed her school, her teaching friends, and above all the kids. Of course, that kindergartner would now be in his fifties.

"Dozen who?" Theo repeated.

Or his sixties. Could it be possible?

Iolanthe took hold of Stella's trouser pocket and shook it. "Dozen who?"

"Dozen anybody want something good to eat?" Stella let go of Theo's arm and hurried away from the group towards the dining room, where Thelma was likely waiting for her. But before she turned the corner, she looked back, and thank all that was good in the world, Theo was smiling.

Throughout her life in the outside world, Stella had liked her breakfasts to be the same each day, and in this one aspect of Fairmount menu planning she was satisfied. Since the morning she had left home in her twentieth year, thus shuffling off the mortal pot of porridge her mother had served throughout Stella's childhood, she had by choice eaten toast with marmalade for breakfast. And, on the side, black tea. She got exactly that at Fairmount. True, there had been an issue with the marmalade supply chain a few weeks back, when the Greek Chorus had surrounded and captured every packet in the dining room for their own table. Since then, a small condiment skirmish had decided matters in Stella's favour, and recently a Nameless Dear care worker had forcibly united the two half-empty tables so that she, Thelma, and the Greek Chorus shared marmalade toast together at Stella's table, far from the window but close to the door.

The Greek Chorus did not like this table. They felt it was badly placed. Iolanthe and Lucille grumbled that they missed the light from the window, but they never looked at the window when they said it.

Instead, they frowned at the table next to theirs, where Rose Corridor residents sat. These women were, every one, rumoured to be incontinent, as if that were anybody's business but their own. And now their bottles of medications had gone missing. Stella thought back to the empty medicine bottles she had discovered in the locked room, with Rose Corridor resident Wanda's name printed on it. Where were the pills that belonged in the bottles? And where were Dolores, Mildred, Wanda, Norma, Florence, and Roberta, owners of said pills and bottles? Statistics argued that they couldn't all have misplaced them at the same time. One thing was certain, though: no matter who was responsible for the pills' disappearance, the Rose Corridor women were clearly victims of institutional bullying and peer resentment, and Stella made it a point to stop by their table each morning with a cheerful greeting.

This morning, she made her usual stop to smile at the lot of them, conscious all the while of the Greek Chorus's scowls against her shoulder blades.

She asked Rose Corridor, "How are we all on this sunny morning?"

From the far side of the table, Dolores said, "We are sick of being in the doghouse, that's how we are."

Next to Dolores, Wanda said, "Mrs Warren wants us all to go to her office after breakfast."

Stella said, "It'll be all right."

The six women looked up: Dolores, Mildred, Wanda, Norma, Florence, and Roberta. Their teacups stood untouched before them, and their hands rested in their laps as if they had nowhere else to go.

It would not be all right. Not unless somebody made it all right. Dolores, Mildred, and Wanda were what Stella thought of as tough birds like herself, but it was asking a lot of any of them to protect a whole corridor of vulnerable women from Fairmount's Director.

She said, "It seems to me that Mrs Warren, our Director, is picking on you six."

"We think so too," Dolores said. "Even before the drugs started going missing, she seemed out to get us."

"She told everybody that we're incontinent," Norma added.

Stella nearly said, *Ich bin incontinent.* She did say, "We are all incontinent."

"We certainly are not," Iolanthe said from the adjacent table.

"Be quiet," Thelma snapped. "It's a metaphor."

"It's not a metaphor," Stella said. "We *are* all incontinent. There's not a person in this dining room who hasn't peed when she laughs or leaked after a long morning in front of the TV. And that goes for Mrs Warren too."

"It happened to me when I was eighteen." Mildred smiled palely. "On West Boulevard, in front of a dry cleaner's."

"I peed myself when I was forty-seven," Lucille admitted. "I was in a crowded elevator, and somebody said something funny."

The six women of Rose Corridor sat up a little straighter.

Residents at the tables around them were listening with apparent interest. Stella didn't want to catch the attention of the care workers scattered here and there around the dining room, pushing residents close to the tables and settling paper napkins on laps, but she said what she wanted to say loudly enough for the nearest tables to hear. "We mustn't let those in charge make us feel ashamed of ourselves."

"What does any of this matter?" Norma asked starkly. "Our lives are over, dear."

"I'm not dead yet," Thelma interjected.

Stella's blood seethed with the desire to climb up on the table and speak her mind out loud. *Listen to me, you residents of Fairmount: We here may have few contributions left to give this world, for we are like the famed lilies of the field, who do not toil anymore; but we have toiled. In fact, over the decades of our rich lives, we've given our share and even more. Therefore, the hours of our lives matter just as much as anyone's.*

Platters of toast were now being placed in the centre of each table, and care workers approached with tea and coffee in stainless steel pots. Stella, bold words unspoken but stirring her spirit nonetheless, took her seat. She accepted a packet of marmalade when Lucille pointedly offered it.

Iolanthe raised her little finger and sipped tea from her mug. "Stella, you're a detective. Why don't you find out why the Warden bullies Rose Corridor?"

"Stella knows why. It's a law of nature," Thelma said. "Rose Corridor women don't do anything mean to anybody, so they get bullied."

Sally snorted, and Lucille shook her head. "The Warden bullies Stella, and Stella does plenty to deserve it."

"That's not bullying, dear," Iolanthe explained gently. "That's battling."

Stella laughed through her mouthful of toast. She had never liked Iolanthe much, but that remark raised within her a bushel of unexpected loving feelings.

Stella asked, "Isn't there a civilization somewhere where the elderly are esteemed?"

Iolanthe said dryly, "Yes, I saw it on a public television documentary. The place is called Cloud Cuckoo Land."

Stella said, "Why must we be bossed and bullied here? Is it really the only way to run a care home?"

"Reliza doesn't bully," Thelma said. "Nor Cheryl, nor Ollie."

"They're the exceptions," Stella countered.

"Apparently, a place full of old people attracts pushy workers," Iolanthe said. "They must get satisfaction out of bossing their elders around."

"That's all very well," Stella said. "But bullying Rose Corridor is exceptionally disturbing behaviour by management."

"Look for the money," Thelma said.

"What money? There's no money," Iolanthe said.

"There's always money," Thelma replied.

"Huh. I can't see it," Lucille said. "What I see is that bossy board woman Audrey something, every time she swans into Fairmount. It's my belief she's watching us so she can pick off the weakest, kick us out of here, and fill our rooms with folks who don't need much help."

Stella thought of Ruby, naked in her chair.

"I wouldn't be surprised." Iolanthe sighed. "We'll have to pretend to be supple fifty-year-olds now. If we show any weakness, they'll ship us off to bed rest in public hospital wards."

Lucille said, "Be careful who sees you with that hip, Thelma."

"What hip?" Thelma scowled. "There's nothing wrong with my hip."

Cheryl, the care worker with the Mona Lisa smile, and her dodgy care worker ex-husband Riley, looked across at them from Rose Corridor's table, where she was touching a napkin to Roberta's long and buttery nose.

She walked over to Stella's table. "How is your hip, Ms Hu?"

"My hip is fine. My hip smells like a rose." Thelma pushed back her chair as if to get to her feet. "Watch me jump up and dance the bossa nova."

"Please don't get up, Ms Hu. I worry about you, that's all." Cheryl moved off towards the tray of toast that Enid the cook was placing on the stainless steel counter outside the kitchen.

"But your hip is giving you so much pain," Iolanthe said, and Sally nodded.

"There is nothing wrong with my hip." Thelma moved in her chair, and her grimace gave the lie to her words. "I am fine."

Thelma's hip was by nobody's measure fine. But Stella couldn't help worrying that for Thelma, a trip to hospital, especially for a hip operation, might be a one-way journey.

Stella shivered. She was unexpectedly overcome by the sensation of being herself on a one-way journey that would end too soon. She imagined herself at the rail of a big shabby boat, lightly crewed and steering straight over the edge of the world.

Here be dragons. But at least on this, her final journey, they were serving toast with marmalade. She took a bite and washed it down with black tea.

The dining room doors opened, and Dr Terry rushed in and pulled Cheryl aside, speaking in low, hurried tones. The two stood not far from Stella's table, where she sat eating her last piece of marmalade toast slowly and with concentration, as if she were being careful of her teeth and not fully engaged as an amateur sleuth investigating the mysteries affecting Fairmount staff and residents. As if eating toast and looking out the window were all she had to do that morning. As if she were not straining to eavesdrop on Dr Terry's every hissed word.

"The Board is coming," he said. "Audrey wants to address the residents. Something about ticking boxes."

"What boxes?" Cheryl asked.

"I don't know. But heads up—they're on the way."

But that was where Dr Terry was wrong because, clearly visible through the glass in the dining room door, a small, fast-stepping group of people was arriving. The door opened. The Board was not on its way; it was here.

The dining room door opened again to admit a small group of casually dressed men and women. At their heels, the ubiquitous new care worker, Riley, pushed an elderly man in a wheelchair into the room. The latter, in contrast to the other board members, wore a linen jacket, and Stella recognized the fellow whose chair and lapel she'd straightened that morning while he slept. He was wide awake now, and, like everyone in the world, far better looking than when he had been sleeping with his mouth open.

So, this was not, after all, a new resident; this was a member of the Board. He looked a few years older than Stella, perhaps Thelma's age, but he was clearly here to tour the facility and observe its residents, not to be toured and observed himself. Stella was about to formally dislike him as a quisling against elderly rights when he partly redeemed himself by jamming one wheel up against the door so that Riley had to squeeze himself on the far side of the wheelchair and wiggle the trapped wheel free.

Residents chewed their toast and watched this bit of drama with evident interest.

Once the door was clear, the Warden bustled in after the board members. She waved for residents' attention. "Let me introduce the Board. This is our chairperson, Mrs Audrey Frederick—"

Mrs Audrey Frederick interrupted the Director with cheerful callousness. "Perdita, I think that's my job, don't you? Thanks so much. And I want everyone to call me Audrey."

"Of course, Audrey." The Warden stepped back.

"For those of you who don't remember your board members, I'm Audrey, and this is my father, Vaughn. You'll all know the sports radio host Kenny, and Rhonda and Todd, both leaders in the world of real estate."

The members of the Board waved like stars and said good morning. Stella studied Audrey, to see whether this middle-aged, suit-clad chairperson might be worth liking, since she'd so firmly put the Warden in her place. But Audrey had a look in her eye and a jut to her chin that was familiar to Stella from her days in the educational system, when folks with similar expressions whipped parent-teacher evenings into submission with lashing resolutions and excoriating votes. Stella decided she had no more love for this bully than she had for the Warden.

Audrey continued, "It's lovely to see all of you here, enjoying the tasty breakfast your Director has planned and your cooks have carried out here for you on spotless trays. I'll bet not one of you misses your cruise ship days when mealtimes roll around …"

Stella sat back to evaluate the board members as a group. The younger members were all tricked out in sporty attire with their well-shod feet planted hardily on Fairmount Manor flooring; in Vaughn's case, his gleaming boots were set wide upon his wheelchair footrests. Stella reminded herself that, Vaughn aside, these men and women with their sturdy poses of command were only a few decades younger than the Fairmount residents. She imagined the Board in thirty years, dressed in fleece leisure suits, the knees of their track pants sagging and their pockets full of lint. Why should simple chronology give these people so much power? They could, with a word and a signature, allow Stella and her associates more food or less; better care or worse; improved facilities or the status quo.

Audrey continued, "I'm glad to see you all well and happy enjoying visitors, trips to the mall, and activities in the activities hall. I think I'd better join you there today, for the sake of my own figure." She laughed. Her figure was fine.

Stella judged that Audrey was one of those speakers who made it her business to make eye contact with every person in the room, from Fairmount's Director — shifting from one foot to the other — to each care worker, and with every resident in the room. When it was Stella's turn for the chairperson's gaze to meet hers, she likened it to a steely grip upon her upper arm.

"And let's not forget to thank your staff, the care workers we call angels among us, who do the heavy lifting so that you can enjoy your sunny days and busy, activity-filled lives …" Audrey's attention moved to Rose Corridor's table, where Dolores, Norma, Mildred, Wanda, Florence, and Roberta wilted under her gaze. Audrey's focus lingered upon them as she spoke, as if she had heard talk about Rose Corridor and had strong opinions about the residents at that table. The contrast between the gleaming Audrey and the limp-haired, sad-eyed, undermedicated women of Rose Corridor gave Stella a flash of unmixed loathing for the person or persons who had placed Rose Corridor's women in this position.

Someone had stolen their medications and left them to fall without a pharmaceutical net into last place in competence among the residents. Had Riley stolen their medicine? She contemplated him as he stood behind Vaughn's wheelchair. Was that a new shirt he wore beneath his tidy care worker's zip smock?

She attempted deduction from this admittedly limited data.

1. His shirt collar was visible, open at his neck, and that might mean a missing button. If so, an old shirt on a vain young man might indicate a lack of disposable income, and thus innocence of drug dealing.
2. But equally, the open neck might just be the fashion or, if not, then possibly a further indication of his lackadaisical attitude, not only to his work here at Fairmount but to his family obligations to Cheryl and their children.

She decided that an open shirt collar was no clue as to whether Riley had or hadn't stolen Rose Corridor's drugs.

Furthermore, she wasn't convinced that drug dealing would or even could occur in a place like Fairmount Manor Care Home. There was no back alley here, no graffitied concrete stairwell as seen on television. More importantly, stealing elderly women's meds was unlikely to bring in a cocaine dealer's income.

And, most importantly, even if Riley did steal the meds, theft was not what most threatened Rose Corridor. Dr Terry could get the women another prescription, and Riley could get himself fired, but Rose Corridor would still be in danger of being singled out by Audrey and the Board and sent away from the only friends and the only home they knew.

Stella was confident that right here before her was that great threat to all the residents' lives and happiness: the Board of Directors. And they were not a distant threat, either, for Stella observed Audrey's gaze return frequently to Dolores, Mildred, Wanda, Norma, Florence, and Roberta, and she deduced that something perilous loomed for these infirm but deserving women.

Audrey gave the Rose Corridor table a final, piercing look and then beamed at the residents at large. "Together with your Board, you'll also want to thank those who helped you find your way to Fairmount — your loved ones who cared enough to send you here where you get the unique blend of care and independence that Fairmount offers. We have today sent each of your families a letter, laying out emerging and developing parameters of care as they will unfold here over the coming months."

Stella sat up. Unfold how?

Audrey's smile widened with the scope of her words. "Independence and respect for all our residents remain paramount for us members of the Board, and we plan to dedicate Fairmount, this homeplace, to that end. That is why now we will be keeping close records of residents who can continue to enjoy Fairmount's free and breezy style of living, and those who would benefit from a move to another facility with a more focussed, hands-on approach. But if you don't need help toileting, if you can get yourself up and ready for the day on your own, if you can walk unaided — walkers are fine, of course — if you know the day of the week and enjoy and recognize your visitors when they arrive to spend precious moments with you, you can be sure that every day at Fairmount will be a great day for you. Thank you."

Stella studied each board member with loathing. These people stood before their elders, chests out, hands in the pockets of expensive sports clothing. They cast condescending looks on Rose Corridor's table and maybe even gloried in their power to send residents to an uncertain future in a palliative hospital. For that was what Audrey's speech came down to. It was a hammer poised over every white-haired and bald head.

Many leave Fairmount for hospital, but few return.

The five ambulant board members gave a final wave and made their way around Vaughn's wheelchair and into the corridor, while Vaughn waited. Once the rest of the Board was through, Riley attempted to manoeuvre Vaughn's wheelchair through the door, but the older man held up a hand. Riley halted and held the door open with his foot as Dolores and Norma helped their less agile Rose Corridor neighbours — Wanda, Florence, and Roberta — out of the dining room. When the way was clear, Riley pushed Vaughn's chair through after them.

At their own table, the Greek Chorus set to dusting toast crumbs off their bosoms and began to get to their feet. Thelma kept a hand on Stella's arm while care workers cleared the tables, and when they were too far off to overhear her, she hissed, "Let's get me to my chair before that Audrey woman sees my limp and has me embalmed where I stand."

Lucille said, "Better than cremated."

Iolanthe said, "I want to be cremated. But not yet, obviously."

Lucille said, "I want to ripen and fall from the branch."

Sally nodded.

Stella held the dining room door for the Greek Chorus to pass through, and then jammed the door open with a chair. She helped Thelma to her feet and out the door, doing her best to shield Thelma's limp from view of the care workers still bussing the dining room. Once outside in the corridor, she found that the coast was still not clear, for here were the Rose Corridor women, Theo Longbourne, Vaughn in his wheelchair, and Riley.

Stella looped her arm through Thelma's. Thelma sagged against her.

"Hold on," Stella said. "Try to stand up straight."

"Tell that to Mr Gravity."

Stella held Thelma upright and did her best to make it look easy while she evaluated the situation. To her right, down the corridor towards the office, the women of Rose Corridor clustered outside a washroom door, whispering together and shooting glances at Stella and Thelma. They were no threat to Thelma, of course; they had enough to worry about with their own troubles, including missing medications.

Theo Longbourne strode around them towards the office, but Theo was a friend, and furthermore spoke so infrequently it was hard to imagine him inadvertently betraying Thelma and her sore hip to the authorities.

No, it was the two men directly in front of Stella and Thelma who were the stumbling blocks. Vaughn, with his back to them, barred their way with his wheelchair, while Riley, also turned away, was busy fiddling with his foot at the chair's brake. He was making quite a business of it, rattling the mechanism with the toe of his shoe (well-worn canvas slip-on, Stella noted, with the mark of his toenail clearly showing through the fabric) and then bending over to poke at the brake with his fist. Vaughn, apparently unaware that Stella and Thelma had emerged from the dining room, spoke.

With a nod towards the women of Rose Corridor, he asked Riley, "Don't you find it extraordinary that, all things being equal in age and infirmity" — Vaughn patted the arm of the wheelchair — "I am on the Board and those ladies over there are not?"

Riley straightened. "Not at all, sir."

"That was a very quick answer."

"Well, sir, when you think about it, you've taken care of yourself all these years, and you've worked hard to earn money so that you can stay in your own home. You can pay for your own home care. Everybody here could have done the same, including all those Rose Corridor ladies."

Stella felt Thelma's grip tighten on her arm. Forty years of teaching school exchanged a look of disbelief with sixty years of twelve-hour days keeping a neighbourhood corner store.

Riley smiled down at Vaughn, man to man. "Life is what we make it, am I right?"

Vaughn nodded. "You'd better go, young man."

"Yes, sir? Can I get you something?"

"Well, you can. After that nasty little speech, you can get going. In fact, you have ten seconds to get out of my sight before I fire you."

Riley started, stared, and walked quickly away with a look over his shoulder at Vaughn. The latter reached down, released his brake with the ease of much practice, and spun his chair around to face Stella and Thelma.

On the far side of Vaughn's wheelchair stretched one of Fairmount's winding corridors, and at a certain point in its vagaries was the haven of Corridor Park. There Iolanthe and the Greek Chorus stitched pillowcases without hope of Ulysses's return, and there Thelma would be free to sit in her chair with her sore hip undiscovered by the authorities. Stella tucked Thelma's small hand around her elbow and pulled her closer. She frowned at Vaughn, willing him to move on so that she could help Thelma to safety.

Why didn't he turn his wheelchair? Why did he stare at her so?

Vaughn said, "Thank you."

Stella answered, "You're welcome. But I'm not sure what for."

"You helped me this morning when I dozed off and nearly missed the meeting of the Board. In my wheelchair predicament, you spared me some embarrassment."

"Embarrassment!" Thelma snorted. "That's an expensive treat around Fairmount."

Stella said, "It was a pleasure." She thought it better not to mention that she'd leaped to the conclusion that Vaughn was a fellow resident. He might be about Stella's age, but he was clearly a man of power who could, with a word, accomplish things of which Stella herself could only dream, like firing Riley and exiting through Fairmount's front door whenever he liked. He was a man, simply put, whom Stella couldn't trust. And therefore, she couldn't let him spot Thelma's infirmity.

Stella placed herself firmly between Vaughn and Thelma and began to move slowly past him along the corridor.

Thelma took seven steps and then stopped. While she rested, Stella cocked an eye over her shoulder to see whether Vaughn had rolled his wheelchair away, perhaps towards the little group of Rose Corridor women huddled by the washroom. His wheelchair was one of those quiet, titanium models you could almost play basketball from. It was not motorized, and it moved so noiselessly that she couldn't simply listen to learn where Vaughn was. She had to look.

He hadn't moved an inch. In fact, he'd turned his wheelchair again, and the bloody man was staring after her and Thelma. She positioned herself still more carefully to hide Thelma's limp, gave him what she hoped was a friendly, valedictory smile, and the two made their way a little farther along the path to Corridor Park. She was congratulating herself on their progress when she heard some among the Rose Corridor women sniffing and others offering words of comfort and dismay. Stella longed to stop, to see whether she could help or at least reassure the beleaguered six that they had at least one champion. And she would. But she had to first get Thelma safely past Vaughn to her chair.

It occurred to her that if Vaughn was really the gentleman he seemed to be, he might turn his attention to helping the weeping Rose Corridor residents. In anticipation of this move, she walked Thelma two more steps towards Corridor Park.

But Vaughn in his wheelchair approached Stella and Thelma from behind, passed them, and stopped, barring their passage.

"I can't help noticing," Vaughn said, "that one of you is having trouble walking."

"Pot," Thelma said. "Kettle."

Stella nudged Thelma to be silent. To Vaughn, she explained, "It's just a little crick in her leg. She'll be better if she can get to her chair to rest."

"Right." Vaughn studied the two of them. "It sounds unlikely, though. I can't help worrying, especially because of my position on the Board."

"Well, if I'm such a problem, why don't you send me off to hospital?" Thelma asked with poisonous sweetness. "I'll never come back, and then you won't have to worry about me at all anymore."

Vaughn blinked. He studied Thelma's face, and then Stella's.

Clearly, this exchange was unsalvageable, and Stella moved Thelma a little more quickly past Vaughn and along the corridor. If she and Thelma could manage to sink anonymously back into the greater community of Fairmount residents, they might well be overlooked. Or even forgotten, for if the gods of Olympus had granted one supernatural power to otherwise powerless people, it was invisibility.

But Vaughn in his wheelchair passed them again and turned the back of his chair to them. "Hop on," he said.

Stella remembered sitting on Theo's lap in his short time in a wheelchair not long ago. It had been rather fun. Something to make her feel special after what, she recalled, was a very challenging day.

But Thelma shot Vaughn's wheelchair a black look. "You've got a nerve. Around here, if you ride on somebody's wheelchair with them, you have to marry them."

Vaughn snorted. "Ride on the back, then. See, there's a little bar there for your toes. My great-grandkids ride on it all the time. Climb on and tell me where I can drop you."

Stella tucked Thelma's cane under her arm and helped her onto the back of the chair. The rear bar of the wheelchair was narrow, and she had to help Thelma hold on. Stella kept her own feet, in their lace-up shoes, firmly on the floor while she struggled along, impelling the chair and its two occupants forward as best she could while Vaughn worked his push rims and Thelma directed the way to Corridor Park. The sound of the three of them, all over eighty and panting like a Victorian train engine, echoed from walls and ceiling.

A ride that involved three active people on four wheels was rather a committee effort. However, unlike many committee efforts of Stella's long experience in the public school system, it succeeded beautifully. The heavily laden wheelchair, propelled by Vaughn's machine-like arm movements, Stella's steady pressure from behind, and Thelma's strength of personality, shivered the three of them into Corridor Park.

The Greek Chorus looked up from their seats near Stella and Thelma's empty chairs. Iolanthe, Lucille, and Sally registered surprise by throwing their needlework down on their laps. On their far side, Theo halted mid-stride in his customary morning ramble. All four gaped as Vaughn's wheelchair decanted Thelma into her own seat. Stella tucked Thelma's cane into her hands so that the rubber-tipped end rested between her red silk slippers.

"I knew it." Lucille shook her head. "I knew that if I sat here in this corridor long enough, a bus would come along."

Vaughn smiled. "Hold very tight, please, and have your fares ready."

At this quip the Greek Chorus moved happily in their chairs. Stella regarded Vaughn with more warmth than she had ever expected to feel for a member of the Board. In his expensive suit and still more expensive wheelchair, he looked rather handsome for a man with quite a bit of hair in his ears.

Stella had not in her long life interacted often with powerful, wealthy people. Certainly, she had never dated anybody more aristocratic than an all-business civil engineer in her first year of Normal School, before she'd started her teaching career. Now, gazing with appreciation at this prince of wealth and influence in his pricey wheelchair, she felt power's attraction. When she was young, it had been acceptable for a girl to dream that a noble might rescue a maiden. She imagined the swoop of Vaughn's limousine up to Fairmount's door, how he would help Thelma and Stella into its lush interior; she could almost feel the cold flute of bubbly wine he would hand to her and Thelma while his long black vehicle drove them off to … where?

Here Stella's romantic imagination abandoned her. She laughed silently at girlish limousine imaginings, and still smiling, looked past Vaughn to meet Theo's gaze. He smiled back.

And that was two smiles from Theo today. With Theo sorted and Thelma settled, Stella moved towards her own chair under the skylight. She brushed away a couple of drops of condensation that had fallen onto its seat from the skylight's frame and was about to sit down when Vaughn turned his wheelchair to face her.

"I could use a guide to the front door," he said. "Will you show me how to get there?"

"I'd be embarrassed to try. Sorry, my sense of direction is a bust," Stella explained.

"You might as well ask Alice to show you around Wonderland," Iolanthe offered. "The farther Stella travels towards the front door, the farther away it moves."

Lucille cackled, and Sally nodded twice.

"We'll find our way," Vaughn assured them.

Stella had, over the past couple of months, trained herself not to say *it's your funeral* to anybody at Fairmount. Furthermore, arguing politely with Vaughn seemed like a waste of her time left on earth.

Stella fell into step with Vaughn in his wheelchair. She glanced down at him and reflected that she didn't have far to look because, even when seated, he was a tall man—nearly as tall, she judged, as Theo. Stella discovered that walking side by side with Fairmount Manor's most senior, or rather oldest, board member was a strangely convivial experience. He rolled; she strolled. And for a few moments they walked in the silence that often settles happily upon old friends. She wondered whether he felt equally amicable towards her, or whether it was an ambience he generated around everybody he met, a sort of aura that would have contributed to his prestige and success in the outside world throughout the years of his life. She felt relaxed and positive in Vaughn's company. In fact, she felt young in his company, for she was at present reminded of her years in high school, particularly of unhurried walks between classes on warm days. As she had done back at school, she placed the flat of her palm against the walls and dragged it along the cool surface, wondering why doing something useless just because one had done it long ago was so very satisfying.

Vaughn broke the silence. "I'm worried about your friend Thelma. She's obviously in pain."

"She thinks her hip will heal on its own," Stella said. "It has before. She wants to give it some time."

"I keep thinking, shouldn't we get a doctor to look at it?"

"X-rays?" Stella frowned. "Possibly an operation?"

"Well, yes. That is, after all, how modern medicine can help."

"You'd think so, wouldn't you? Unless you lived here at Fairmount."

"I don't understand."

"Exactly." Stella smiled tightly.

Vaughn frowned. He set his brake and gazed down at the corridor floor. Stella recognized this as the sort of power pause a certain school principal of her acquaintance employed: a moment of silence that worked to strengthen his point of view without raising hackles or voices. Often staff members or parents, overcome by the power pause, would begin babbling requests or excuses, but Stella was an old hand with the strategy. Since Vaughn was staring at the floor, Stella gazed up at the ceiling and, as had been her practice in staff meetings when the principal pulled such stunts, she began to count silently to herself.

She had reached twenty-three when Vaughn spoke.

"Please explain why you won't try to get Thelma to proper care."

Stella recited, "*Those who leave Fairmount seldom return.*"

Vaughn blinked. "Is that true?"

"It's a tenet around here. Therefore, it doesn't matter whether it's true. They ..." She corrected herself. "I mean, we at Fairmount believe it, and believing it makes it true enough to frighten us sparrows off the power lines."

"So, what if we absolutely need to send a Fairmount resident to hospital, for example for a heart attack or stroke? Or if they ask to go? You say we should keep them here?"

"Certainly not. You do have to send them to hospital. You must."

"But?"

"But they — we — often don't return. Unless it's to Palliative, upstairs. That means ..."

"I know what palliative means."

Did he? Stella doubted he knew Fairmount's palliative floor the way she knew it, or as Theo did, as a place of oblivion from which they both at different moments had narrowly escaped. For Thelma, a palliative care ward was a mortal peril she had yet to face.

Stella said, "Well, given that we all feel that those who leave Fairmount seldom return, you might make an effort to imagine why Thelma is being stubborn about wanting to deal with her hip on her own."

"Yes." Vaughn's lips tightened. "You must think we're monsters."

Stella said, "Monsters might be going a bit far. I don't think you board members want to bite us with your sharp teeth."

"Of course not."

"But you might accidentally trample us with your big unthinking feet."

Stella had hoped to make Vaughn laugh — Theo would certainly have laughed at the thought of board members stomping like sportswear-clad Godzillas along Fairmount's corridors. But when she met Vaughn's gaze, she was startled to see a real warmth there. Not the sense of humour that Theo's watery blue eyes communicated, but something almost as nice. It was the look of a man who liked and respected her. Increasingly over the decades, and thanks to social evolution, Stella had met men who spoke to her in that respectful manner. She wondered whether, if she'd met Vaughn fifty or sixty years ago, he would have treated her with the same high regard, or if he'd learned to appreciate women as equals along the way. There was a third possibility, however, because having a hardline daughter like Audrey might well have forced him into an egalitarian outlook. She thought a little more kindly of Audrey and gestured towards the end of the corridor.

"So be it. Let's carry on." Vaughn flipped off his wheelchair brake. "But I reserve the right to check back on Thelma in a week or two."

"*I'll* check on her," Stella said briskly. She began walking, and he joined her, but this time Stella set the pace for both of them. She knew perfectly well that her sense of direction hadn't improved any in the last ten minutes, but she was not going to show Vaughn the great and powerful exactly how disoriented she could become. She added, "I'll make myself responsible for Thelma's health."

Vaughn sighed and spoke words that gave away the truth of his generational attitude to women. "You're the kind of gal who gets her way."

"Am I?" She remembered a vice-principal who had said the same thing to her and how she had replied. She answered Vaughn now as she'd answered her administrator then. "Or am I a *person* who gets her way?"

Vaughn laughed. "Sorry. *Person*. Fellows our age are guilty of enough misogyny. I'll try not to add to it."

"Oh, you're not doing so badly, believe me. Between ageist visitors, a heartless administration, and racist old fools everywhere at Fairmount, I'm becoming quite tough-skinned."

Vaughn frowned, and they rolled several steps in silence.

At last, in a soft voice that made him sound much younger than he was, he said, "This place must be different from what you yourself are used to. What did you do before you retired?"

"I taught school." The phrase was inadequate to communicate the decades of laughter, worry, intellectual challenges, small sacrifices, and big joys her career in the school system had brought her. The years of her happy employment stretched out in memory as long as Fairmount's corridors, but straight rather than winding, so that she could see every classroom in her old school: the seating arrangements, the art cupboards and classroom sinks, her library shelves neatly rowed with fiction and non-fiction volumes, and all her thousands of students, bright faced still in her recollection. She felt as if, should she try, she would remember each of their names, the ring of their voices, and the stamp of their shoes as they tore past her door out to recess. "I taught in an elementary school. All subjects, and I administered the library."

"Good for you," Vaughn said. "I haven't formally retired, but except for being on the Board, I haven't done a lick of what my daughter calls 'lawyer work' for seven and a half years, come June."

"Not that you're counting," Stella said.

"How long since your last day of work?"

"Seventeen years," Stella said. "They made me go at sixty-five, of course. I understand the rules have changed."

"Rules, maybe. Attitudes, no. How long have you been here?"

A thousand years. "A few months," Stella told him.

"I can't help thinking, here but for the grace of God. I hope that's not offensive."

"Of course it is," Stella said. "But as I said, you'll have to work pretty hard to be offensive enough to get under my skin in this place."

"I don't think I'd like living here."

"Then don't."

"I won't. I don't like the idea of you living here either."

"Don't worry your head." Even to herself Stella sounded a bit fresh and flirty, but why not? "I'm all right."

"Are you?" Vaughn said. "You're still sharp. Why aren't you bored to death?"

Stella couldn't resist. "I'm a member of the bored, and you're a member of the Board."

"See? Still sharp. I wish there was something I could do to make things better for you."

"I have a roof over my head and food on my plate. Family if I want it, just like you."

"Not like me. I order my carers around like dogs."

Stella remembered his treatment of Riley and smiled. "I would never do that to Ollie and Cheryl. And Reliza wouldn't last a day."

"Don't change the subject. You live in a building that smells like urine and cleaning fluid. Isn't there anything I can do for you?"

"You can go to the board meetings. Vote for better funds for the cooks and more care workers. You know the drill. You must have dealt with union demands in your time."

"Sure, that's ongoing here, for all the residents." Vaughn shook his head. "I mean you, Mrs Stella Ryman. What do you need? You personally?"

Stella stopped at his side. She looked down at the toes of her good lace-up shoes, the ones she'd inherited from a dead woman, lined up evenly with the toes of Vaughn's gleaming boots. Were they Church's? Ingeldew's? Italy's best leather product? Her own lace-up shoes were the one thing she'd needed before she got them.

Now, what was her great wish? A handbag. She missed the feel of her handbag on her arm.

"Freedom," she said. "That's what I want."

"Freedom." Vaughn tapped the padded arms of his wheelchair with the tips of his index fingers. "That's a rather loose term."

"And I'm sure it's different for you and me."

"Keep talking. What's freedom for you, Stella?"

"I suppose it's the power to leave Fairmount and walk outside, along the sidewalk, and into a corner store to purchase six cold beers for me and my friends and a bag of Hawkins Cheezies. To wear my own good clothes, linen and cashmere, and then return with my purchases to my own home. Can you give me that, I wonder?"

Vaughn didn't answer.

They passed the office where the secretary's desk used to stand. Stella looked back at the Warden's office door. Nearby was the spot where she had first seen Vaughn, bumped up against the wall and left alone with his wheelchair askew, an old man left to his slumbers while the younger members of the Board discussed issues vital to the administration of Fairmount Manor.

Vaughn rolled his wheelchair along with one arm while he fumbled in the pocket of his jacket and then contorted his torso to dig into his trouser pocket. He twisted to reach deeper.

Stella was so fascinated with his searching movements that she almost missed their arrival at the front door, where the nurses' station stood empty.

"Here we are," Vaughn said.

Stella thought at first he meant *Here we are at the door.* But he was holding out a fistful of something. She took it from him in her two hands and looked down to see whether it really was what it felt like.

"Freedom." Vaughn shrugged. "Power."

Stella's hands were so packed with paper money that it was all she could do to hold on to it before it scattered about Fairmount's foyer like autumn leaves across a school playground.

Her mother's voice in her head said she ought not to accept such a gift from a man. The Warden's voice twitted her that she would never have anything on which to spend this money.

She ignored them both and thanked him.

"No problem. Flowers in my garden," Vaughn said circumspectly. "Soup in my cupboard. Money in my bank."

Stella wasn't sure what he meant by these eccentric remarks and was even less certain that she wanted to ask. She gazed down at the paper money in her hands. The thick wad appeared to be made up primarily of twenties and fifties. *Fifties.* Vaughn pressed the buttons on the keypad at the front door to exit. She decided that if his fingers trembled, or if he got the keypad numbers wrong, she would stop him and return his gift.

But his fingers were steady, just as steady as Theo's when he pressed those same buttons. Also like Theo — and unlike Stella herself — Vaughn got the numbers right the first time. Stella stepped forward, her hands still full of fifties and twenties, and held the door open for him with her elbow. Vaughn nodded his thanks, but he was already looking ahead along Fairmount's entry path to the large grey SUV waiting there. He rolled his wheelchair through the door and onto the path.

Stella stood and stared after him. She gripped the wad of cash between her hands and wondered where she might safely conceal it. For nobody had to tell her that she would not be permitted to keep cash in this amount. The saying you can't take it with you applied to entering a care home the same way it applied to death. Furthermore, the Warden's imagined sneer would be accurate, for there was not a darned thing she could buy with all this money at Fairmount. Still, the fact that she had it felt like a small but toothsome victory. She divided the bills into two thick wads and shoved them into her fleece trouser pockets.

Job done, and still holding open the foyer door, she breathed in the outside air, rich with the odour of Fairmount's laurel hedges. Their leaves were nearly yellow where the sun touched them, such a bright and heart-lifting hue that she was tempted to follow Vaughn outside and then stroll away down the sidewalk to even a short-lived freedom. The chances of real escape were few, and the prospect of capture and ignominious return a daunting one. Still, might it not be worth risking humiliation to step out into a world of clear May skies, budding roses, and the green tips of new conifer growth? She might have gone, too, swift as lines from Poetry of Departures—with a wink at Philip Larkin in poet's heaven—if she'd been alone. However, she wasn't alone.

The shuffle of slip-on shoes creeping up behind heralded the arrival of several Fairmount residents. Perhaps they could all escape together? She turned and recognized the women of Rose Corridor bearing down upon her at the open door. Rose Corridor residents, outside? Much as it pained her to think like the Warden and the Board, she worried that a car might hit one of them.

Stella stepped away from the foyer door, and it closed with the shushing noise that Stella hated. It sounded as if the building were telling her, *Shh, you're all safe at Fairmount, so you've no reason to complain. After all, you have everything I want you to have.* And then, the click of the lock.

The six women of Rose Corridor crowded into Fairmount's foyer. Dolores, Mildred, Wanda, Norma, Florence, and Roberta gathered around Stella. Together they stared out the front windows at Fairmount's walkway. They had a perfect view of Vaughn being helped out of his wheelchair by his driver and into the back seat of the SUV. Stella took a step back to let Florence and Roberta, always the shyest of these women, get an excellent gander. The group stood close to one another, close as six fairy-tale sisters, and she remembered with a pang that she was meant to be solving the mystery of their missing medications.

Although, taking collective stock of the Rose Corridor residents, she observed with some surprise that they looked far more cheerful than they had at breakfast. More alert. Their colours were higher, and they chatted quietly among themselves about the sunny day and what might be for lunch (the consensus was packet chicken noodle soup). What had brought on such a change in their demeanour? There had not been time for replacement medications to arrive.

The driver folded Vaughn's wheelchair and set it inside the rear door of the SUV. He tugged shut the back hatch and climbed into the driver's seat, and the car pulled away.

Stella turned to the Rose Corridor women. "I'm sorry I've been so slow to discover what thief took your medications."

"I can tell you." Norma pointed at the departing car. "He did. The man in the wheelchair."

A moment's silence followed Norma's pronouncement. All eyes turned from the windows and fixed upon Stella.

With deliberate calm, Stella asked, "Are you telling me that Vaughn, a board member, took your meds?"

"He did." Dolores frowned. "Did he? Are we sure?"

"Oh, yes," Mildred agreed. She nudged Wanda and Roberta on either side. They nodded.

Florence said, "What? Yes?"

Norma nodded. "He said he'd bring our pills back, but he never did."

Stella gazed at each of the Rose Corridor women, friends to the end. Stella was grateful to have Thelma as a girlfriend, and she knew the Greek Chorus members were as happy in each other's company as three snappish witches could be. Still, she wondered how it would be to have six chums who could count on each other day and night.

Stella had always felt sorry for Rose Corridor residents. These women were always the slowest to begin and finish meals, holding up the advent of cups of tea and coffee while they nibbled crusts and spilled soup from their spoons back into their bowls. They were the butt of all incontinence rumours and, as of this morning, the evident targets of the Board's crackdown on unreliable residents. But now, seeing these women's united front, she envied them.

"Vaughn took the meds, you say?"

"Do you believe us?" Norma asked anxiously.

"It would be useful to have proof," Stella explained. She had for evidence only the testimony of the women of Rose Corridor. Stella read in their eager gazes a heart-tugging certainty of her fairness, regard, and consideration of their words. She wished she were actually an investigating police officer so she might respectfully thank them and call in Vaughn for questioning. But she knew something that a police officer might not know: that Vaughn had everything—had so much of everything, in fact, that he was giving it away. Witness the money he'd given Stella, now bulging the pockets of her fleece suit. Vaughn didn't need Rose Corridor's medications, because he could buy whatever he needed.

But if she were completely, even robotically, objective, she had to admit that when Vaughn gave her all that money — thrust it, unasked, into her hands — he'd demonstrated such an inappropriate generosity of spirit that she was not entirely certain he was as *compos mentis* as he appeared to be. Though he wasn't feeding yesterday's tuna fish to a secret cat, of course. Yet.

Still, her deductive instincts told her Vaughn would not have stolen Rose Corridor's medications. (The phrase *deductive instincts* was arguably an oxymoron, like genuine Naugahyde, but she had long ago learned in her teaching career that, with practice, one gained intuition for any challenging work.) Therefore, if:

1. Vaughn were indeed innocent, as she believed, then it followed;
2. That these apparently fragile and put-upon women from Rose Corridor were the classic detective's challenge, the test of any accomplished sleuth: lying witnesses.

Stella would have to break them somehow, and she had to do it without browbeating them or making anybody cry.

"My dears," she began, "you seem very well. Much better than I feel, in fact."

Norma blinked. "Oh, that's nice of you to say."

Stella added, "I feel like an old rubber band. Or a holey sock."

Wanda rolled her eyes in agreement. "I used to get that feeling all the time."

Florence ventured, "I feel just like that when I've not had my yellow pills."

"Yellow pills, yes. You should try them, Stella," Wanda said.

Dolores suggested, "You might ask Dr Terry if you can take them."

"The red pills are the real firecrackers, though," Norma added.

Wanda said, "Maybe. I must say, though, I can't even get out of bed without my yellow pills."

Stella asked, "Are they round or oblong?"

Wanda dug in her pocket and brought out a screwed-up bit of tissue. "Look, they're round."

Wanda pulled at the tissue and revealed several yellow pills.

Stella nodded thoughtfully. "Is that the best one? The yellow one?"

Now Dolores dipped into her pockets. "Oh, no, that's for blood. Inflammation's the best one, the red one, but you must build up to it for a few days."

Norma nodded. "Oh, yes, that's true. Once you start you can't stop, or you have to build up again."

Here was another thing a real police detective might not be aware of: every Fairmount resident was proud of his or her medications, a little the way Stella remembered being proud of her high school back in the day.

Now all six of the Rose Corridor women were digging in their pockets.

"Now, the orange pills …"

"Yes, still, you know, the yellow …"

How Stella longed for the traditional unmasking of a mystery culprit. She wished she could produce an *aha!* And wave it about like a flag.

J'accuse, mes amies de Rose Corridor. You stole those medications from yourselves and kept them and are now waiting on the new batch from Dr Terry.

She watched the Rose Corridor women, feeling more love for them now than she had even before she knew they'd lied and accused an innocent man in a wheelchair.

Mildred was saying, "Take the blue ones at bedtime, on an empty stomach, no matter what the instructions say."

"Oh, the instructions!" Dolores laughed indulgently. "I take those with a pinch of salt."

"Still, you must be careful. You don't want to take more than your dose, or you'll run out."

Now the Rose Corridor women spoke together, one overtop the other.

"You don't want to run out."

"Keep some of your medications aside."

"Riley lost ours. Then he found them, so we got extra."

Aha. Stella asked, "Riley lost your medications? Or said he did?"

"And then he talked about, you know …" Wanda coloured.

Mildred was made of stronger stuff. "*Incontinence.*"

"And then we weren't, you know, because we hardly ever are."

"Except a few times for …" There was a pause, and everybody looked at everybody else, except Florence and Roberta. "But none of us told."

"And then Riley gave the pills back."

"Why?" But Stella knew why. She had witnessed Riley with the bouquet of flowers he'd given her, to soften her, and then, imagining she would forget, had given the same flowers to Reliza, to ease his way with her as well. It was the sort of thing he would do—withhold Rose Corridor's medications unless they stayed continent or cleaned up after themselves. To make morning chores easier for him.

"So, we kept the pills. In case he did it again," Mildred said. "We kept them all. I don't think he noticed, really."

Stella said, "Riley is an incompetent fellow."

"Oh, he's like all the care workers. They lose everything."

"Or the doctor. You know he's in love."

"With that Reliza."

"Nobody can get things right when they're in love."

Stella said, "I'll write the pill colours down, so I remember."

Nodding and helping one another as they moved, the women of Rose Corridor shuffled away from Stella, past the empty nurses' window, and along the corridor.

She called after them, "Thank you very much indeed. Where are you off to now?"

They didn't answer. Nor could she blame them for their non-response, for where was there to go? The activities hall, their own corridor, and soon enough the dining room for packet chicken noodle soup and, eventually, a warmish cup of tea.

You had to hand it to Rose Corridor for nerve and cool. Because Riley threatened to withhold their medications, the women had stolen their own meds, lied about their disappearance, and hoarded more.

Stella grimaced. She had solved a mystery, and what was her reward? Was it, as for Hammett's amateur sleuths Nick and Nora Charles, a flute of cold champagne and dinner on the town? No. Not even a cold beer and Cheezies with her friends.

Her reward was likely to be lukewarm tea. Sometime in the future.

But that would not do at all. Her prize for solving the mystery of Rose Corridor's stolen medications must be a nice mug of properly hot tea. And she should have it now. Or as close to now as a raid on the care workers' staff room could be. She smoothed the bulges in her trouser pockets and decided that once she had stolen a nice mug of tea from the staff room, she would take it with her into the storage room, under the shelter of the art table with its green plastic tablecloth. She would enjoy her solitude, count the cash Vaughn had given her, and see how unnecessarily rich she had become.

Perhaps Mad Cassandra Browning would find her there, as she had done once before. Company, even the company of a woman who had in all probability died years ago, would be acceptable. Better than acceptable, really, for although Mad Cassandra was unlikely to be much help counting money, she would certainly enliven the morning. She would probably toss hundred-dollar bills around the storage cupboard and spill the tea. Stella laughed aloud at the thought. She might be just a bird in a Fairmount cage, but some of the company here was not bad. Not bad at all.

Stella turned a corner that she was certain would lead into Daffodil Corridor near the staff room and its supply of tea and clean mugs. Instead, she found herself in Corridor Park.

The Greek Chorus sat scowling at their needlework. Stella had seldom seen them look fiercer. Sally held her little golden thread-snipping scissors before her face and snapped them open and shut upon the empty air.

The air was not all that was empty. For, next to Stella's seat under the skylight, Thelma's chair stood unoccupied.

A care worker might have taken Thelma to the washroom. Or … Stella tried to imagine where else Thelma might have gone. She could not. Thelma was limited in her movements, for nothing would stop her taking every opportunity to rest her hip and get well before anybody noticed the problem.

"Where is Thelma?" Stella asked.

"That young fellow took her off," Iolanthe said. "Thelma didn't want to."

"Want to what?"

"Go in the wheelchair he brought."

"That Riley man helped her in," Lucille said. "Some help. Bumped her knee."

Stella steadied herself against her chair. "Where did Riley take Thelma?"

"Nowhere. Dr Terry took her."

Iolanthe added, "He rolled her away, and she waved goodbye. That was not very much like our Thelma, was it?"

Stella swallowed. "How long ago?"

Iolanthe murmured, "It's hard to say, isn't it?"

Lucille nodded. "One minute is exactly like another."

"First, Dr Terry made a phone call, didn't he?"

"Oh, yes. For the ambulance."

Stella wanted to sit down in her chair so badly that her knees were doing it for her, but she straightened up. "Why didn't I see them in the corridor?"

"Oh, our Stella, never knowing which way is up." Iolanthe sighed. "I suppose we all have to admit that it's about time Thelma had that hip of hers looked at, isn't it? But I did hate to see her go."

"If you don't want to be next off to hospital, Stella, take a load off your heart and give your rear to your chair," Lucille advised her. "Otherwise, it could be you in the ambulance."

"True, true," Iolanthe hooted softly.

"Which way did Dr Terry take her?"

Lucille and Iolanthe glanced at each other. Before they could make a further reference to her poor directional instincts, Sally turned her gold scissors so that their sharp little blades indicated her left and Stella's right. Stella set her sails, turned right, and hurried off along the corridor. Left, and then right. At this junction she ran straight into Reliza, who was travelling at a fast clip herself. Stella caught hold of Reliza's arms and steadied them both.

"I'm looking for Dr Terry," Stella said, thankful to have run into the one person in Fairmount who was in love with the doctor, for no matter how rocky the road of love might become, the young care worker was certain to know where in the building the doctor was. "I'm looking for him and for Thelma."

"You two are such friends." Sympathy shone from Reliza's bright eyes. "Did you not say goodbye?"

Stella wanted to say, *Not good-bye! Au revoir, until we meet again.* But this was no time for semantic denial. This was a time for inquiry and action. "No. Where can I find her? Where's the ambulance picking her up?"

"At the front door. I've just come from there. But I think ..."

Stella didn't wait to see what Reliza thought. She headed at full speed in the direction from which Reliza had come. Straight on and then where? Some emergency-inspired sense of direction must have descended upon her like a gift from Olympus, for she turned right and found herself in the foyer where she had recently stood among the women of Rose Corridor to watch Vaughn's big car pull away. Now Dr Terry stood alone with hands on hips at the foyer door, handsome and dog-tired as always. On the other side of the glass, at the end of Fairmount's laurel-edged walkway, an ambulance idled with open rear doors. An emergency worker in a white shirt with red piping on his collar slammed the doors shut and then peered inside the back windows.

The ambulance was too far away and at too narrow an angle for Stella to see what the emergency worker was looking at. But she knew: Thelma. Stella's great friend would be lying on the ambulance cot, strapped in for safety, small and silent as a fallen bird in her fleece suit and red silk slippers. She would be staring back at the emergency worker with her wise brown eyes.

She would be terrified, but she would not show it.

The emergency worker secured the back lock of the double doors that shut Thelma inside. He tested the doors with a tug and disappeared around the far side of the vehicle. Stella knew that she had only seconds before he did what he was paid to do, viz. drive away with Thelma, likely never to return.

If only Stella could go too. But she knew it was useless to ask. Even Dr Terry, sweet as he could be when not too exhausted or lovelorn for good manners, wouldn't allow it. There were nasty and sometimes mortal illnesses that elderly people caught in hospital, she knew, and there would be no place there for her to rest, sleep, or even sit and wait without a care worker. And anyway, nobody ever seemed to say yes at Fairmount.

Certainly, there was no time to argue. *If only I could have a stroke,* she thought. They could bundle her in with Thelma in the back of the ambulance. Two birds, one bigger, one smaller, to be managed with one stone, if only she would fall senseless right this moment to the floor.

All this passed through Stella's mind in the second before she turned to Dr Terry.

He touched her shoulder. "Are you feeling well, Mrs Ryman?"

Unfortunately, yes.

But how was he to know? She drew down one side of her mouth and waved her right arm. She let her left arm dangle, the way they showed you in stroke awareness commercials on TV.

She fell to the floor and heard her own fall rather than felt it. She lay on the gritty foyer tiles, the noise of Thelma's idling ambulance large in her head. She couldn't see the doctor or the ceiling above her. The little room turned grey and then black.

Stella remembered with odd, swift logic, her wedding day so long ago. And she remembered her mother, Tanis Marie Seton, saying, *Be careful what you wish for, Stella, because there's always a catch.*

Stella heard the heavy click of a car door and felt it was safe to open her eyes. She was lying along the back seat of the car, awkwardly strapped in place with a seat belt, her feet on the floor.

She made out the top of the driver's curly head in the front seat. The car moved forward, and Stella strained to look out the back window.

She asked, "Where's Thelma?"

The driver didn't answer. Perhaps she hadn't asked the question out loud. She heard music and understood that the driver was humming along with the radio.

She twisted and pulled against her seat belt until she was able to sit up and see out. The car was pulling away from Fairmount's driveway and driving south. She made out the back side of Thelma's ambulance, travelling north, heading downhill towards the first turning. It flashed its brake lights, indicated, and disappeared around a corner.

"Follow that ambulance," Stella urged the driver. "Don't let it get away."

Riley spoke cheerfully from his spot at the wheel. "Don't you worry yourself, Mrs Ryman. I'll get you to hospital emergency in two shakes. The doctor phoned ahead for you, and he's sending you to the hospital a ways south of here, with the shortest waiting time for emergency."

Riley, too, put on his blinker. Stella closed her eyes and felt the turn take them farther from Thelma in her ambulance.

"Where are they taking Thelma? Why didn't they put me in her ambulance instead of you driving me?"

"She's going somewhere that does hips and legs, I guess," Riley said. "You're a different kettle of fish, medically speaking. But don't worry yourself, Mrs Ryman. It's my bet that a few days with the expert medicos will sort you out nicely."

Stella said hurriedly, "I feel better." But she did not feel better. Her heart pounded, and dizziness knocked her against the passenger door. She pulled herself up and tugged at her seat belt. "Please take me back to Fairmount."

"You'll get me in trouble with the Director. I'm to take you to emergency, and no funny business from you, Mrs Ryman. Those were Mrs Warren's exact words." His indicator clicked again, and she leaned against the door as he took the next turn.

She felt cold, despite the warm May noontide.

Outside the car windows, mansion gates flashed by, and a small beater of a car that must have belonged to a maid or a caretaker pulled out in front of them. Riley merged into a long line of cars moving steadily away from Fairmount. *Be careful what you wish for, indeed.*

Stella was outside now, wasn't she? She had tricked the doctor and escaped Fairmount. But here in Riley's power, she was less free than she had been before she pulled the stunt meant to reunite her with Thelma.

Those who leave Fairmount seldom return.

A green light ahead, at a busy crossing that Stella had never thought to see again, turned red. Riley swore and thumped on the brake. The light turned green again, and now Stella saw bridge rails flicker outside the car window.

She deduced that Riley was driving them south across the river. What river? Stella, attempting to recall the city's geography, thought of the River Styx. Riley was too handsome and feckless to make a good Charon. But then again, what did anybody know about the appearance or personal habits of the boatman of the River Styx? Only that one must pay to cross into the tunnels of the dead. One also recalled that, with few exceptions, no systems were set in place for a return journey from Hades.

She tucked her cold hands into her trouser pockets. There she found the lumped-up twenty- and hundred-dollar bills Vaughn had given her. Charon's price, and more. Outside, the river flashed sunlight, and she saw crows darting across a cloudless sky as the car sped southward.

Chapter Three
The Curse of Youth

Stella unbuckled her seat belt and moved to the right along the back seat of Riley's car. Once settled, she refastened her belt. From here she could keep Riley in her line of sight. Riley was proving to be something of a darter in driving style, and she had never respected these swift in-and-out-of-lane drivers who put everybody's nerves on edge just to save a moment's travel. Back in her driving days, she had quietly enjoyed passing a seething darter forced to wait at a left-hand turn.

Stella peered through the back passenger window at the moving city, an exceedingly grand view when compared with Fairmount Manor's sponge-painted walls and wood-tone doors. She had once known these roads on the city's west side well and now observed a few changes in the expensive section of town they were passing through, mainly pretty houses of which many were fenced for demolition.

Still, the ornamental cherry trees shaded the streets the way they'd done every May while she'd been among the living and working. She felt a little like an astronaut returning from space, stunned by the relativity of time. She'd been gone for only three months but felt long forgotten by the world.

She reminded herself that she must try to appreciate the drive. Her mother had been of the generation that enjoyed a car ride, especially on Sundays. If Stella hadn't been so worried about Thelma, she would have enjoyed this ride far more.

She asked Riley the time, and he told her ten thirty. She could hardly believe how little time had passed since breakfast with the Board. Now here she was, on her way to hospital, driving in apparently the opposite direction from Thelma's ambulance. Stella's fake stroke, meant to allow her to join Thelma in the ambulance, had failed, and the sense of moving farther and farther away from her friend in this time of need sent up a flare of panic inside her. Before anything else, she had to narrow the distance between them. She told herself not to show her distress, for it wouldn't help her with Riley. He could be friendly, and he might do a person a favour if it was in his interest; apparently, he liked to be liked. But he was not kind.

Stella wished she had pretended to break her hip, but it was too late now. She tried again to turn Riley back.

"I am one hundred percent better." Was she? Stella took inventory. Heart beating at an appropriate rate, breathing consistent. Everything else was gravy.

"That's very good news," Riley said. "You can tell it to the doctors when they check you out."

"I'm certain that I don't need to go to hospital after all." She felt the urge to apologize, but if there was anything one learned in eight decades on this planet, it was not to grovel before an unkind person. "I don't want to waste your time. Let's go back to Fairmount, shall we?"

"Can't do it. You've got to be checked out, my beauty."

Stella silently acknowledged his charm. "There's not a thing wrong with me."

"Let the doctors do their jobs. That's why they get the big bucks, right?"

"Yes, of course," she said. Doctors and lawyers and entrepreneurs, oh my.

A thought struck her. Even though Thelma's ambulance had driven off in the opposite direction from Riley's car, many drivers, especially those who drove for a living such as ambulance drivers, had arcane knowledge of vastly differing routes around the city to reach certain destinations. "Do you think that Thelma might possibly be on her way to the same hospital we're going to? Perhaps the driver has taken an alternate route?"

"Sure, could be," Riley agreed cheerfully.

A careless reply. Nonetheless, she might be right. All things were possible, or else how was Stella out of Fairmount Manor and sitting in the back seat of Riley's car? Furthermore, at the start of the day she'd not had a penny in her pocket, and now, since rich, elderly Vaughn's gift, Stella had wads of money. Even at eighty-two, one's life took unexpected turns.

Riley swerved into the left lane, back into the right, and swung over again. The traffic on Granville slowed, then stopped short. Riley cursed, nipped between braking vehicles into the right lane, and turned into a parking lot.

"Are we stopping?" she asked.

"Nope. This parking lot leads into a back lane." He steered a hard left that swung Stella sideways in her seat, against the door. The turn onto a side street brought the nose of the car up against a temporary no-entry barrier. Riley huffed and backed into a private driveway, nearly hit a boat trailer, and swung around to drive down another lane. He turned right on a residential street, right again, thumped over a speed bump, and on the third light turn met the same no-entry barrier again from the other side.

"What are they doing with the traffic flow around this city?" he said. "I'm getting angry, and I don't like to drive angry."

Stella said, "Let's take a moment to get our bearings."

"I know where we are," he said.

"I don't." She did, actually; she had known a learning assistance teacher who lived on this street. "But if we don't stop a moment, I'm afraid my blood pressure will go through the roof, and things might end badly."

Riley pulled over to the curb, put his elbow round his seat, and regarded her closely. "Your colour is good," he said.

Now look who's the hobby doctor, Stella didn't say. "Let's chat just for a minute. Calm me down."

"Chat about what?"

"Well, this is a very nice car." Stella touched the seat cover. The stitching was ripped, and the piping well worn, but it appeared to be real leather. "What make is it?"

Riley's expression brightened. "It's an old Saab, quite a great car if you know anything about older models. It's equipped with one of the early computerized systems, actually."

"You must have sold your pretty SUV, then?" Stella asked. "It must not have been easy to give up a luxury car even for a classic vehicle like this."

Riley nodded. "I'm saving my pennies—want to take the kids on a road trip when school lets out. Give Cheryl a break."

That was unexpectedly responsible of him. Was it possible a family man's heart beat within Riley's shiny exterior? Perhaps he was something like the tough kids she had sometimes taught, the ones who only wanted to read books on racing cars. She had noticed that doing this sort of student a favour went a long way. She remembered the battered copy of a book on the 24 *Hours of Le Mans* she'd given a tough boy to keep. It had made a new child of him.

What might she give Riley? What would he like? The question was easily answered. She took a twenty-dollar bill out of the sheaf of Vaughn's money she had stuffed in one pocket and pretended to pick it up off the floor. "Did you lose this? I found it under my foot just now."

Riley reached over the seat to take the bill from her. His smile shone in his handsome face. "Money is magic, isn't it? I tell my kids, if they ever find some money, they can make a wish."

He pulled into the street, made an illegal U-turn, and the Saab was back in traffic and heading south again. The car passed a series of bright façades of fast-food places.

Stella frowned. "Make a wish on money? What a pretty thought. Well, what do you wish for?"

"Gas in the tank! I'm running low. But we'll make it to the hospital, never fear."

"That sounds like a wasted wish to me, since neither of us really wants to go there."

"I guess so, but then I'm not the one who found the money. You found it, Mrs Ryman, so you get to make a wish."

"I wish to turn around and go back the way we came."

Riley's eyes met hers in the mirror. "Now, there's a wasted wish if I ever heard one. You shouldn't use up a wish wanting to drive back to Fairmount. That will happen, anyway, after you see the doctor and get some tests done."

Stella sighed. This was the second time today she'd been asked to make a wish. It might even have been the second time in her life.

"Well, then, I wish for …" She thought about all the things she'd missed at Fairmount. Hamburgers. Her handbag. Her collection of Colin Dexter's Inspector Morse novels. But no. If she were going to play with magic, she felt a duty to ask for the grandest and most unlikely outcome.

"I wish to be younger."

"Don't we all! How much younger?"

Don't be greedy, Stella. "Thirteen years."

"Done." Riley laughed. Did he mean it to sound mocking?

Stella studied the passing buildings until a traffic light paused Riley's car outside a pub.

Riley nodded towards the green-fronted business. "That's the best pub in the Lower Mainland," he said. "They pour their Guinness slowly and know their correct temperatures."

"I've never seen so many shamrocks on a building, even in Ireland," Stella said. "I prefer a crisp lager myself, but when I travelled there, I saw the pubs with a few old fellows drinking their breakfast Guinness."

"They say Guinness drinks like a meal."

"I'll bet the pub serves coffee. Maybe we could go in and get a cup." And maybe she could talk Riley out of checking her into the hospital.

Riley peered ahead towards the apparently static red light. "Are you trying to get me fired, you temptress? Anyway, I have a rule—I never order coffee in a drinking establishment. I'd have to order a beer. And then who would drive? Anyway, look, the pub is closed until eleven."

"Too bad. I'd like a beer." Stella was surprised to find that her statement was true. She also wanted a bag of salt-and-vinegar chips to go with the beer. She remembered the tang of vinegar against her tongue, the full round saltiness of the potatoes. As a child, she had put chips in her sandwiches when she could get away with it. She remembered the crunch of chips against lettuce and cheese, and the soft sweetness of the bread, which contrasted with her mother's hard look when she saw what Stella had done to her sandwich. Tanis Marie Seton was not one to alter a recipe.

Stella smiled. "A beer in the middle of the morning? I'm imagining what my mother would say."

"Your mother?" Riley glanced at her in the mirror. "Is your mother still …?"

"No, of course not. She died many years ago. But her opinions on drinking beer live on."

"You can buy me a brew some other time, then." The light changed at last. Riley drove through and darted between two cars in the left-turn lane.

Stella looked back at the pub. The sign on the door read *Closed*, but even so, a woman stood in the window with a pint glass in her hand. The reflections of shining shamrocks and the whisking shadows of cars on the window glass obscured the details of the woman's appearance beyond her narrow frame and long tangled hair. Stella wondered whether Mad Cassandra Browning might not have expanded her haunting territory. Possible, but unlikely.

A break in the oncoming traffic sent the woman in the window out of sight as car after car turned left in swift arcs. Riley swerved left with the rest. Stella had hardly taken breath before he turned left again, drove into a covered drive, and set his brake.

"Here we are," Riley said.

To the right of the Saab, the road leading to the bridges and downtown flashed with sunlit vehicles lined up at a red light. To the car's left, the hospital's glass double doors slid open, and a uniformed medical worker exited and walked off along the roadway, for lunch or maybe the end of a shift. Above the doors, a large backlit sign read *Reception, Drop-Off Only.* Stella thought of the old fairy tale, Mr Fox. The sign over Mr Fox's basement door had read *Abandon hope, all ye who enter.* She could easily picture those very words under *Drop-Off Only.* Furthermore, Riley had the same sort of slick good looks Mr Fox was said to have.

Riley put the car into neutral—he was hard on the gears, Stella noted without surprise. He rested one hand on the steering wheel and turned to address her. "I guess I'd better take you inside."

"The sign says *Drop-Off Only.* Shouldn't we park somewhere else?"

"I want to get you in line at Emergency."

"But this isn't an emergency. Look, the sign says *Reception.*"

"Oh, for god's sake." Riley grimaced. "But maybe they can check you in here and you'll avoid the Emergency wait. Dr Terry did phone ahead, but I don't know exactly how it all works. I'm sure I can leave the car here for a little while without any problem."

Stella peered at the doors and the big plate-glass windows to either side of the entrance. She saw a queue of people inside, one of them a man in a uniform that had nothing to do with health care.

"There's a police officer inside the lobby. You'll have to drop me off and find short-term parking or else you'll likely get a ticket."

Stella heard her own steady tone of voice and marvelled at it. She'd not wanted to let things get this far, but the adventurous heart that still beat inside her thrilled at being out on her own in the greater world, even if it was only a hospital lobby and just for the few minutes it took Riley to find parking. But another part of her — the institutionalized part that had spent three months at Fairmount, plus the part that had shut herself into her house and watched box sets of *Ironside* and *Mary Tyler Moore* for a year before checking herself into Fairmount — wished cravenly that he'd refuse to leave her alone in the hospital.

While Riley idled the engine and peered through the windows, apparently considering his parking options, Stella watched a droopy-trousered elderly fellow limp through the sliding glass reception door and turn towards the main road. He was not quite as old as Stella was, but she was clearly a better walker. If that fellow could go to the hospital on his own, why couldn't she? Wasn't she the woman who had thought nothing of ordering five-thousand dollars worth of books to support curriculum and student interests over the course of an autumn term, of reorganizing library shelves for a more efficient layout of information, and of designing units of study for her research skills program? Or was she a mouse?

Was she a cowardly, irreversibly institutionalized rodent?

Two cars pulled up behind Riley's Saab, so silently that they almost seemed suspicious, like creeping footpads approaching from behind. Of course, they were electric vehicles. Was it only six months ago that she had considered buying one, had imagined gathering the courage to leave her house and drive boldly to the supermarket and liquor store? To a movie! But she hadn't done it. She had not valued her opportunities for independent travel, and now they were lost to her. She reminded herself that regret peeled no potatoes, that what was done was done, and at least she was no longer the television-watching hermit she had been a few months before.

Now she was a sleuth, with a job to do and friends who counted on her for help. Today she must follow — no, pursue! — Thelma. And even though this particular hospital was almost certainly the wrong hospital, it was not impossible that Thelma had arrived here after all. For amateur detectives such as Stella, lacking backup and surveillance vehicles, it was vital she not bypass any arena worthy of investigation.

The two cars idling behind the Saab let out their passengers and drove around Riley's car. Both vehicles followed an arrow indicating long- and short-term parking. The patients they'd decanted onto the walkway made their way to the reception door, one with help from a younger person and one, limping, on her own. A police officer appeared momentarily in the open door, glanced at the Saab and down the street. He moved back inside, and the big entry doors closed behind him.

Riley said, "I just feel like Mrs Warren would say it's better to leave the car here and go in with you."

"She won't like it much if you incur a parking fine. Unless you plan to pay it?"

Riley said, "Like hell I do."

"Then, when a no-parking area is this well policed, you'd better park somewhere legal."

How on earth would she be able to investigate the hospital with Riley at her scut? "As well, you're low on gas. What if you go and top up the tank?"

Riley bent down to pick something up off the floor. Stella leaned forward to see him place a slim sheaf of papers on the empty seat beside him.

Stella said, "If that is my medical paperwork, I'd better take it in with me. Go and get gas before you park. There was a station near that Guinness-pouring pub of yours, just round the corner. Maybe you could have some coffee."

In the rear-view, Stella saw Riley's eyes brighten, perhaps at the thought of coffee. Or gasoline. Or even the pub.

He handed her the paperwork. "I'll hurry back," he said.

"Please, take your time." Stella set her papers down on the seat and unclipped her belt. She opened the passenger door and got herself up and out onto the sidewalk. Another car pulled up behind them, and Riley drove away with the back door still open.

Stella called, "Oy!" and he stopped. She slammed the door shut for him. No sooner had he driven away than she realized that she'd left her medical paperwork in his back seat. She shrugged. She was not here for treatment, after all.

The hospital loomed before her. Stella straightened her fleece jacket and walked towards the entrance.

The glass reception door was well pasted with stickers reminding folks to have medical papers ready and hands washed, to phone this or that crisis number, and not to bully staff or engage in violent behaviour. To Stella these messages were refreshing, even stirring. After three months of Fairmount Manor's inane and insulting posters banning residents from climbing stairs and taking baths, Stella welcomed rules that applied to everybody, young and old.

The doors parted and she passed into the reception foyer. This area extended in a wide rectangle of ordered spaces, rather like a parking lot if the chairs were cars. The big streetside windows cast a generous light across the waiting area. The seats were perhaps two-thirds full of patients and accompanying friends or relatives, most engaging with their phones.

Stella noted a single receptionist behind glass at the intake kiosk. This might have been a recipe for a long wait, but a queue of only six patients waited on painted footsteps for the mother and son at the kiosk to finish their business there. Behind Stella, the doors whisked open and two women, the younger supporting the elder, walked past her and joined the line, bringing the total to ten. Stella knew Riley wanted her to wait for him, but she was feeling a very human desire to join the queue. She checked the window to see whether Riley was approaching. He was not. When she turned back, she accidentally locked eyes with the police officer. She smiled at him, and he nodded. *Nothing to see here, Officer.*

She took her spot in line and gazed about her. How interesting a person would find the people waiting in this room depended entirely upon how long that person had been trapped in a down-at-heel care home. A woman in a seat near the queue wore a camel-hair coat that matched its owner's hair. She opened her top-grade red leather handbag and rummaged inside it. Stella remembered the fiendishly expensive handbag she'd bought herself the year she retired. It had been a sort of going-away present to herself, and it coordinated with the rolling travel bag her fellow staff members had given her. She'd taken these with her overseas several times in her sixties, trips she'd enjoyed mostly on her own, although once she'd signed on for Petra with a group of retired teachers. She remembered the line-up at Petra in the heat, and how she had hated the delay. It seemed she had evolved since then, because today she was enjoying herself, standing and staring as the poet William Henry Davies advised the world to do. Enjoying, in fact, the view from the queue.

The windows offered a panoramic vista onto the busy road beyond, and Stella thought of Riley on his quest for coffee and gasoline. Her own quest was trickier, for she had to investigate Thelma's possible presence at the hospital without revealing the fakery of the stroke that had brought her here.

Beside the kiosk, the police officer and a nurse chatted quietly. Inside the kiosk, the receptionist paid close attention to the teenaged boy who spoke at length, holding his arm close to his chest, while his mom hovered, interjected, and corrected him. Stella couldn't make out their words, but she didn't need to; Stella had been in that mother's place a few decades back. Her daughter Junie had taken a bad tumble while ice skating. Stella remembered the blood stiffening Junie's flesh-coloured tights, and how Stella had felt compelled at the hospital to command help and healing from all possible sources.

This mother-and-son confab no doubt meant Stella's wait would be a long one, and judging by the sighs and shifting from one foot to another in the line-up, she was not the only one to have deduced it. The elderly woman in front of Stella leaned on her younger companion. She met Stella's eye and offered a tired but bright-white smile. Stella was aware that there were some advantages to false teeth in old age, like whiteness and easy access for brushing, but she remained grateful to her long-dead dentist, an early advocate of flossing.

Stella told the older woman, "I'm happy to save your place if you'd like to sit down."

"I was going to offer you the same." The woman nudged her younger companion. "You have nobody to lean on, but I have Sharon here."

Sharon grimaced. "Aunt Bethie, I should have thought of

that. What if I hold both your places? You two ladies can rest your feet."

Stella glanced downward. She noted the younger woman's swollen ankles above worn suede shoes.

Stella said, "Thank you so much, but I'm not tired."

"Don't be silly, dear," Bethie said. "We're all tired, aren't we?"

"And the whole world has sore feet," Sharon added. "I've been standing on mine a few years less than you have, so I'm happy to stay in line. Please, go and rest yourselves."

"Listen to the experience of youth," Bethie said.

"That's funny," Stella said, "because I'm sure it was the other way around when I was younger."

"Everything was simpler then, wasn't it?" Bethie said. "Now Sharon's the only one who can operate my television set."

Sharon laughed. "My nephew taught me. He's six and sick already of turning on devices."

"It's tough to be young," Stella joked, thinking of her grandson Derek and his impatience with unsavvy elderly users of technology. She'd never have been able to watch all those box sets of seventies television shows without his phoned-in guidance.

Stella offered Bethie her arm, got her comfortably seated near the woman with the expensive handbag, and returned briskly to the line where Sharon stood wiggling her toes in her shoes. Stella guessed this exercise would bring little relief to Sharon's sore feet and swollen ankles.

"Sharon, how do you do? My name is Stella Ryman. Please go and sit with your aunt."

"I couldn't," Sharon said. "It wouldn't be fair. I'm only sixty."

"The curse of youth. It isn't fair, is it? Anyway, I'm only sixty-nine," Stella lied recklessly. After all, she had wished to be thirteen years younger. "And you'd be doing me a favour, letting me do you a favour."

Sharon sighed, said thanks, and left the line-up to join her aunt. Stella felt a tap on her shoulder. An elderly fellow behind her said, "As you're only sixty-nine, would you be willing to watch my spot too?"

"Happy to," Stella said.

The woman now ahead of Stella, since Sharon and Bethie had left the queue, tossed Stella a wishful look. Stella jerked her head towards the seating, and after that, the last four behind the teenager and his interjecting mother at the kiosk took quick advantage and followed the others over to the chairs.

"They ought to have a number system," a young fellow with both knees bound up with tensor bandages muttered from behind her.

"There's a little screen up there for appointments, I'd guess, but it looks like it's out of order. I don't mind holding your place. Do go have a seat."

He hobbled off, and Stella found herself standing all alone in the middle of the floor. Despite William Henry Davies' well-known poem, standing and staring was not a conventional delight in the modern world, and she had not forgotten the urgency of her quest to find out where Thelma had been taken. But impatience had never moved a queue, and it was so long since she'd stood among strangers, in comfortable anonymity, that she let herself relish the moment. She hoped that Riley would take his time gassing up and parking the car. She willed the woman—still insisting on something beyond the call of medicine for her son—to carry on, like a good mother should. Stella felt a youthful sunniness of spirit, for she was up to her favourite brand of mischief, the kind that hurt no one and thus was acceptable even to career educators like herself. For nobody could deny that among the crowd were several people who actually believed Stella was sixty-nine years old.

While the mom ahead in the queue spoke her volumes to the receptionist, Stella remembered how in earlier times she would have taken a book from her handbag and passed the time reading. Since she had no handbag and thus no book, she mused upon the poet William Henry Davies, and then upon Wallace Stevens, who wrote that he was the world in which he walked. Today in the reception queue, Stella was the world in which she stood. She was also an amateur sleuth with a keen intention to ask subtle yet probing questions of the receptionist when she reached the head of the line.

Meanwhile, she decided to practise her sleuthing. She set herself to take inventory of her surroundings. In front of her:

1. By the kiosk, the police officer accepted from the nurse a brown waxed bag with what must have been lunch inside.

She wondered at a police officer being stationed in a hospital reception area: was his assignment because of some kind of a crime wave, or was this simply police outreach in the community? Whichever it was, the police officer did not appear to be tense or even very alert, and there was some serious legal-medical flirtation going on now at the kiosk, but there was no way to know why he was here without … Stella cast her mind back to *Ironside* … listening to a police scanner, so she moved on with her observations:

2. To her left, scattered around on the waiting room chairs, a number of old folks dozed, hands on chins or heads tipped back, mouths open.
3. Among them lounged a youngish mother in tight stretch pants and black bucket boots worn to grey at the seams.

The outfit was not attractive, but Stella, in her fleece suit, felt she must not judge anyone who chose comfort over style.

4. The woman in stretch pants had with her a little girl who wore a red hoodie that lent her a storybook air.

The child swung from side to side on her mother's chair back, and Stella followed the girl's gaze back to the police officer eating his sandwich.

For anyone who had spent decades in an elementary school, sandwich smells resonate strongly, and Stella was beginning to feel peckish. She hoped that Riley had bought himself a mid-morning snack. Perhaps he would even bring her one, if miracles happened among us, and he thought of it. Stella's stomach growled, and it struck her that all institutions counted out the last hour of the morning by the multiplying odours of sandwich fillings. Fairmount Manor certainly did. And at the school where she'd taught for so many decades, noontide burst from every child's brown bag or lunchbox.

Here in reception, the police officer by the kiosk, demonstrating good courting form, was eating his lunch slowly and gazing at the nurse, who was bent over a tablet, tapping at paperless paperwork. Meanwhile, the mother had worked through her son's issues, and they'd left for the seating area. One by one, the receptionist dealt with the others until at last she concluded her dealings with Bethie and Sharon of the swollen ankles.

"Step right up." Sharon waved Stella to the kiosk window. But the receptionist held up her hand to wait and picked up her phone.

"Stella, thank you for holding our place in line," Bethie said. "You're the angel in this waiting room."

Sharon nodded. "I can't thank you enough. Sometimes it feels like I've got cranky puppy dogs instead of feet, chewing away down there."

"You're very welcome," Stella said. "I'm happy to help your feet any day."

"I hope we see you again, Stella," Bethie said. "Are you often out this way?"

Stella grimaced. "Not often, no."

"Gosh, we were lucky to meet you."

The receptionist hung up her phone and nodded to Stella.

"Good morning. Services card?"

Medical services card. Intake papers. Stella had left her Fairmount Manor medical paperwork on the back seat of Riley's car—the same car Riley had driven off to gas up and park somewhere on the hospital grounds. She stole a glance at the reception doorway in case Riley was for once where he might have been helpful.

But of course, he was not. And anyway, she didn't want to show her paperwork for two good reasons:

A. She had no wish to be admitted to hospital, for that would put the stopper on her search for Thelma Hu.

B. Her paperwork showed her true age, which was not sixty-nine.

"My goodness, I've just realized that I don't have my number and the papers from my"—she eyed Sharon and Bethie, who were listening to this exchange—"papers from my doctor, but I think my driver has them, and I don't see him yet."

Sharon groaned. "You're going to have to go to the back of the line again. That's really unfair. Can she come right up to the front when the papers arrive?"

"Depends on the length of the line-up," the receptionist said. "And how disagreeable everybody is."

"Maybe you could find Stella's information on the computer," Bethie suggested.

The receptionist asked, "Name? Date of birth?"

"Meet my hero. Her name is Stella Ryman," Sharon said brightly. "And she's sixty-nine."

The receptionist turned to the computer. Riley had said that Dr Terry'd called ahead, and thus Stella's true age would soon be revealed. She steeled herself for the embarrassment of having her birth date read out. *How the Greek Chorus would delight in seeing me caught out,* she reflected wryly. And even Thelma would chuckle if she knew of Stella's little white lie. Chuckle with sympathy? Stella sighed. Probably not. Rightly not. How she missed Thelma. She yearned to know whether the ambulance had brought her here.

Stella waited for the receptionist to finish typing in her inquiry to reveal her age and circumstances. *An eighty-two-year-old resident of Fairmount Manor Care Home.* It was very much like being one of the soldiers in *The Great Escape,* seconds away from recapture. She vowed not to let them admit her into this hospital. They'd never take her alive. She smiled grimly to herself: a Steve McQueen smile.

The receptionist looked up from her keyboard. "I don't have a record under the name Stella Ryman."

Had Dr Terry failed to call? In the silence that followed the receptionist's statement, Stella felt inspiration's hand upon her shoulder.

She asked, "What about Thelma Hu?"

"What's Thelma Hu got to do with anything?" The receptionist's eyes softened into something dangerously close to pity. "Aren't you Stella Ryman?"

"Yes, but ... I'm very sorry." Stella scrambled to cut a logical path to a cogent question. "My mind was wandering, and I'm afraid I wasn't clear. I'm hoping to visit a Miss Thelma Hu, if she's here. Here in your hospital."

The receptionist frowned.

"Or any hospital," Stella added hopefully.

"You don't need a Services card to visit a patient." The receptionist peered upward at Stella.

Stella felt certain that her cover was finally blown. Next would be the phone call back to the Stalag—or rather, Fairmount Manor—and the disappointment in Sharon's and Bethie's eyes when they heard her real date of birth and saw Stella clapped into the gyves of old age and driven back to captivity.

Sharon asked, "Can you find out on the computer where Thelma is?"

"What family name again?"

"Hu? Thelma Hu?" Bethie said. "Was that it?"

"H-U," Stella spelled out. "Thelma is a resident of Fairmount Manor, and her hip was quite seriously hurt."

"No, I see no records for a Thelma Hu," the receptionist added. "And an elderly patient with hip problems might well be sent downtown if the care home is closer to that side of the city."

"Thank you very much indeed."

Downtown. There was only one important hospital downtown. Stella took the result of her investigation, chewed it, and swallowed it down.

Sharon and Bethie walked with Stella over to a seat in the waiting area. She had stood in line for at least half an hour. Riley ought to be back soon, his car gassed up and Stella's medical papers in hand. When that occurred, she supposed that all would be revealed to the receptionist, Sharon, and Bethie. It would happen soon, but not yet.

Sharon checked her watch. "They told me Cardiac is running late today, and we've got an hour's wait. I could eat a walrus and it's getting on for lunchtime."

Bethie nodded. "Let's get a sandwich in the café downstairs. Stella, will you join us?"

"I'd like to, certainly, but …" But …? What was stopping her? Only a creeping sense that the longer she talked with these two nice, unsuspecting women, the more certain it was they would find out she was lying to them. Still, she wished wholeheartedly to join them for lunch. To order a sandwich—no! Not a sandwich. She'd had nothing but sandwiches and packet soup at midday since she'd arrived at Fairmount. Sandwiches be damned. She supposed it was too much to hope for a café to carry her preferred lunch selections from long ago, viz. patty melts and cottage cheese with pineapple chunks. But quiche? Yes, there might very well be a slice of quiche. *Pastry beneath the egg and cheese filling*, she thought, and possibly bacon. And, lest she forget, Vaughn had gifted her with a pocket's worth of paper money.

She could buy a whole quiche. A dozen quiches. Every quiche in the city.

"Let's go before noon hits and we're lined up out the door," Sharon said.

Bethie added, "I'd bet my sister's cat you've had enough of line-ups, Stella."

"You'll win that bet," Stella joked, just like anybody who wasn't trapped for the rest of her life in a care home. "And a good thing, too, because what would I do with your sister's cat?"

She thought of Dottie and her illicit cat, Percy, back at Fairmount. And of the Rose Corridor women, the Greek Chorus, and Theo. She swallowed. Always Theo.

She said, "In fact, I will join you two."

"Hurray," Bethie said. "It's a treat to have you along."

"This way," Sharon said.

Stella moved to follow. But what if Riley returned and didn't find her where he'd left her? She imagined the alarms, the blared announcements over PA systems, and her public disgrace. She said, "You two go on ahead."

"What is it? We'll wait," Sharon said.

"No, you go and order. I'll try to join you in a few minutes. Please."

Sharon gave Stella a hug, and Bethie squeezed her arm. They moved off, and Stella watched them go, as grateful for the sudden affection of strangers as for the fact that the two women wouldn't witness her reunion with Riley. How long did she have until he returned to her? As long as it took him to find gasoline, coffee, and a parking spot.

But at least Stella had discovered the hospital where Thelma had likely been taken. And until Riley arrived, it was her privilege to stand in the sunny reception area, with freedom in her gullet, and an appreciation of time and place that likely exceeded everyone else's.

To all the seated visitors, the police officer, outpatients, and staff behind glass, it was a day just like any other under the aegis of the health system. But Stella felt keyed up. Here in reception, as she never had done at Fairmount, she perceived the ephemerality of belonging with these strangers in the greater world. Here, windows opened to the pavement spreading outward into the gasping traffic. She imagined the air above the roads, coloured by collective exhausts and the blended breaths of a large city's inhabitants. Just for today, she was a part of this population. And today must be enough for her, because she couldn't stay in Reception forever. And maybe she wouldn't get to eat quiche or visit that nice-looking pub they drove past on the way to hospital, where she thought she saw Cassandra Browning, of all people.

Then again, maybe she would. But of one thing she was certain: if Riley came and tried to check her into hospital, he'd find himself in a fight. In the meantime, in this period of calm before his return, she might as well continue to reap the pleasures of independent anonymity. For this might be the last opportunity she ever had to breathe in the sights and sounds of a place away from Fairmount, as if she were taking in a grand bazaar on a senior's tour. She noted:

i.   music over the speakers, a jazz mix that would have suited a coffee shop;

ii.   the magenta bobble-wool jacket draped over a woman's shoulder;

iii.   the receptionist, attending to the line of visitors and patients; and

iv. an old fellow in baggy trousers, seated with his empty pockets hanging open and his zip fly puckered and pilled.

Stella took a seat near the door Sharon and Bethie had left through, whence she could watch the entrance in case Riley drove by. She smiled at the woman with the camel coat that matched her hair, who was still waiting with admirable patience. The woman took off her coat and hung it over the back of her chair so that it covered the red leather handbag Stella so envied.

Also still waiting, but without the same placidity, was the young mother in stretch pants and bucket boots engaged in following her daughter protectively around the waiting room. Stella noted the padding under the stretch pants' rear, which she identified now as protective cushioning for bicycle riding. She gave the mother extra points for environmental as well as parental responsibility. Just so did Stella used to follow her own daughter Junie around the park where she played. However, Junie had been a well-behaved paragon compared to this little girl in the red hoodie. The child tore around the waiting area at a pace no grown athlete could match. Stella marvelled now, as she'd always done, how children's short legs moved with swift power, light as a bird, muscles firm as a fish.

The little girl darted up and down the aisles, put up her red hood and took it down, brushed with her shoulder the top of the empty-pocket man's grey fringe of hair, knocked the camel-coat woman's red leather handbag off her chair, and then ducked behind the bobble-jacket woman. At last, her trailing mother appeared to lose energy, stopped still in her bucket boots, and walked towards the doorway. Two cars pulled up, and new patients and family members climbed out. The police officer, now near the door, stood aside to let them through. The stretch-panted mother stepped aside to let the new patients and their small entourages pass.

Once they'd cleared the door, she stared around the waiting room and called, "Maxie?"

Patients and visitors around the waiting area straightened a little in their seats.

"Where are you, Maxie?" The woman spoke in loud, worried tones to the waiting area at large. "It's my daughter. She was here, and now she isn't."

Everybody craned and twisted to look about them. Stella studied the spot where she'd just seen Maxie hiding behind the woman with the camel-hair coat, but if the child was still there, Stella couldn't see her.

The camel-hair woman appeared not to see her either.

The bobble-jacket woman said, "You know, she was just here, running around. She's probably down the corridor."

The mother turned fiercely to reply. "She wouldn't run off. That wouldn't be like Maxie at all."

Stella privately felt that Maxie was exactly the sort of independent-minded kindergarten-aged child who ran off on her own, the sort of child who, in her experience, darted among the bushes at recess time while teachers coaxed them in firm tones back to the classroom. However, Maxie's mother no doubt knew her daughter.

Her child was missing. This was a real problem that put Fairmount's mysteries in the shade. It was not a crime. Not yet. And perhaps Stella could be of assistance. Forty years of dealing with little children like Maxie, along with her more recent experience investigating problems and crimes at Fairmount Manor, made her uniquely qualified to investigate the little girl's disappearance.

"My child is missing." Maxie's mother sounded more worried still. She held out her arms towards the seated patients and visitors. "Can't you people look around you?"

Stella hurried towards Maxie's mother. Out of the corner of her eye she saw that despite a growing queue in front of the kiosk, the receptionist was also on the move, exiting her station, one palm raised to keep in place the waiting patients.

Stella moved more quickly, still in her good lace-up shoes (heaven knew how difficult those big bucket boots would be to walk in) to reach Maxie's mother before the receptionist could.

"I'll help you look." Stella squeezed Maxie's mom's arm comfortingly. "How old is your daughter? That will help us find her. That and her red hoodie."

"Maxie is only five."

"Oh, my goodness, they're so adventurous at that age, aren't they?"

"Not Maxie."

"Of course," Stella murmured. But her sleuthing mind remembered the way Maxie had darted about, swift and bright, with a complete disregard for bumping into older persons on their chairs. Once again, she recalled a top tenet of all investigations, which declared that most witnesses, including relatives, were entirely unreliable and sometimes even dishonest.

The receptionist approached. If Stella weren't so grateful to the receptionist for the information she'd given Stella regarding Thelma's likely whereabouts, she might have felt an even deeper chagrin at having her investigation interrupted so swiftly.

The receptionist looked from Stella to Maxie's mom. "Did I hear you say your child is missing?"

Maxie's mother covered her eyes. "I came to visit my Aunt Linda, but she was asleep. We were waiting, and now this happens ..."

"We don't know that anything has happened, but we'll get on this immediately, of course. Where have you looked?"

"Just here." Maxie's mother covered her face with trembling hands. "Just around here. Maxie wouldn't go far."

"You haven't looked anywhere else?"

Maxie's mother shook her head behind her hands, and the receptionist directed an irritated look at Stella. Stella deduced from the glance that hospital receptionists held the same low regard for witnesses that sleuths did.

Stella said, "Maxie is wearing a red hoodie, and she's five."

"Oh, that kid. Sure. I remember her. I'll put out a heads up on the address system. Dr Dupray is our code for a lost child. We take this very seriously. Maxie will be fine."

"Easy for you to say," Maxie's mom muttered.

Stella thanked the receptionist, who stepped smartly away back to her kiosk and picked up the phone. Even though all address systems broadcasts were difficult to grasp when one's ears were over eighty, Stella made out *Dr Dupray* and *red hoodie*.

The police officer re-entered reception, a few crumbs from his early lunch dotting his jacket breast. He strode past Stella and Maxie's mother to the sliding door and fiddled with an electrical box next to it, which, Stella supposed, locked the door. He pulled out a cell phone and spoke quietly into it.

Stella decided she could hardly have improved on the hospital's organization in the face of a sudden if uncertain emergency. In fact, she felt the same sort of satisfaction Hercule Poirot would have felt when Scotland Yard, despite its reluctance to cooperate with a private detective, covered the basics while he made the profound discoveries and deductions necessary to the case. She had noticed that a great difficulty with being a sleuth outside the legal system was getting the authorities to do one's bidding. But here stood the police officer, a little dozy perhaps after his sandwiches, but chock-full of authority and so big he would have made a good hockey goalie. Stella hoped the nurse appreciated his charms.

While the police officer locked down reception, Maxie's mother searched the far reaches of the area, beyond the seated patients. She peered around drinking water machines and under several tables spread with medical information booklets (*Dementia: What Can You Do About It?* caught Stella's eye) while patients and visitors stood to help her or twisted in their seats to watch her search. Stella followed Maxie's mother, thinking hard about the mystery of the child's disappearance. For, although it was likely that a simple search would turn up Maxie in whatever hidey-hole the child had crawled into, it was not a certainty. What if the child had been taken? What sort of a crime would this be? That obvious worry came to mind, as it undoubtedly had occurred to everybody here.

But Stella, as a career educator, was perfectly aware of the statistics regarding abductions by strangers. They were extremely rare. Furthermore, the obviously well-trained staff members searching the hospital (courtesy of *Dr Dupray*) were best placed to rescue Maxie if such were somehow the case. She considered the possible reasons for Maxie's disappearance.

Thesis: Kidnapping for money was out of the question, for Maxie's mother was obviously not in funds. You only had to look at those seedy, too-big bucket boots to know that.

However, the child might have been abducted by a family member, for example, Maxie's estranged father, if such a person existed. Even so, why would a parent kidnap his own child from a hospital, of all well-staffed places? And the clincher against this possibility was that if there was the slightest chance of such a family-based crime, Maxie's mother would certainly be broadcasting it widely.

Therefore, either the child had left on her own, or she'd been taken somewhere by somebody. Stella tried to think of a third option but could not.

Stella trailed Maxie's mother, who was now bent over, searching the waiting room at a knee-level view. She pulled back coats hanging on chairs and shoved handbags aside, peering under seating and between shoes. This was not a bad bit of searching.

After all, the child was only five, and it was just possible that she'd curled up under one of the longer coats hanging there. She might even have fallen asleep. Maxie's mom crawled on the carpet and left handbags swinging as she passed, while patients and visitors stood up out of her way.

Stella stopped following Maxie's mother around the room. Instead, she stood and studied the woman's progress. If Stella didn't know Maxie's mother was searching for her little daughter, she might have thought something rather different was going on. Witness that red handbag, expensive as all get out, swinging back and forth behind the camel-coated woman. It was not the only handbag hanging off the back of a visitor's chair. Stella walked closer to the camel-coated woman.

Yes, if Stella didn't know Maxie's mother was searching high and low — especially low — for her daughter, Stella might have thought the woman was rifling through handbags and maybe even coat pockets.

Maxie's mom returned to the centre of the room. Tearful and distraught, she turned towards the corridor leading to the café and elevators.

And it was from this direction that her child's voice piped up, calling for her mother. The little girl in her Red Riding hoodie skipped into reception. She held the pretty nurse by the hand, and at the sight, the police officer's face lit up as brightly as Maxie's mother's.

"There you are," Maxie's mother said.

"There I am." Maxie laughed.

"You're very naughty to run off. Come here."

Maxie ran to her mother, who took her in her arms. The child settled on her hip, looped an arm around her neck, and smiled around the room. The room smiled back.

Stella leaned down to the camel-coated woman. She murmured, "Better just check your handbag, don't you think?"

She checked her own pockets for the wads of bills Vaughn had given her and was reassured to find all as it should be.

The camel-coated woman looked sharply at Stella and reached for her bag. Several other visitors looked up and had obviously overheard; the advice would spread without any further input from her.

Stella approached Maxie's mom, Maxie, and the police officer.

She smiled at Maxie. "Just a little girl's hide-and-seek game, I'm relieved to see."

Maxie's mom shot her a frazzled glance. "I'm going to take this kid home and put her to bed."

"She says it," the little girl said, laughing, "but she doesn't mean it."

The police officer smiled at the pair. "I'm sure your mother will have a talk with you about running off."

He turned to open the door. Stella took the opportunity to look back and see how the women with their handbags were coming along. Several had pulled out wallets and were leafing through them. So, wallets had not been taken. But then, where would the woman have concealed such bulky items?

Stella said to Maxie's mother, "But you haven't had your treatment yet?"

Maxie's mom frowned. "Treatment …?"

"Not a treatment, then?"

The police officer pressed buttons and unfastened the door.

It whisked open, and Maxie's mother thanked the police officer.

"You say thank you too, Maxie."

Maxie, merry-eyed, did as she was asked.

Stella stepped between the woman and the doorway. "Or did you say you were here to visit somebody?"

"Aunt Lena, but she won't mind."

"Didn't you say Aunt Linda?" Stella smiled. "I probably got it wrong—my memory isn't my very best friend. Would you like me to give your aunt a message? What's her last name?"

"Don't bother, please. I'll phone her from—"

A wordless shout of discovery from the visitors' seating interrupted. The police officer turned to look.

The woman in the camel coat held up her wallet. "They're gone—they're not here."

"What's not here?" the police officer asked. "Is there another problem?"

Maxie's mom attempted to step through the door.

"It's always something, isn't it?" Stella stepped in front of Maxie's mother. "I'm so glad you're both all right, dear."

"Thank you so much." Maxie's mom sidestepped Stella.

Stella stepped back and had a little stumble. She held on to Maxie's mother's arm for balance.

The woman with the bobble jacket stood up. Her handbag hung open. "Mine are gone too."

"What's gone? Your wallet?"

"Not my wallet," the bobble jacket woman said.

"That woman took my credit cards," the camel-coated woman said. "Maxie's mother. She was playing around with the handbags."

"I did not take anything." Maxie's mother attempted to remove Stella's hand, but Stella held on tight and tottered again for good measure.

"She took mine too." The woman in the bobble jacket gazed around the seating area. "Everybody, check your bags and pockets."

Maxie's mother freed herself from Stella's grip, but by this time the police officer had the door shut and locked again.

Maxie's mother set her child down on the entry mat and turned around to show no pockets in her bicycle pants and no handbag.

"See? I haven't got anything."

"That's quite a trick to travel so lightly," Stella said. "Don't you have keys and licence for a car? And money for parking?"

"I have a bicycle. What's that got to do with anything?" Maxie's mom demanded.

"It's interesting, that's all. And may I say, good for you for saving the environment. But, heavens, where do you keep your bike lock keys?"

"It's a combination lock. May I go now?" Maxie's mother asked testily.

"In a minute." The police officer was nodding at a third woman, waving her wallet above her head. "You too, ma'am?"

"She was right behind me, flinging my coat around."

"I was looking for my child," Maxie's mom insisted. "You can see that I have nothing. Maxie, turn out your pockets."

Maxie did so.

The police officer, Stella, and the rest of the room watched Maxie retrieve a cell phone, which she handed to her mother, and which the police officer took in his turn. Maxie pulled her empty pockets inside out and shook them.

Stella said, "You did that very well, Maxie. Not every five-year-old knows just how to turn out their pockets when asked, do they?"

"Not without some practice, I guess," the police officer said.

He looked from Maxie to Maxie's mother, and to Maxie's mother's capacious bucket boots.

Stella followed his gaze. She said, "I don't think she'd be carrying anything in her boots, do you? She wasn't walking with a limp."

"Take off your boots," the police officer said.

Maxie's mother complied with rather good grace, Stella thought.

The visitors and patients watched with increasing restlessness, and Stella overheard the receptionist calling security.

"See?" Maxie's mother shook her boots upside down. "Now are you satisfied? Please be good enough to open that door."

Stella stepped between the three of them and the door. "You might want to check those stretch pants. They're very tight, and I'm sure it's the sportive fashion, but, with apologies for my tactlessness, the padded backside could hide quite a few small flat items."

"Nothing shows." The police officer peered at the rear of the woman's stretch pants.

"Those are bicycle pants," Stella clarified. "They are tight, and they are padded. The cards wouldn't show, would they?"

Maxie's mother paled. Maxie took hold of her leg and stared at the four newly arriving, uniformed hospital personnel nearing the little group at reception's doorway. The camel-coated woman appeared intent on joining them, along with several others. Stella couldn't blame any of them for the intensity of their feelings: not Maxie's mother, or her victims, or the uniformed staff who would transition all of them into the legal system. Her own feelings were equally intense, if differently focused.

Mystery solved, she wished now to escape the drama and be out of the way before names were taken and statements required. And birth dates written down.

But escape would not be easy, for the women Maxie's mother had robbed assembled now around Stella like bridesmaids around a bride, if the bride wore a fleece warm-up suit.

The camel-coated woman and the woman with the bobble jacket hugged Stella. "You are certainly the smartest person here today."

The former nodded fiercely. "I would have been home before I noticed my cards missing if you hadn't spoken up."

"I'm so glad." Stella backed a step towards the door. "It's very nice of you to say so."

"Not at all …"

"We're in your debt."

Stella took another step towards the door. "Anybody would have done the same. I just happened to notice what was going on …"

Laughter from all around Stella.

"… did you just happen to notice …?"

"... observed, that's what you did ..."

"... like some kind of detective ..."

"... lots more than the real police did ..."

This last came sotto voce from the camel-coated woman.

Sharon of the swollen ankles and Aunt Bethie reappeared in reception, eyes agog, and joined Stella's crew of admirers at the door.

"Did we miss some fun?" Sharon asked. "What happened when we were gone?"

The camel-coated woman said, "If you were here earlier, you should check your bags to see if your credit cards are still in your wallet."

"Mine are." Bethie held out a brown waxed paper bag, a little spotted with oil or butter. "I just used one to buy Stella this. To say thank you for holding our place in line."

Stella took the bag. "How nice of you. What is it?"

Before Bethie could answer, the camel-coated woman brought the new arrivals up to date with the tale of Maxie's mother, Maxie, and the credit cards. The group watched the police officer enlist a female member of staff security to address the issue of the swag-concealing stretch bicycle pants. She put on disposable gloves. Without violating any laws of decency, she rescued several cards from their padded hiding place just below Maxie's mother's waist.

Maxie's mom snatched her cell phone back from the police officer. "I'm calling my lawyer."

"Your first good idea, miss. Ask him to meet us at the police station."

"You just keep your hands off my bum."

And at the word *bum*, Maxie giggled. Her laugh was so infectious that the robbery victims giggled too, along with the staff, police officer, Sharon, and Bethie.

Stella sneaked another look at the door in time to see Riley's car tear up to the door and stop.

She murmured, "The clock strikes midnight, Cinderella."

If Ollie had been here, he would have named her *Cinder-Stella*.

"What did you say?" Sharon asked.

"Just goodbye, and how much I enjoyed meeting you two. And thanks for this." Stella held up the paper bag Bethie had given her. She turned her back on the milling visitors, patients, staff, and Maxie with her criminal mom.

The police officer opened the door for her, and as she passed through to the drive where Riley was lowering the window of his car, she felt no longer like an astronaut, but rather like an outer space traveller leaving one world for another, blasting from the pull of civilization towards the heavier gravity of Fairmount Manor. She didn't want to put herself back into Riley's sphere of control. But where else could she go? Thelma was still in a hospital, which the receptionist had told her was very likely downtown, forty minutes away with average traffic. She had to remove herself from the pull of hospital reception. Even then, Riley was not Stella's first choice for a chauffeur.

But needs must. She finished the old saying to herself with a chuckle.

Just now the young devil of a care worker had one arm hanging out his window, and he was looking at her with disfavour.

She said, "Well, here you are. I guess you had to go quite a ways to find a gas station."

"Sure. Why aren't you inside? I said I'd meet you inside. We've got to get you checked in."

"Well, I told them not to bother, because I'm feeling much better now."

"Like hell. I'll need to find parking again. Get in. Next stop: Emergency."

"I'm completely fine again."

"That's beside the point. We'll do what we were told to do, you and I." He huffed an impatient breath.

Stella caught a hint of something in his tone, and then a hint of something else in his exhalation that had not been there before.

Before she could be certain of its provenance, the reception door opened again, and the accompanying rush of air dissipated the suspicious smell. Sharon and Bethie stepped outside and joined her on the sidewalk beside Riley's car.

"Oh, good, we caught you," Sharon said. "That police officer wants to talk to you before you go."

"Police officer?" Riley stared from Sharon to Bethie and then past them at reception's doors. "What happened with a police officer? What did you do, Mrs Ryman?"

Bethie said, "She didn't *do* anything. Is this your ride, Stella?"

Bethie and Sharon leaned close to the open driver's window to peer inside. Close enough that, when they pulled away, they exchanged a knowing look.

Sharon said, "Stella's a heroine, actually. Come and talk to the police officer."

Stella said, "I don't think I need to —"

"No, she doesn't," Riley said, but he said it to the backs of the two women who were hurrying into reception. Sharon had a hand raised towards the police officer.

Stella leaned closer to see whether she had or had not imagined the new odour emanating from Riley.

Riley said, "Please, Mrs Ryman, let me take you to Emergency."

"Just a minute, please." Stella had not, after all, imagined it. And now, having smelled what she smelled, she would not need to convince him, trick him, or trap him into helping her.

She could blackmail him. What a relief.

She said, "I have somewhere else I'd like you to drive me now."

"Excuse me?" Riley put his head out the window. "I'm not driving you anywhere except Emergency—and then back to Fairmount when the doctors are finished with you."

"You've been to the pub, haven't you?"

"For a sandwich and coffee …" His eyebrows rose, which body language Stella recognized; it meant he was telling a lie. In this case, a lie of omission.

She said, "And beer. More than one, I'd guess, from your breath."

"I haven't."

"You have. Don't argue. It's as plain on you as if you'd painted your nose purple. Are you able to drive properly?"

"Of course, I am."

Stella nodded. "Well, I'll have to take your word for it."

"Thanks for nothing, Mrs Ryman."

"You're equally welcome, Riley. Now, let's not fight. I need you to drive me downtown."

The door behind them opened again, and this time Sharon and Bethie had the police officer between them.

The police officer said, "Mrs Ryman, I appreciate your help with those credit card robberies. Good observation, well done."

"Help is hardly the word," Sharon said. "Stella solved the whole thing for you. Maxie's mother must be playing that little scam in waiting rooms all around town."

"Stella gave you the thief on a plate," Bethie added.

"I said thank you. Now, Mrs Ryman, I want a word with

your driver." The policeman walked over to Riley's car. Sharon and Bethie stood next to Stella with their arms crossed, and the look they gave Riley was anything but pleasant.

The police officer said, "Please get out of the car, sir."

Riley said, "Damn."

The police officer opened the driver's door, and Riley climbed out. He didn't look at Stella or the two women beside her. He looked at the sidewalk, as if he were measuring it for a drunk test.

"Did you drive here, sir?" the police officer asked.

There was no other way he could have arrived on the scene in his car. Riley sighed and nodded.

"I'll have to ask you to come with me," the police officer told him. "You'll take a breathalyzer."

Riley said, "But what about my passenger? I have to take Mrs Ryman to Emergency."

Sharon spoke up. "You're not taking Stella anywhere, you day-drinker driver. Here's where you get towed."

Riley gestured to the car. "This is a classic Saab. Let me take off the brake, or you'll wreck it if you tow it."

"I'm sure Mrs Ryman can drive it for you," the police officer said.

"That's a fine idea," Bethie said. "You don't need this fellow at all, Stella. Imagine him offering you a ride and then drinking beers."

Sharon said, "There are laws about that, I think."

Riley said, "Mrs Ryman can't drive."

Now it came.

"She's over eighty and demented. Although not as demented as some," he added in an apparent attempt to be fair. "She lives in Fairmount Care Home. She can't be out on her own."

Bethie said, "What a crock. She's sixty-nine."

"What?" Riley said. "She's not. She's never—"

"She totally is. You're so obviously over the limit, guy." Sharon turned to the police officer. "He's not allowed to drive Stella anywhere, is he?"

"Not in his condition. He can wait inside with the credit card thief."

"You're all nuts. I wash my hands." Riley let the police officer lead him away.

Bethie opened the car door for Stella. Sharon handed her a business card. "Call us some time, won't you?"

Bethie nodded at the paper bag in Stella's hand. "And have a good lunch."

"But don't eat and drive," Sharon joked.

Stella climbed into the driver's seat of Riley's old Saab and set the bag Bethie had given her down on the passenger seat beside her. She had always driven standard—it had been a point of pride with her throughout her life to drive only standard cars—but today she was not unhappy to see that Riley's car was an automatic. She had three bridges to drive over to reach downtown, and honestly, she'd never thought to be behind the wheel of a car again.

Soldier on, Stella.

Stella imagined Thelma, all alone in a hospital bed, her small body pressed nearly flat by heavy white sheets folded back at her neck. Thelma, tiny and fragile, hot in temper.

She would be terrified that she would leave the hospital with her hip repaired—but feet first in her red silk slippers, deceased, and soon forgotten by the world outside Fairmount, if not by her friends there.

Stella adjusted the rear-view mirror of Riley's Saab. A police car pulled up just behind her, warning lights flashing. Two police officers climbed out of their vehicle and entered the hospital. Stella saw the handcuffs clipped to their back pockets, shiny and circular, looking like odd kitchen gadgets that measured, perhaps, large servings of spaghetti. She peered up through the driver's window at Sharon and Bethie and returned their farewell waves. Inside reception, a small crowd milled around Maxie's mother, Riley, and the police officers that had joined the group. What a flurry of justice she'd helped to loose upon the hospital. She should have felt victory, or possibly guilt. But she did not, for it was all in a day's work for an amateur sleuth.

Now. Hang on, Thelma. I'm coming.

Stella checked her side mirror and reached down for the lever that pulled her seat closer to the steering wheel. It was all coming back to her now.

She touched her brake with an experimental toe and moved the transmission to drive.

Chapter Four
Stella Takes the Wheel

Stella leaned forward over the shabby leather-covered steering wheel of the somewhat stolen Saab she was driving northward through the city in her search for Thelma Hu. Ahead, a red light turned green above the northbound lane, sending a few lucky lunchtime drivers through the junction that should, in the fullness of time, lead her to the first of the bridges, and then downtown. It had been several years — and one institutionalization into Fairmount Manor Care Home's driverless culture — since she had last travelled this road. It was no wonder she felt shaky; she was an elderly, rusty driver who'd eaten no lunch. However, even an escaped care home resident was no worse than this fool on her left, who was tailgating a purple van while signalling right. Such a move would, if she read his intentions correctly, take him directly into the Saab's driver-side door. She frowned out of her window and waved the driver away. He responded by steering closer to her. She waved again, with the more imperious wave she had used in her days as an elementary-school teacher and librarian, when the end of recess found a few students still swinging from the monkey bars, oblivious to the movements of others and the passage of time.

Ahead, the light turned red again. The driver on her left buzzed down his passenger-side window. Stella opened hers.

The driver grinned at her. "Are you going to let me in, darling?"

Darling. Some things in the great world she'd thought she'd left forever didn't change. Some she missed, like hamburgers and garlic soup, but she did not miss fellows like this one, who snapped endearments at you like elastic bands off a ruler.

She said, "You will observe that our two lanes are moving at about the same rate of speed. I can't see why I should let you into this lane. Unless, of course, you're turning right up ahead. Are you?"

"No."

"Then you're exactly where you should be." She rolled up the window.

The light turned green, and she and her neighbour moved ahead perhaps a dozen car lengths. He gestured at her to roll down her window again, and she did so.

He said, "I think I will turn right after all. Let me in now?"

She shot him an even look. "I tell you what—let's switch places."

"What, in line?"

"No," Stella said. "I'll get out and drive your car, and you can drive mine. Then you'll be in my lane. What do you think?"

The driver rolled up his window.

Stella drove the old Saab towards the first bridge with the irritating driver just behind her left bumper. It was the perfect spot for him, out of her sight and hearing. Four cars ahead of her, the next stoplight turned red again, leaving her perfectly placed for the next green light. It was warm in the Saab, and Stella hung her elbow out the open driver's window in the manner of James Dean.

The obnoxious driver pulled up beside her. Clearly, he'd had time to think up some new jibe, for he rolled down his window again.

"Are you all right in there?"

"Yes, thanks," Stella said. "One more green light and I think we're good to go over the bridge."

"I only ask because your car seems very much past its prime."

"It's doing very well, actually."

"I only ask because it's so very *old*."

Stella blinked.

He continued, "It's just that I worry that you're going to break down in traffic. Because, you know, of very old age. For a car, I mean."

Stella tightened her hands on the Saab's distressed leather–covered steering wheel. This fellow was a bit too accurate with his barbs.

She said, "Thanks for your worry. Really, I'm fine."

He said, "A car as old as that ought to be called by her first name. Have you named it?"

"I suppose I ought to name it," Stella said peaceably.

"Here's a good name — the *Old Grey Mare*," the other driver said.

When on earth was the light going to change? Stella squinted at the road ahead where cars still raced across the east-west route.

But was that the walk sign winking orange? Hope rose in her heart. She felt like Daedalus, poised on the ledge, preparing to fly.

"This Saab is a he," Stella said. "His name —"

"How about *Oldstermobile?*"

"His name …" Stella ransacked her brain for a name of glory. "This Saab's name is *Icarus*."

"Icarus?" The driver raised his eyebrows. "I saw that cartoon. Didn't he drop dead out of the sky? What a loser."

The light changed. Traffic moved, and the Saab pulled a little ahead of the rude fellow before he passed her again. She called out, "Icarus is a story of success, actually, not failure. He flew, didn't he?"

She would have added, *and every story ends in death eventually, just like every success,* but by the time she thought of saying this to him, he was darting in and out of the lanes ahead of her, rather like Icarus himself, if Icarus had been a snappy, discourteous middle-aged man.

She powered through the green light and drove along the causeway towards the next bridge that lay between her and the downtown hospital, where she intended to seek out Thelma Hu and take her home.

Traffic on the feeder road for the second bridge was no speedier than the first, and Stella's (and Riley's) Saab moved ahead in stops and starts. Warm air, heavily scented with vehicular odours, was augmented by the midday sun's warmth through the window. Nonetheless, Stella felt grateful for Icarus's comfortable leather seats, and for the fact that her driver's licence had not yet expired. She had the right to drive, then, although not the card that proved her right. She had no idea where she'd left her licence. Maybe in the rubbish bin, where she'd tossed away all the other paperwork of her lifetime, a few months back when she sold everything to live at Fairmount Manor. But, if she understood the internet correctly, her right to drive was somewhere out there in the ether, ripe for reclaiming anytime she liked.

She roared the engine, jumped forward a metre or so, and remembered that the Saab was an automatic and ought not to roar. She remembered the time, thirty years past, when she'd been rear-ended on this same bridge by a drunk who'd stopped, apologized, and then driven off into a lamppost. She had climbed out of her smacked Fiat and awaited help with her back to the bridge rails, while the rush of traffic tugged at her skirts. Which all went to prove that there had always been worse drivers than Stella out on the road.

Her stomach growled. Breakfast was a distant memory of brown toast and packet marmalade shared with Thelma and the Greek Chorus back at Fairmount. Now her appetite was out in the real world and demanding real-world sustenance. She hadn't been this hungry since the autumn of 1973, when she'd done the eggs-only diet, and she could almost smell the corned beef Kaiser bun with which she'd broken that diet once and for all.

Traffic stopped, and she looked out the windshield at a low-flying seagull with a bit of food in its beak. She smelled corned beef again and remembered that during all the red-hooded and Riley-flavoured kerfuffle back at the hospital, Sharon and Bethie had brought her a gift from the café. They had handed her a waxed paper bag just before the police officer had led that feckless, beer-soaked, occasionally well-meaning care worker Riley away for his DUI testing. She risked a glance to the seat on her right and, sure enough, there was the brown bag she'd been given. The oily spots on the paper promised stains on the upholstery. Happily, they heralded as well an exuberant, fatty feed of the sort not to be found on Fairmount Manor luncheon plates.

With her left hand ready on the steering wheel, she reached inside the bag, pulled out a toasted baguette, and glimpsed a red flash of corned beef within. And just at that thrilling moment, somebody behind Stella honked.

She saw that the cars ahead of her were merging left. She set the baguette down and fumbled with her left turn signal. In the distance a police siren keened, and she checked the Saab's speedometer, but Icarus was travelling, like everybody else, at a prim 32 kilometres an hour.

A moment later she saw the reason for the slowdown: a police check at the end of an HOV lane. The midday sun shone down upon the black brim of the police officer's cap so that it glistened like the patent-leather pumps she had given her daughter Junie for her eighth birthday, many decades ago. And then, in its happily unaccountable way, traffic sped up and cars lapped and were in turn lapped, all of them moving together northward, with Icarus the Saab pulled along like a bead on a string.

Stella made a conscious effort to lower her shoulders and breathe slowly. She eased her grip on the steering wheel and pressed her toe harder on the gas pedal.

At the far end of the second bridge, Stella steered Icarus the Saab down the off-ramp in a glory of competence at the wheel. The nearly shadowless noontide darkened as she descended, and she noted as well that her bones felt rain coming, and coming on fast — as fast as the cars, speeding to either side of her now that they were off the bridge. Stella felt pure driver's delight at the ease with which she and Icarus kept pace with those around her.

Even better, her sleuth's mind deduced a swift path northbound to Thelma Hu, who waited for Stella without knowing that she was waiting for Stella. Thelma, who would be cursing the delay in her rescue and return to Fairmount Manor.

Stella changed lanes and passed a bus.

"Well done, Icarus," she murmured.

It made her feel a little giddy, talking aloud to a car without any worry that a care worker with rubber-soled shoes might slink up behind her, as so often happened in the serpentine corridors of Fairmount Manor. If care workers could hear her talking to Icarus now, they would think her gaga. Even Reliza, the kindest of them, or Cheryl of the Giaconda smile, would think she was losing her mind, chatting with a car.

"But I'm not losing my mind," Stella told Icarus the Saab. "I always used to talk to my cars — to my Chryslers, my Toyotas, my Hondas — and I would point out sights of interest. Or sing to them. Chryslers like Crosby, did you know? And Toyotas and Hondas enjoy Doris Day and Dinah Shore. What about Saabs? Do you like a little travelling music?"

She patted the radio knob, which came on with the local news, and patted it off again. Icarus's steering wheel slipped under her hand, and she narrowly missed winging the car next to her. She accepted what she considered a well-deserved bird from its driver.

"Sorry," she told its taillights.

On her right, three buses passed, big and noisy as aircraft on runways. And then the speed feast ended and the first of a busy series of traffic lights on the northbound avenue turned red.

"I'll sing to you while we wait for the light to change," she told Icarus. She sang 'Moon River' because, like everybody, she knew the words, and because it was a song about people who were stuck in their lane in the traffic of life. On the other side of the dashboard, beneath its battered hood, the Saab contributed a rattling percussion. It sounded as if something might be wrong with the motor, but not too wrong, because when the light changed, she and Icarus moved forward ten car lengths while 'Moon River' ran wide, and the Saab hummed and flammed along. Another police siren sounded nearby, and it fit the descant pretty well.

The sky opened over the city. The rain added its own rhythms as it drummed the windshield. Signs and traffic lights merged into smears of colour against the grey city sky and street.

"Where do you keep your wipers?" Stella asked Icarus. She flipped a switch, inadvertently turned the emergency blinker on and off, beeped the horn, and found the wiper lever, all in a crazy five seconds. "Life with you is never dull," she said.

Icarus waved its windshield wipers at her like a fevered warning signal. *Stop, stop, stop.* Meanwhile, the traffic light showed green.

She was almost through the intersection when she observed that the cars to the front, back, and right of her were all police vehicles. Her neck stiffened. She wished to see whether any of the police officers in their squad cars and vans were looking her way, but the rain poured down harder and there was no way to tell.

Her heart pounded, and her vision dimmed. She followed the blurry vehicle ahead of her and went through the light at the end of the yellow. The police cars travelled with her, and she and Icarus were boxed in. Lights nearby flashed red.

She was certain she'd be pulled over. But the uniformed drivers were only indicating a change of lane and a right turn. No siren sounded. In her relief, she wondered whether she should turn right with them. She liked a right turn.

She was shaking with more than hunger now, and it was all she could do to keep her eyes on the police car bumper and her hands on the wheel. Once all the police cars had turned east, she decided that she must pull over. It was all parallel parking along this section of shops, nail bars, and sushi cafés, but she spotted two empty spaces together and nosed towards the curb. She set the parking brake and leaned her head against the steering wheel.

Footsteps approached the passenger-side window, and the sound of rapping on glass brought Stella out of her funk. She jerked her head up from the wheel and peered at the window. The downpour had stopped. Sun poured into the Saab through the rain-streaked windshield. The rapping sounded again. She wondered who might be anxious enough to demand her attention on such a busy street. Did somebody want a ride? She fervently hoped not.

Who would tap on a stranger's window, anyway? If only it was not a police officer. The tapping grew louder. But not loud enough for the law.

Stella felt dog-tired and about a million years old. She longed to close her eyes and let the tapper give up and move off, but she had learned early in her life that the true test of character was behaving agreeably towards others when all you really wanted was to get a cup of tea and pull the afternoon in around you. So, she wiped her face with the collar of her shirt, rolled down the rain-smeared passenger window, and said hello to the figure outside on the sidewalk.

Two figures, rather: a man and a woman. The man bent down to look across at Stella. Behind him, the young woman's wet hair fell into her eyes, and she pushed it back. She wore a big black raincoat that didn't disguise her very advanced pregnancy. Was the woman at her full nine months? One couldn't inquire, of course. Stella recalled that she had recently driven away from a hospital. She tried to remember where it was. She supposed she could find it again, if this young woman needed her to transport her there.

Stella asked, "Do you need help?"

The man said, "I was going to ask you the same question. Are you all right? You looked like you were ... upset."

"Crying," the woman added. "My husband and I wondered, are you hurt?"

"I wasn't really crying," Stella said. Her answer sounded untrue even to herself, and furthermore her cheeks were wet. "I must just be very tired indeed. Thanks for your concern."

She expected the young couple would move away from the car, but they didn't.

"I don't want to intrude," the man said. "It's just you're parked about a foot and a half from the curb."

"It doesn't seem safe," the woman added.

"And you're in danger of stepping directly into traffic."

"It's scary parking in this kind of traffic," the young woman said. "I park too far out all the time too."

Stella looked at the traffic outside the driver's window. The cars whiskered by her side mirror. She blinked, and her vision went blurry as it so often did under stress. A bus rattled the Saab as it passed, a hand's width away, and she heard the hiss of big tires on the wet blacktop. Stella peered into her rear-view at the stream of traffic.

She said, "You're thoughtful. And correct. It doesn't seem safe. I'll just pull back into the empty space behind, I think, and narrow the gap ..."

She put the Saab into reverse.

The young man and his wife uttered simultaneous shouts of warning. "Stop! The space isn't empty."

Stella looked over her shoulder and saw they were right. She felt herself colour. "Oh dear, I'll just …"

She opened the driver's door to climb outside, and the two shouted again. Traffic whizzed by. It could have taken off the Saab's door.

The young man said, "You could have killed yourself stepping into traffic. Wait a minute." He walked around the front of the car and stood until the traffic flow stopped. He helped Stella out of the car and led her around the Saab and onto the sidewalk to his wife. "Would you like me to park your car for you?"

Stella had experienced the effects of morphine when she long ago gave birth to Junie, and the surge of cool relief at the young man's offer felt much the same. "That would be kind, thank you."

He returned to the Saab and sat behind the wheel.

The young woman took hold of Stella's arm in a comforting manner while her husband manoeuvred the Saab with swift jagged reversals closer to the curb. Once the car was pulled up tight and straight, he waited while a bus pulled into a stop a little farther along the street, then took advantage of a break in the traffic to exit the car. He came round the back, Stella's keys in hand.

The young woman said, "I don't think she's well at all. Maybe we could call someone."

Stella said, "No, thank you."

"Okay." The pregnant young woman and her husband exchanged a glance.

Stella said cautiously, "I have an idea that I'm not myself because I'm hungry."

"Let's get you something," the husband suggested. "Do you like sushi, dear?"

So soon after being *darling*-ed by the lane-changing elder-baiting fellow, Stella noted with surprise that just now the word *dear* didn't sting. Perhaps the explanation was that, at this moment, beside the great buzzing insect that was city traffic, these two strangers were a little bit dear to her too. In a we-are-the-world, hands-across-the-generations sense. This thought ought to have cheered Stella, but she felt too weak to be happy. And her fatigue made her too fuzzy to be certain she was not asking too much of this kind couple of strangers.

"Goodness, I couldn't possibly take advantage, but thank you."

"You must eat something, though."

The husband nodded at the Saab. "What about the lunch bag on the passenger seat?" He leaned into the car, partially unwrapped the baguette in its paper bag without touching the food, picked it up, and sniffed it. "This smells fine. Corned beef?"

"I thought it might be corned beef," Stella said cautiously.

"You'd better take it, hadn't you?"

"Heavens." Stella took the sandwich in its wrapping in her two hands. "It's enormous. Would you like some?" She held it out.

"No thanks." He looked at his wife. "What about some coffee?"

His wife nodded. "Good idea." She darted off, graceful for a pregnant woman. Stella wondered if she'd taken dance lessons when young. She was going to ask, but instead took a bite of the sandwich. She chewed and swallowed.

The young man asked, "How's that?"

"Very good indeed. And it's going straight to every cell in my body," she said.

"Coffee will do you good too. Here. Sit on your passenger seat with your feet on the sidewalk."

Stella let him help her sit inside on the bucket seat with her feet resting on the sidewalk. She worked on her sandwich while the young man watched, dangling Stella's car keys from one hand. The young woman returned with two small paper cups that smelled of dark-roast beans. She gave one cup to her husband and set the other on the sidewalk within Stella's reach.

"Where's yours?" Stella asked.

The woman laughed. "I haven't been able to bear coffee for the last eight and a half months."

"For me it was eggs," Stella said. "It was very difficult, because I like omelettes, but then after my daughter was born, I liked eggs perfectly well again. If you've gone eight and a half months without coffee, then have you only two more weeks until the baby comes?"

"You're right on the mark," the woman said.

The husband said, "Can't wait for the day."

Stella wanted to ask what they meant to name the baby, but she had observed that over the last couple of decades, many young parents appeared to dislike the question. She conjectured that they preferred to make the infant's acquaintance before settling on a name. So, Stella kept her curiosity to herself.

She chewed some more of the superb corned beef baguette and sipped the coffee. Shoppers passed along the sidewalk, ran for the bus, and took their own cups from the coffee shop.

Stella ate and drank, at first like a child, but she sat up straighter and grew a little taller with each mouthful. The rain had thrashed about and confused her, and hunger had obfuscated her goal. Now she bent her thoughts again to finding and rescuing Thelma.

She said, "This was just what I needed. Thank you for your kindness, and for the coffee too."

She nodded at the car keys.

The two young people exchanged another look.

"Where do you live?" the husband asked. "Do you trust us to drive you there?"

Stella imagined pulling up to Fairmount Manor in Riley's car, without Riley, and facing the unwelcome explanations that would ensue. Worse, any further escapes from Fairmount would necessitate what Stella had come to think of as the long game.

She didn't have time for the long game. Thelma was alone, in hospital, and in some ways nearly as vulnerable as this woman's baby would be when it was born.

"Thanks, but I think I'll be all right," she said. She folded the last quarter of her baguette back into the bag and reached up for the Saab's keys.

The young husband exchanged another look with his wife. He glanced down at the keys in his hand.

"I don't know," he said.

"We don't want you to be hurt," his wife said.

"Why would I be hurt?" Stella asked. She tried not to show that she was irked at the suggestion. The overcautious signs around Fairmount were bad enough, with their *Residents must not climb the stairs, Residents cannot bathe alone,* without hearing the same kind of doubts here on the city street from people who didn't even know she'd had herself committed to a care home.

A man in a cap walked out of the coffee shop with a paper cup in each hand. He chuckled as he approached the tableau the three of them made and shook his head as Stella reached out to take the keys from the young husband's hand.

The man in the cap said to Stella in jolly tones, "If you want my opinion, lady, you'll do the world a favour and hand in your licence. Over eighty, you shouldn't drive."

Stella said, "You might discover you feel differently when you're eighty yourself."

"I think when I turn eighty, I'll trade my car in for a chain-saw," he answered. "That way, if I lose my mind in a senior moment, I'll only kill myself and not a bunch of people at a bus stop."

He nodded at a bus that pulled up a few yards farther along the road to downtown.

"Yeah, okay," the wife said. "You've made your point."

Her husband added, "Thanks for your concern, guy." He shot Stella a glance that might have been sympathy or possibly a warning to keep still.

"Just a word to the old and wise . . ." The man tapped his nose with one of his cups of coffee. His gesture knocked the lid off the cup and spilled coffee down his shirt. He cursed and walked off.

Stella looked up at the two young people. "I don't drive much, I promise you, but I absolutely must drive downtown. I have to fetch a friend who's alone and afraid in hospital."

"Have you phoned to make sure your friend is still there?"

"I have a phone at home but not with me. It's rather an old model. But I'm almost sure she's there."

"What's her name?" The young woman reached into her raincoat pocket and brought out her phone.

"Thelma Hu."

"There's only one hospital downtown, right?" The young woman talked into the phone and then replaced it in her pocket. She said to Stella, "They have workmen everywhere at the hospital this week, and with all the work on their networks, boxes, and cables, their computers are down again. You can phone back in an hour . . . How's our time, sweetie?"

"We have about ten minutes to spare."

"That won't get us downtown to her friend in the hospital and back."

Stella said, "I'm fine to drive now."

"Well, see, that guy was a jerk, but he was a jerk with a valid point," the man said.

"I do still have my driver's licence." This was starting to feel like one of those school meetings where a kindly administrator was leading the discussion towards extreme cuts to her library budget. Stella talked cheerfully on, as she had always done when the rumour was that all spare funds would go to team uniforms and not to books. "I don't have my licence with me, but it will still be on record."

"Well, sure. But we're just worried that you'll get into another fugue state."

Fugue state. The foggy condition was disconcerting and embarrassing, but Stella decided that overall, she liked the appellation *fugue*. It was certainly better than *senior moment*. *Fugue state* sounded like something Mozart might have experienced if he'd lived to be an elderly genius. Stella pictured Mozart at eighty, or even ninety, his white hair tied back, driving a four-in-hand along a Paris boulevard.

She said, "I promise, no more fugue states."

"I don't think that's something you can promise, though."

"Good old Icarus will get me there."

"Icarus?"

"Because he can really fly. But I won't go too fast. You see, I'm very careful." Somewhere, she supposed Mozart was laughing at her and urging his team of matched horses to greater speeds.

"Didn't Icarus fall?" the young woman asked. "It's not a happy story."

"On the contrary." Stella smiled. "It was a very happy story, except for the bit at the end."

"The bit where the father watched his son fall to his death?"

The wife touched her belly with the flat of her hand.

Stella deduced the young people's message. It was the same old warning. The imprecation many folks felt compelled to offer, but she disliked to receive. *Be safe. Death can and must be avoided.* Their attitude was understandable and even sound. Still, she wished that she in turn could communicate to them what death looked like from her view, away out here towards the end of life. From here, you didn't fear death as a sort of kidnapping or blow. Death was more like a mysterious darkness kept at bay by the fiery torch of life, a flame that might or might not keep burning, and around which you gathered with those companions who saw it too: Theo and the Greek Chorus back at Fairmount, for example. The Rose Corridor women. And Thelma Hu, somewhere in this city, lying in a strange hospital bed, practically blind and entirely alone, with no friend to wake her at sunrise and sit with her at night.

But Stella couldn't say that. Or she wouldn't. Not with the exact opposite occasion coming up so soon for these two young people. She thought of this young woman's baby, and of her own Junie, tiny in her arms long ago. It occurred to her that she might never hold a newborn child again in her lifetime. She had noticed since arriving at Fairmount that endings happened without her noticing: the last newborn she'd held, the last milkshake she'd sucked through a straw, the final time she'd read her favourite book.

"You know, I might just take the bus downtown."

Relief broadcast itself from both young people.

"That's a really good idea," said the mother of the unnamed future baby.

Her husband helped Stella up. He peered inside the Saab. "Is your handbag in here, or anything you need?"

Stella had no handbag. It was a point of pain with her. But she touched her right-hand trouser pocket, full of the cash Vaughn had given her. "I've got everything I need right here."

"Will I put the rest of your baguette into the trash or leave it in the car?"

Stella considered the question. It would be pleasant for Riley to find a half-eaten baguette on the passenger seat of his Saab, but hardly kind to the Saab itself.

"Into the trash, please."

The young man binned the baguette and closed and locked the Saab doors.

"Good luck," the young woman said. "Do you want me to telephone the hospital downtown to let somebody know you're coming?"

Stella observed the woman check her watch and said, "Let's not give them any advantage. I'll take them by surprise."

They laughed, and the husband said, "We've got to leave you right now if we're going to make our appointment. Here are your keys."

"Thanks." Stella tucked them in her right-hand pocket.

"Thanks for all your help. And my good wishes for your new life with your lovely child."

"It's a girl," the woman said. "We asked."

"Oh, how wonderful," Stella said.

The couple waved, turned, and walked away. Before he'd gone ten steps, the husband turned back, and his wife looked up at him. He called out, "What's her name?"

"I'm Stella," she answered. "Stella Ryman."

"No, what's your daughter's name?"

Stella blinked. "Junie."

"June or Junie?"

"Junie." She smiled at them, remembering the sunlit inspiration that had sent her that name. A sunny day, much like today.

"Good name," he said.

"Junie," the woman said.

They waved again, and Stella watched them walk along the sidewalk. She would have watched them walk out of sight, but she spotted a bus at the light. Its sign read *Downtown*.

Once the young couple had left her alone on the sidewalk, Stella took a moment to stand casually beside the Saab and jingle the car keys in her pocket, as one did. She felt an unexpected sense of quiet confidence in her role as an escapee, acting insouciant beside a stream of passers-by. Most of them walked quickly past her and out of view along the sidewalk, north or south; several passed into the coffee shop. A few entered the sushi place to the left of the coffee shop, and one person entered and then exited the Dollars4More store to the coffee shop's right. She smiled to see on display in its window the same Canadian-themed tea towels that students had from time to time given her for June thank-you gifts. Her own national icon tea towels had, of course, worn out over time and finished as cleaning rags, their bright patterns unrecognizable by the end. But here they were again, miraculously and delightfully unchanged except in price, and available for purchase if, like Stella, one had money in one's pocket. Stella could buy a lot of tea towels with the money Vaughn had given her. She smiled to think what flabbergasted expressions Annie and Enid, the Fairmount Manor cooks, would wear if they took delivery of crates of matching moose-emblazoned tea towels for their institutional kitchen.

But daydreaming about a glorious return to Fairmount wouldn't bring Thelma home. Stella needed to move her quest forward if she were to find her friend this afternoon. Car keys in hand, she watched another bus pass the parked Saab. Now that her two young rescuers had left her with the keys, it would be simple to pull out into traffic and drive downtown. The obfuscating rain showed no sign of returning anytime soon. She felt a twinge of self-reproach and swiftly banished it. After all, she had not promised them that she wouldn't drive. She hadn't stated outright that she would take the bus. All she had said was that she was thinking about it. And she was.

The bus for downtown stopped a few yards up the way from the store. Passengers stepped off and passengers stepped on. Stella hadn't ridden a bus in about twenty years, but the passengers made it look easy. The bus doors flapped and closed, front and rear. Nothing new there. The steps to the doors were lower than she remembered, and much closer to the curb. Back when she was a girl, well before she got her driver's licence, bus steps had been cliffs of high black rubber, which, more often than not, let her out to leap a small blacktop chasm beside a leaf-clogged gutter.

The bus pulled away. Stella took the Saab keys out of her pocket. The sun shone nearly straight down on them, and they flashed like a warning light.

A second bus whooshed past without stopping, and Stella put the keys back in her pocket. She moved towards the bus stop and joined a queue of four people. She had no idea how much fares were now — like the moose and beaver tea towels, they must have climbed in price — but she remembered bus drivers very well: they did not suffer gladly making change from large denominations, and they did not hesitate to order people off the bus. She dug in her pocket and pulled out a fifty-dollar bill. When she tried again, she saw it was a hundred. Stella registered the curious glance of a young fellow ahead of her, tucked her money away, and stepped back from the queue. The young fellow got on the bus, and she returned his stare through the window as it pulled away.

The young man's interest in her cash was a clear harbinger of fiscal complications. She must get change for at least one of her large bills. She turned on her heel and walked into the Dollars4More store. The first observation Stella made at the Dollars4More store was that there was not much priced at a dollar except for candies and sparkly pencils. A lucky thing, too, because she needed to break a large bill into change for the bus. She couldn't pay for a sparkly pencil or a bag of candies with a hundred-dollar bill. Nor could she carry ninety pencils around with her. She could bin them when she left the shop, but that seemed a mean trick to play upon sparkly pencils, a small evil act without consequence, ethically repugnant to her. She needed to buy something small, portable, and more expensive. Further, it was a moral imperative that she buy something she desired, or else why had she accepted Vaughn's cash gift? She studied the goods set out upon shelves and display tables around the store and thought that it was rather like Woolworths long ago, with its open-top cases of lipstick, key chains, and fragile plastic toys.

In the here and now, the crookedly stacked cat-shaped candles seemed as unlikely to sell today as forty years ago. She was struck by the sight of dozens of crazy rainbow wigs on stands skirting the walls, for she remembered a time when wigs were serious business and one thought hard about which style to purchase for, say, a trip overseas, when one's standing weekly hair appointment must be missed.

The fellow behind the cash desk gazed at her across displays of impulse-buy chocolate and chips. He gave her a charming smile, but no matter how friendly his presence, he'd never have been hired at Woolworths, not even in the seventies, with his hair so long and tied up in a topknot.

He asked, "Looking for anything in particular, or something at large?"

Stella answered, "Not really. I guess I'll know what I want when I see it."

"You're my kind of customer. Likely to buy, unlikely to shoplift. Have at it."

He took out a paperback book and bent over it. It was a classic English-language edition of Voltaire's *Candide, ou l'Optimisme.*

"*Candide?*" Stella said. "I'm impressed."

The cashier looked sheepish. "Well, to be fair, I finished a werewolf YA this morning."

"Maybe werewolf YAs will turn out to be the great classics in the twenty-third century," Stella said.

The cashier laughed. "If I live that long, I guess I'll be all studied up."

Stella strolled off to find something among the Dollars4More store wares that she could buy to make change for the bus. As she moved among the shelves and tables, she noticed the convex mirrors at various corners and angles of the merchandise space.

And the cashier glanced up from his book every ten seconds or so. As an amateur detective, she considered this an efficient method for the cashier to enjoy his book while in sole charge of a business where much of the stock was shiny and of a size to fit up one's sleeve. She wandered among the glittering merchandise, while in the clerk's book — and Stella's memory — Candide pursued his Cunégonde across the shark-infested seas. Stella too was in pursuit of a woman, and her friend and care-home co-conspirator Thelma Hu was, in Stella's opinion, far more deserving of rescue than Voltaire's feckless and inconstant heroine. Cunégonde would have liked this store, though. Especially when she perceived that some of the gimcrack necklaces were actually lavalieres. And only eight dollars.

Notwithstanding this excellent price and the attractive symmetry of buying a lavalier from a clerk reading Voltaire, Stella had long ago rejected the lampooned philosophy of *L'Optimisme*, and so she decided on principle not to buy eight-dollar necklaces. She searched the shelves for something less glittery but equally portable. She found the best of all possible items in a shopping section that she had never thought to buy from again: the travel section.

Here were foam neck pillows she might have appreciated the last time she flew to Voltaire's Paris, and here also hung travel handbags that looked quite a bit like leather — genuine Naugahyde was a joke that never aged in Stella's mind. One of the bags reminded her heartbreakingly of her old leather handbag with embossed sides that she'd brought back from a school vacation in Mexico and which, when opened, had always smelled of pack animal.

A rack of travel security accessories caught her eye and brought her back to the exigent present. The boxes were labelled *Krownkind Security Triple Pack*. She picked one off the shelf and peered at the contents through the translucent box top. This pack of three items might have been designed for her own personal use. However, it was priced far higher than the surrounding merchandise. She patted her pocket where she carried the money Vaughn had given her back at Fairmount. Why not use her cash power and buy herself some security? In fact, why not have a little spree and buy two boxes? Stella was certain that she wasn't the only one at Fairmount who could use a Krownkind Security Triple Pack. She picked a second box off the rack and walked with one in each hand towards the register.

She was about to set her purchases on the counter for the topknotted young man with the book to ring up when the front door opened, and a police officer entered.

There was no reason a police officer should not enter this place of business. Equally, Stella had done nothing to invite even casual detainment for questioning except steal Riley's car. Nevertheless, Stella felt an almost primal need to pay and escape. With swift movements, she placed her selections in front of the cashier and fumbled with the folded bills in her pocket. A hundred came free and, along with two fifties, fell onto the floor, out of the cashier's view. Stella held on to the counter to keep her balance while she snatched the hundred, but the fifties slid away and under a nearby display table.

Footsteps approached behind her, and into Stella's limited view came the police officer's comfortable black shoes and trousered legs. With swift dispatch, the hand of the law reached down to pick up Stella's errant fifty-dollar bills. The police officer waited as Stella straightened up and handed her the money.

Stella thanked the officer and tucked two of the bills back into her pocket. She handed the third to the clerk to pay for her security packs. It did not escape Stella that all the while she was keeping an eye on the police officer, the police officer had her eye on Stella as well, or rather on Stella's lumpy, cash-filled pocket.

While she waited for the cashier to ring up the Krownkind Security Triple Pack, Stella avoided the officer's gaze by scanning the merchandise in the innocent manner of a frequent consumer of dollar-store merchandise. When her eye settled upon the travel section, she was rewarded with an idea so excellent that she wanted to kick herself for almost missing it.

"Please cancel the sale," she said. "I want to add to my purchase, if you don't mind."

"You changed your mind?" The cashier set down his book.

"Sorry," she said. "I just thought of something I've been needing for a long time."

"Don't apologize. You're adding to the rich pageant of my day," the clerk said. "Furthermore, they pay me to just do that sort of thing."

He cancelled the sale, and Stella walked past the police officer back to the travel section. There she took down from its hook the travel handbag that looked so much like her own Mexican bag and returned with it to the desk. It was the most profligate purchase she had made in at least a year, but she still got change back from her hundred—certainly enough change to get her onto the bus.

The cashier filled a plastic bag with the two security packs. Stella told him that she wanted to carry this excellent handbag right away, and he removed the wadded-up paper inside it and handed it to her with a flourish. She thanked him and dropped the change from her transaction into her new handbag, which was so empty she could almost hear an echo from the rattle of coins and rustle of small bills.

She glanced at the police officer and caught the woman still staring at Stella's bulging pockets.

The police officer addressed the clerk. "Is there a washroom I could use?"

The clerk pointed at a sign on the wall behind the cash desk: *No public washroom.*

"Do I look like the public?" the police officer asked.

The cashier nodded acceptance and indicated a door beyond the necklaces section that read *Employees Only.* Stella decided that she would ask to use it after the police officer. But in the event, she didn't need to ask because the police officer turned to Stella and said, "Ma'am, would you please come with me?"

Stella gripped her purchases against the front of her fleece jacket and followed the police officer into the small, barely serviceable staff washroom. With her arms full and the public representative of the law standing so close, the lumps of money in her pockets felt enormous.

The police officer took the handbag and the two Krownkind Security Triple Packs in their plastic bag and set them carefully upon the back of the toilet.

She said, "It's about that money in your pocket."

Stella put her hand into her pocket and pulled out the wad of cash. It filled her two hands. Such was the quiet power of the officer's tone that it was all Stella could do not to hand the lot of it over.

"It's mine," Stella assured her. She couldn't help adding, "I haven't declared it on my income tax yet, as it will be for next year's return."

"I know it's your money." The officer grimaced. "I'm afraid this is a very common problem."

"Elderly ladies with money?"

"Always. My aunt was the same. She kept at least a thousand dollars, in cash, in her fridge freezer. And sometimes she kept it in an old men's jacket on her hat rack. And somebody came into the house, found it, and stole it."

"Oh, dear, how awful for her," Stella said. She thought, *What an idiot your aunt must be to keep money in places like that.*

"We get lots of complaints about cash stolen from pensioners. Sometimes we catch the thief."

"I would think that it would be difficult to prove somebody had stolen cash."

"Usually, the victims don't even know how much they had," the police officer said. "Which brings me to the point. I'm worried to see you walking around with all those large denominations bulging in your pocket. You're a real target for thieves."

Stella was about to say that in her experience most people were honest, but it seemed a foolish thing to say to a police officer; as well, she remembered the young man in the bus line-up who had eyed her high-denomination cash with such interest. She said, "What should I do?"

"Don't worry, I know better than to tell you to put it in the bank. There are only so many brick walls I'm willing to talk to. Let's see."

The police officer took Stella's new handbag from her and looked inside it. "Not bad. Anti-cutting strap, so it would be difficult to snatch. And a side pocket for most of your money. Too bad this one doesn't come with a wallet …"

Stella, almost giddy with triumph, produced one of the two Krownkind Security Triple Packs from her shopping bag. "What do you think of this?"

She was rewarded by a look of reassessment from the police officer. The officer opened the plastic box and pulled up the first of the three items. This was a wallet, the kind that stops thieves from reading and copying your cards electronically. Stella had no cards, of course, but she took back her new handbag and pulled out her change in small bills and coins. The police officer held the wallet open, and Stella placed this money inside it.

The police officer looked from the remaining bundle of money to the slender neoprene wallet. "Well …"

Stella placed the wallet inside the handbag's interior zip pocket. "Look in the box again, officer."

The officer looked, blinked, and pulled out a long bit of folded nylon. It was beige, and it had a zipper.

"Goodness. That's a money belt. And wide enough to take all that cash, if you don't mind the inches around your middle. Right. Let's strap you up."

She folded the money and tucked it inside the belt, which expanded in unflattering directions but contained the mass of notes of large denomination.

"Will you please fit it around me?"

"Okay, lift up that jacket." The police officer negotiated the clipping of the money belt around Stella's waist.

"Thank you." Stella tugged at it to make sure the clip would hold.

"Tuck it inside your underwear as well, don't you think?"

This rarely referenced travel tip was not new to Stella after her many foreign adventures in the real life she'd left behind when she sold everything to move to Fairmount Manor. Back in her travelling days, and again now, she would rather her assets fell into her underwear than onto the ground.

"I'm tucked," Stella said.

"What's this third thing?" The police officer held up the articulated invention that had first attracted Stella's attention and then her imagination. Stella knew the item's purpose, but she didn't want to explain it — or her excitement at having purchased two of them. The last subject she wanted to visit with this figure of legal authority was Fairmount Manor and its mores and red tape, nor how these purchases would help with her ongoing mission to put wrenches into the machineries of institution. So, Stella shrugged and kept silent while the police officer packed the remaining travel items into the new handbag, which plumped it out nicely. She looped the handbag's cross-body strap over Stella's head and settled it onto her shoulder.

"Now, where are you off to?" the police officer asked.

Stella considered the question. She wondered whether she ought to tell this helpful and apparently under-occupied officer of the law that she was on a mission to help a blind friend in the hospital downtown. She had an idea that a ride in a police car might be a swift and direct flight to her goal, so much so that she was reminded of Icarus and his joyful, daring rise and fatal descent. If she were to fly too close to the law, she might find herself falling amidst the scattered feathers of her goals and independent decisions to land not at Thelma's side in hospital but back down in Fairmount's corridors and the roiling sea of restricted movement and paucity of options. If so, as with Icarus, her trip would have been a success right up to its inevitable failure. And Thelma would still be alone in the hospital.

When Stella didn't reply to her query, the police officer frowned, and the atmosphere in the little washroom changed subtly. "Ma'am, are you going home?"

"Of course. Look, I'm so sorry to ask," Stella said, "but we're in the washroom, and I need to use it. Do you mind?"

The police officer's expression cleared. "Not at all. I'm going to buy that candy bar I came in for."

"*Bon appétit.*" Stella locked the washroom door and was happy to remain completely honest in her dealings with the law by using the facilities.

Then she waited. Like a spy, like the sleuth she was, she listened from behind the locked door. Distantly, she made out the sound of the policewoman answering her phone and then the clacking noise of a door opening and closing. Had another customer entered, or had the police officer left? She could detect no further sounds of conversation, nor any other clues to the situation in the store itself. The police officer had been kindness personified, and yet if Stella emerged too soon, the officer's helpful hand on her shoulder would undoubtedly reveal itself to be the implacable hand of the law.

Stella decided to give it another ten minutes and passed the time inspecting her new wallet and handbag. She was adjusting the cross-body strap buckle up a notch when a knock sounded at the door. "Hello?"

Stella held her breath.

The cashier spoke through the door. "Sorry, but I need to use the washroom."

"Of course." Stella washed her hands and exited. The police officer was nowhere in sight.

Stella asked the cashier, "What do you do about the store when you're in there? Do you have to lock the front door?"

"I lock the register," he said, "and I, um, hurry."

"Sorry. And thanks for your help."

"Welcome." He disappeared inside.

Stella exited what she now considered to be a Panglossian ideal of a shop.

Out on the street, she adjusted her new handbag and experienced a peculiar desire to show off her purchase to Icarus the Saab parked neatly at the side of the road. She opened the car door and considered climbing in. But, without warning, her conscience struck her a stunning blow. She dropped the car keys into her new bag and remembered that the car was not hers. Thus, she tucked the keys under the seat, pushed the lock home, and closed the passenger-side door. With one hand on Icarus's sun warmed hood, caressing it as she might a dog or a child before letting it roam free, she scanned the sidewalk for the police officer, without result.

Passers-by walked swiftly north or south and didn't glance in her direction, apparently lost in thought or checking their phones. Somebody came out of the sushi bar with a plastic box, and somebody else went into the Dollars4More store. Stella decided that this area of town had nothing more to give her. Even Icarus the Saab couldn't help her now.

A bus heading downtown approached, and Stella moved into place in the short queue. She had just enough time before boarding to take a handful of change from her new wallet, confident that some combination of coins would get her where she was going.

She climbed up after the first three passengers and held out the coins to the driver. He looked from the coins to her face. He pointed to the small notice posted at the front of the bus.

Stella read the warning, apparently meant for thieves, that no money was kept on the bus.

The driver said, "I need your card, please."

Stella wondered what card.

"Did you forget it?"

Soldier on, Stella. "I suppose I did."

The bus driver sighed. It was not an angry sigh, more a *seen it all before* sigh. He closed the door behind her and pulled out into traffic. "Hold on, please."

She said, "I forgot the card's existence, if I ever knew it. I haven't actually ridden a bus for twenty years."

He asked, "Is it an emergency?"

"That's perceptive of you. Yes, I have a friend in the hospital, and she's blind, and …"

"If it's an emergency, and you can't pay, then please take your seat."

Stella was gobsmacked. "But you could lose your job, transporting people for free."

She felt a tug at her sleeve. A grey-haired woman in the front seat of the bus nearest the driver gestured urgently at the seat beside her. "They do have to let you ride if it's an emergency, so don't worry about him."

The bus driver pulled over again, and a couple of people got on. One of them was a girl with a knit hat and a tattered backpack.

"It's an emergency," she said in earnest tones.

The bus driver waved her on board. Stella wasn't sure whether it was proper to hope the youngster was lying and there was no real emergency, or whether to hope she told the truth and so justify her generalized faith in the younger generation.

She glanced at the friendly passenger beside her. The woman appeared to be at least as old as Stella and perhaps older. But, unlike Stella in her washed and worn fleece warm-up suit, this woman wore crisp trousers, a buttoned tunic not made of fleece, sensible shoes, and a silk scarf tied in the French manner and tucked into her tunic.

Stella asked, "Do you know, does this bus stop at the hospital downtown, or will I need to transfer?"

The woman smiled. "I took the bus to that exact stop every day of my working life. Yes, it does stop at the hospital. I hope you're not ill?"

"I've a friend alone in hospital," Stella said. "I'm hoping to find her there."

"Good for you," the woman said.

"Thanks. You look like you still have a vigorous life going," Stella said. "What's your secret? So many of us are in care."

"You're not, obviously."

Stella hesitated. "I've thought about it."

"Those thoughts come to everybody. But not everybody should listen to them. At least not too soon."

"What, then?"

"Philosophy, that's what. When I first retired from nursing, I said to myself, 'Try not to get old, but take all the perks of age that are going.'"

"What a good motto."

"Well, it's just what I thought up — not much of a motto, really. You've obviously got your own philosophy, or you'd be in one of those care homes, wouldn't you?" She rose and touched a button on the upright pole by the driver's seat. "But sometimes a person can't care for themselves, and then I guess it's a care home or nothing. I hope your friend feels better."

"I hope that too."

The woman moved towards the door. "I'd have thought it more likely she's in General than downtown, with all that's going on there."

"What do you mean?" Stella recalled with a start the pregnant woman's attempt to call the hospital downtown and the report of computers being down. "Is something wrong at the hospital?"

"Not at all. It's just progress, isn't it? I'm sure you watch the news …"

The bus driver opened the door, and the woman thanked him and stepped down.

Stella rode on. She puzzled at the retired nurse's mention of the hospital in the news but got nowhere. Outside the bus window, the storefronts flashed multicoloured reflections at her, and the May afternoon sunshine warmed her bones. The bus moved slowly on, making stop after stop, purring and rocking along the long road downtown so that Stella had to pinch the inside of her arm to keep from nodding off. If she slept past the hospital stop, Thelma might never know, but Stella would never forgive herself.

Chapter Five
The Labyrinthian Puzzle

When Thelma Hu was eighteen and all alone, she stood on her sea legs on the Coal Harbour docks, in spitting distance from the boat that had brought her on a two-week journey out of China. She had a full purse in her pocket and was dressed in her best green silk dress with covered buttons at the neck. Even so, she knew she appeared an unlikely bride. The picture her grandmother had sent to her prospective husband had been, at best, optimistic. Furthermore, Thelma had seen a photo of her bridegroom. She knew he could do better.

Above her, seagulls shrilled like old aunties, and beneath her feet, between the dock's grey planks, sunlight flashed off water. The air smelled of fish, engine oil, tar, and sweat.

A pair of stevedores pushed past her; the box they carried off the ship she'd sailed in on emitted a whiff of sandalwood, but it was gone before the aroma could break her heart for home.

Two hours' wait dockside supplied Thelma with all the evidence she needed to deduce that her fiancé must have arrived early, taken in a good view of her disembarking in her best dress, and decided that she would never look better than she did today. He must have said to himself, *No, I don't think so.*

Or perhaps … She laughed aloud, and a passing labourer scowled at her. Perhaps her fiancé had been so filled with the prospect of lifelong joy with a bride from his Chinese home that he felt dizzy with bliss and stepped under a bus, Thelma's name the last word on his lips.

Whichever it was, no one had come to meet her at the dock. Therefore, she had a choice. She could stay in this possibly accursed foreign city, herself an accursed foreigner, or else she must return home. She had the money for a return fare in her purse, slipped to her by her father before she walked up the gangplank at departure. He, at least, would be glad to see her return.

Thelma stood on the dock, her duffel resting against her knee. On her right, an oily slick washed between the great boats, their taut ropes singing against the bollards. On her left, wood and metal crates towered over stacks of sandbags, buckets, and barrels. Between them lay the smoky, untried city.

She put her hand in her pocket and took hold of her purse, because anybody with a head on her shoulders knew that city docks were excellent spots to be robbed. She turned her back on the ship and walked alone across the creaking docks, beneath the screaming gulls, above the greasy waters, away into the city.

It didn't take Thelma long to realize that life was all about money. People could be shipped away by family and abandoned by fiancés on docks, but money met you open-handed, stood by you, and sustained you. It fed you and sheltered you. It warmed you with a coat in winter and bought you flowers in the spring. Money didn't praise, but neither did it argue or bully. To get some, she took employment as a laundry girl and then found a job with a bad-tempered old mom and pop who disliked 'Chinese' but came to depend on Thelma to run every aspect of their corner store. Money she saved over twenty years bought them out when they grew too tired to carry on complaining; ten years later, money bought her a house. When, at nearly eighty, her eyesight began seriously to fail her, she wasn't bitter. If money could have bought her new eyes, it would have.

The neighbours' girl, Cindy, walked with Thelma around the town for several years while her vision narrowed. Arm in arm, they strolled together down Quesnel Street so that she could, with effort, make out the cherry blossoms that bloomed in a long white arbour, lacy and streaming in the wind like a bridal veil.

At last she took herself to Fairmount Manor, because it was close to home. Once again, she stood alone—or rather mostly sat, with few doings at the care home to spend her time on and no use for cash at all. Then Stella Ryman arrived with a new currency, one of intrigue and mysteries to be solved. Of confidences and jokes only best friends can tell. So it was that, until today, death—that second uncaring bridegroom—still had not come to meet her. Of course, she knew death had the run of this hospital, but trapped as she was by post-surgical immobility and excellent nursing, all she could do was lie low and attempt to recover before death discovered her. She didn't fancy her chances.

Thelma lay in her hospital bed and dreamed she stood outside Emergency at a taxi stop, wearing her green silk dress with covered buttons at the neck.

Stella thanked the bus driver. She stepped onto the sidewalk by the taxi stop across the street from the hospital where she hoped to find Thelma Hu. It was a large, shambling, elegant edifice that reminded her of certain women she had known, those few who could pull on any baggy old clothes and appear ready to be photographed for *Vogue*. This hospital also reminded her of the day she'd given birth to Junie. It was a memory of not unmixed joy.

Soldier on, Stella.

She and her early-afternoon shadow crossed the busy road amidst a train of nurses, identifiable by their white footwear, and downtown residents, distinguishable by their coolness. Odds and sods like herself were most likely visitors or, like Bethie earlier today, outpatients heading to hospital for treatment. Nobody was noticeably pregnant, and she remembered that for several decades now the dedicated women's hospital handled most labour and deliveries. Women today were unlikely to do what Stella had done so long ago, viz., turn up alone and in labour at this same hospital bus stop because she was saving her pennies and wouldn't fork out for a taxi. Stella, in labour, had waited under streetlights and outside the open gates. She'd braced against a brick wall mid-contraction and waited for her husband to join her. In the end she'd gone in alone, but the beds had been full up that night, and reception sent her to general, a half-hour drive away across the bridge. She wondered, then and now, whether her husband had ever arrived here at all.

Back then, she'd longed to be inside this hospital to safely birth her baby Junie. Now, she was here to rescue Thelma and bring her home to Fairmount. Stella knew she was walking into peril to do so, for she was herself one swift professional diagnosis away from being drawn into the same protective mechanisms of eldercare that held Thelma here, far from her friends. For even though the police and helpful passers-by had not managed to stop her in her quest for Thelma, her own vulnerabilities remained in play. To illustrate:

1. Stella might tumble into a fugue state, and a medical professional could shoehorn her into dementia observation of some kind.
2. A terrifying diagnosis in unfamiliar surroundings might send Stella into a spin — a *fugue* — from which she wouldn't return. Stella might even forget her own name, and she had no identification, just a handbag full of travel accessories and a money belt stuffed with cash.
3. Thelma might, after surgery, meet with serious complications and be sent to palliative care. Would Stella then have to feign dying to follow her?

Stella caught sight of her reflection in the hospital's front door. She could perceive no outward sign of agitation or uncertainty. She didn't look as put-together as the elderly woman next to her on the bus, but even in her pilling warm-up suit, her new cross-body handbag gave her an appearance of self-sufficiency and connected her visually to the world outside Fairmount Manor.

She took a steadying breath and walked towards the hospital entrance as if upon a razor's edge. A nurse in a smock bumped her on his way to the front door. He apologized.

"Not at all," Stella said.

"Are you all right? Can I help you find the front desk or anything?"

Since the invitation to inquire was wide open, Stella said, "Can I ask you a silly question?"

The nurse blinked. "Okay — if you promise it's extremely silly, ma'am."

"Could you tell me, please, upon first glance, what you think I worked at before I retired?"

He laughed. "I used to play a drinking game like that."

"Sounds like fun. Now, if you don't mind, please tell me what you see." Stella stood tall with her thumb looped through the strap of her handbag.

He looked her up and down in her fleece warm-up suit.

"Ma'am, I'd say you probably ran a department at a nationwide sporting goods store. Senior staff."

"Gosh, you're good." Stella decided that if she was going to do a lot more lying — lying to good purpose, almost surgical lying, she assured herself — she might as well start now. "Very close indeed. It was an independent sportswear outlet, though."

"Score one for me," he said. "I guess I haven't lost my touch."

Me neither, Stella said to herself.

She gestured to the hospital entrance. "After you, for I'm sure your patients await."

"Please, ma'am, after you."

He held the door for her, and she passed into a dingy reception room that possessed in the way of charm only its obviously distant construction date: the post-Edwardian wall sconces were half-concealed by 1960s suspended ceilings. There were a lot of labourers rolling trolleys filled with boxes and bits of unassembled metal shelving. Despite all the work going on, any progress here appeared rather bargain-basement in quality. However, Stella supposed that even a cheap upgrade would benefit patient care and staff efficiency. It was too bad this entry didn't get the sort of good, cheerful light enjoyed by the reception area Stella had observed earlier; however, they'd have to tear the place down to get that kind of open-concept look, and if they wanted sunshine as well, they'd have to demolish all the tower blocks surrounding the hospital to get it.

A woman in whites behind the laminate reception desk scowled at her computer screen.

"It's about time," she said to the computer. The computer beeped a warning back. The woman's frown deepened.

Stella recalled that when the young pregnant woman, whose husband had helped her park Icarus, had phoned from her cell earlier that day, the hospital computer had been down for some construction-related reason. What a bit of luck if it were indeed working properly now. She needed all the help she could get to find Thelma, because these hospital corridors, stairwells, and elevators were likely to be even more of a maze than the ones at Fairmount Manor, which was saying rather a lot. If the computer was again functional, she might be able to pinpoint the location of Thelma's bed in this big rambling building, and even get directions.

Stella walked up to the desk. She tucked her thumb into her handbag strap. "I'm here to visit a patient with a hip problem."

"Name?"

Stella blinked at the receptionist. Normally, she was happy to give her name, but normally she hadn't escaped from a care home, ditched her driver, and stolen said driver's car. But these were small-time crimes, so she did what any small-time criminal would do: she gave her mother's name instead of her own. "I'm Tanis Marie Seton."

"I mean, what's the patient's name?" The receptionist glanced up at Stella and then back at her computer screen.

Stella flushed. "Thelma Hu."

"Date of birth?"

Stella was ready this time and gave Thelma's birth year, which was six years earlier than her own.

The receptionist whistled. "Not bad, not bad at all. Hope I live so long."

"Indeed," Stella said politely.

The receptionist shook her head at the computer and picked up a thick sheaf of papers that appeared to be a printout of names. Stella, with her librarian's love of order and her sleuth's impatience for progress, hoped to heaven the names were alphabetized.

They must have been, for after a pause the receptionist nodded. "Third floor. Bones, Muscles, and Joints. Ask again at BMJ reception."

"Thank you." Stella looked about for the elevators.

"But with all the work going on, I'd better phone ahead and make sure the corridor is safe for visitors." She picked up the phone, listened, and set it down again. "Nobody is answering. I'll phone again in a few minutes. In the meantime, you'd better wait."

"Oh dear. Thelma needs me, you see." Stella looked around the chaotic reception area. "Can I wait in Bones, Muscles, and Joints' reception?"

"Not possible, sorry."

"That's rather disappointing."

"We're in such a state, as you can see …" The receptionist gestured at the workmen coming and going with trolleys and gurneys.

The receptionist would never guess from Stella's cooperative nod that she was secretly thinking up a plan to infiltrate Bones,

Muscles, and Joints. Might not all this noise and movement of furniture, crates, and stacks of cardboard boxes provide cover for a stealthy raid past the receptionist and up to the third floor?

Perhaps walking past the receptionist, hidden from her view of the far side of a big crate, in the manner of the Hope and Crosby *Road* films, would do the trick. Or maybe the receptionist would go to the washroom, and then Stella could make her break.

The receptionist—unwary soul—continued. "The café isn't even open, sorry."

"Thank you, anyway. You're very kind. I'm just worried about poor Thelma."

"We can't allow visitors, as you can see."

"Nobody?"

"Almost nobody."

"What's almost?" Stella asked politely. "Just so I know for next time."

"Well, you could go up if you were her registered carer."

Stella started. "I *am* her carer."

"My goodness." The receptionist's eyes scanned Stella from head to cross-body handbag to toe. "I'm so sorry. Of course you can go up. I should have asked first."

Stella regrouped. "I should have told you."

"Not at all. I'll have to enter your name."

"I'm Tanis Marie Seton."

The receptionist wrote it down on her printout. "Right. I'll phone again to say you're on your way, so they'll be expecting you, Mrs Seton."

"Ms," Stella said.

"Ms Seton. Follow the blue arrows and take the third elevator in the second bank of elevators you come to. And do watch your step. There's so much debris around, and you don't want to end up in Bones, Muscles, and Joints along with Ms Hu."

"I'm certainly walking the razor's edge today," Stella said.

"Pardon me?"

Stella shook her head and thanked the receptionist. She followed the blue arrows past the first bank of elevators. However, when she rounded the second corner, the blue arrows vanished as if arrow guides had never been thought of. Instead, there were several colourful lines, none of them blue, stencilled along the grubby tiles.

Stella followed the receptionist's directions as best she could remember them. She peered down the side corridors for banks of elevators but saw none. The new painted guide lines led along the hospital flooring, side by side, but instead of indicating the elevators, they took her straight to a rank of three metal chairs set against the wall and bolted to the floor. The seating reminded her of the chair arrangement in Corridor Park, where she and Thelma, along with the bitter crones of the Greek Chorus, passed their time.

In the first of the three seats sat a man about Stella's age. He wore the sort of cheery white moustache favoured by elderly sports coaches, and a crisp blue and green tartan shirt beneath a three-season-weight tweed sport coat. A metal cane leaned against his knee. His hands rested flat on his thighs, and his slip-ons pointed straight along the coloured lines at Stella.

His face lit up. "There she is! Nice to see you."

Oh dear. Stella said, "Nice to see you too. You look like you're waiting for somebody."

He looked up and down the corridor. "I guess I'm waiting for you. Come and sit down, won't you? I'm expecting coffee, and maybe the nurse will bring two cups."

Stella revised her assessment. Here was not a demented person, but a gent of the loquacious sort she'd met so often in her youth and middle age. Generally, as they matured, these sort lost hair and physique but continued to score strongly in banter. She enjoyed his type and moreover was grateful to them. In her young days, they had made up approximately eighty-five percent of the fellows who asked quiet girls to dance.

"Coffee sharpens my eyesight," he said, "so I can notice pretty women and offer them something to drink."

"And the possibility of a caffeine boost tempts us to comply." She looked along the corridor, feeling the full thrust of the day's exertions but wanting to get on. "Do you know the hospital well?"

He held out his hand. "My name is Wallace."

She shook it. "Stella. Pleased to meet you. Do you come here often? Of course, I hope you're well and just here visiting."

"No, you won't get rid of me as easily as that," Wallace bantered.

"Oh, you," Stella bantered back. These exchanges with this familiar type of fellow gave her the oddest feeling that a jazz combo somewhere nearby was about to kick in with 'Green Onions', and that somebody would bring her not coffee, but a Singapore Sling. "I'm a bit lost. I'm looking for a friend, and the directions the receptionist gave me ran out just about here."

"I'll have to write the receptionist a thank-you letter," Wallace said.

This guy was pretty good. Stella smiled but kept her hand on the steering wheel of investigative procedure. "I'm looking for a friend in Bones, Muscles, and Joints."

"It's a small world, Stella. I've just come from remedial therapy in Ambulant there. Was it your friend's hip as well?"

"Yes."

"And is this a woman friend?"

"Indeed."

"Well, well, so my luck is holding."

She laughed, as one did. "Do you have any idea how to get to Bones from here?"

"I do, as a matter of fact," Wallace assured her. "I have a clever way to get up there."

"That's wonderful," Stella said. Relief was a pick-me-up, better even than a coffee or a Singapore Sling or a Blue Hawaii, Stella's one-time alternate favourite. "Can you tell me?"

"Anything for you, Stella. Well, the corridors here are ridiculously convoluted, and when I was in for my hip operation—I got a pin, you know, and there were a few complications—"

"I'm sorry to hear it," Stella said.

"Well, I'm tip-top now, I assure you." He slapped his hip.

"But for recovery, they send me out to walk, and the boldest outdoorsman would get stumped in this labyrinth. Even Daniel Boone."

"Or Davy Crockett," Stella added.

Wallace tipped his head back and sang 'Davy Crockett, King of the Wild Frontier', which had been ubiquitous in the mid-fifties. Stella joined in the second time round, but on the third iteration, she added, "Or Lewis and Clark," because there was no song known to her with those explorers' names in it.

"Sure." Wallace was a little pink in the face from singing. "Anyhoo, I made it a little game. Want to play?"

Stella felt that she had already been playing quite a lot, but she said, "I sure do."

"Well, go round the corner" —he tipped his head to the

right—"and find the next bunch of elevators. Come back when you spot them."

Stella rounded the corner, and the next, and saw three elevators. She returned to Wallace.

He said, "Get it?"

"Got it."

"Good. Now the next part is kind of tricky, but I think you're up to it."

"Think of me as Colonel Bowie," Stella said.

"Okay, Colonel, you're going to take the left-hand elevator and press the number three. Then, when you get out, you'll turn left again. You'll walk briskly for seven full seconds, then turn left, then right, then left, and you're there. Get it?"

"No."

Wallace burst out laughing. His delight was so obvious, and so entirely free from malice, that Stella laughed along with him.

At last Wallace wiped his eyes and said, "I'm sorry. That's not the clever method, that's the ridiculously complicated method, which I simplified with my clever method."

"Wallace, you are a card. Now, let's have the clever method."

"It's a kind of a mnemonic." He raised his eyebrows in a gesture that invited her to ask for a definition of the word.

But Stella was a big fan of mnemonics. "I like those. I use them to go to sleep."

Wallace nodded. "You're my kind of gal, all right. I knew it the moment I laid eyes on your lovely self."

"Thank you very much indeed. The mnemonic?"

"It's a marching song, actually. You might know it. *Left, left, left a wife and seventy children in perfect condition with plenty of groceries left, right, left.*"

Stella did know it. "I learned it as *starving condition and nothing but gingerbread left, right, left.*"

Wallace frowned. "Do you know, it works no matter what the children eat. You go to the elevators, take the one on the left, press three — that's the only trick — then you've left the second floor, and you get out at three, turn left out of the elevator, walk for as long as it takes to say *a wife and seventy children in perfect condition* — or," he added fairly, "*starving condition …*"

"I do prefer your *perfect condition*. But go on, I think I see the cleverness of you."

He crowed like Peter Pan. "'*The cleverness of me!*' That's a good one, Stella. And the rest of the marching song …"

"*… with nothing but groceries …*"

"*… left, right, left.*"

"Exactly. You turn left, right, left, and you're there. Say it with me?"

"I don't need to. I've got it." She had. "Thanks, Wallace. It's been a pleasure."

"Will you come back this way ?" he asked. "Can I see you again?"

Stella hesitated. She wasn't sure she could easily reverse all those lefts. "I'll try. Thank you again."

Wallace raised a hand in farewell, and she left him alone in the waiting area. She was sure he was sincere in wishing to see her again, upon her return from the third floor, but she hoped (mostly for his sake, and a little for her own) that somebody would give Wallace his coffee and take him wherever he was going. With a guilty pang, she realized she'd not even asked him where that was. But it was too late now, for here were the elevators, and there was the one on the left.

The doors of the left-hand elevator opened. Stella stepped inside, and the doors shut quietly for an old elevator in a decrepit hospital. She touched the button for three. The doors opened again, and shut, the elevator floor moved sideways, and presently she felt the slow rise of the ancient machinery.

Left, left, left a wife and seventeen children …

The doors opened onto a corridor and a big, blue-painted number three. Stella stepped outside.

She murmured, "*Left*— check! *Left*— check! And now, *left …*"

She turned left again. She made a rough calculation of Wallace's probable speed of movement and paced along with the next section of the mnemonic.

"*… a wife and seventeen children in perfect condition with nothing but gingerbread …*"

Left. Right. Left.

She made the turns and found herself exactly where Wallace had said she would be.

There, the black-and-white melamine sign reading Bones, Muscles, and Joints.

Here, the handwash gel station.

And next to it, the buzzer to press for entry into the department. But Stella saw at once that she wouldn't need to buzz, for the double doors stood open, propped back by cardboard boxes. Through them, the semi-gloom indicated that the hospital fluorescents were switched off. She detected the spicy odour of antiseptics and the sweet pine scent of cleaning fluid, so cleaners had been through Bones, Muscles, and Joints recently, possibly that day. But the silence and half-light here spoke to her sleuth's heart. They said, *Here's a mystery.*

Stella stepped between the cardboard boxes and through the open doors into Bones, Muscles, and Joints.

She walked along the central corridor past several empty rooms, each with four stripped beds. She passed nursing desks, where black-screened computer monitors stood.

If there had been computer monitors on the *Marie Celeste*, when the ship was found derelict and stripped of its crew, they would have looked like these. She peered about her for Thelma Hu, or indeed any patient or staff member. The *Marie Celeste* began to seem less of a joke and more of an antecedent.

A keen interest expanded within Stella, and with the practised eye of an experienced amateur sleuth, she surveyed the quiet aisle that ran between the patient rooms. She observed nothing out of the ordinary aside from the mysterious disappearance of every single person in the ward, including Thelma Hu. There was nobody to ask where everybody was, nor any living soul from whom she might elicit the reason for the abandonment of these rooms and the missing patients. Therefore, the investigation was wide open, and there were several ways in which she might approach it, some more difficult and demanding of hard thought than others.

She decided to begin at the basic investigative level and move from there to the most sophisticated deductive strategies. After that, if she still hadn't made any progress, she would pass to the middling methods of the gumshoe investigator. She would leave gumshoe to last because, as its title suggested, it would require physical exertion, and she was quite tired. So tired, in fact, that she would very much like to curl up on one of these stripped-down mattresses, pillow her head on her hand, and sleep, like Ariadne on the island of Naxos. But she was not Ariadne. She was Theseus, and like Theseus she would soldier on with her search.

1. Stella determined to begin with the most basic strategy of any search, employing methods that were obvious and not very sleuth-like, but which would be foolish to bypass out of any Holmesian deductive arrogance. She called out, "Is anybody here? Doctor, nurse, or patient?" Nobody answered.

2. She moved on to the most expert or extreme level of observation, a hyper-professional line of attack that required sub-numbering.

   2.1 First, she must design a sturdy yet flexible theory.

      2.1.1 But what theory? Stella struggled to see any reason why all the patients and staff would disappear from what was, in an increasingly long-lived population, a high-use medical ward. Bodies outlived their joints these days, and nearly everybody she knew in the outside world had some Bones, Muscles, and Joints procedure done once they hit seventy.

      2.1.2 Moreover, Thelma had been listed as present in this ward. So, it wasn't just a slow day in Bones, Muscles, and Joints.

      2.1.3 Therefore, the only logical reason to separate patients from their beds and nursing staff from their desks and monitors was because every patient had simultaneously gone for tests, physio, or procedures, and the staff had taken them there.

   2.2 Therefore, Stella would lurk in the shadows until their return.

Stella paused to consider the positive and negative aspects of this articulated theory and its conclusion, viz. that all patients and staff had gone to testing and would return in time. On the positive side, her logic was sturdy, for patients and nurses did go for testing and procedures. Moreover, it was flexible because she had set no artificial timeline for their return. Nevertheless, the extraordinary coincidence the theory required — that everybody was somehow absent from the ward at the same time — was too much for a seasoned amateur sleuth like Stella. In fact, her study of Holmes, Poirot, Marple, Wolfe, and McGee showed that none of them believed in coincidences. Neither did Stella.

Parallels, yes; coincidences, no. The implausibility of everybody vanishing at once glared at her like an investigative red herring.

Therefore, she moved to:

3. Medium-level gumshoe investigation, which didn't start with a theory but instead required her to gumshoe around the place to make observations regarding the scene of the crime — or the disappearance, at least. Above all, she had to keep an open mind. She must examine every tiny detail to see whether the puzzle came together. No elaborate numbering was required for gumshoe investigation, just a keen eye for detail and the discipline to draw no premature conclusions.

Observe. Note connections and anomalies. Draw no premature conclusions.
Stella smiled. Gumshoe was her favourite investigative technique when she had the energy for it. She marshalled what vigour she could, polished her glasses on the hem of her fleece

jacket, replaced them on her nose, and gumshoed into the first patient room on her left.

Even though the overhead fluorescent lights were not operational and the window blinds hung closed, there was enough natural light from between the slats to see what clues might be discovered in this unoccupied room. The heavy blue curtains dividing the space from the corridor had been pushed back on their rails so that they bunched against the wall. The four beds, one per quadrant of the room, stood at odd angles, stripped to their impermeable pale blue covers. There were no stacks of laundered linens visible to the investigative eye. The floor had been mopped to a shine. The beds appeared to have been wiped down as well, and on the bed to Stella's left, near the windows, lay a spray bottle of disinfectant. She peered at it. The white plastic bottle had only a small, printed label and was evidently not a spray cleaner you could purchase from the supermarket or even a hardware store. An in-house hospital brand, it seemed. This deduction was unlikely to add to Stella's understanding of the scene, but she made it, anyway, without fear or favour.

More informative, perhaps, were the twin objects lying on the bed to her right, where the corridor opened. These were a pair of white boxes, free from dust, but slightly grey around the edges, like plastic kettles after long use. Their cords hung loose over the rail of the bed. A number of coloured buttons, including off, on, reset, and call, gave no hint of the electronic mission of these boxes. However, the lack of dust was inarguably a clue. Stella ran her finger along the bed rail and the blind slats. There was not much residue here either. Stella nodded.

Her first useful gumshoe clue: *these hospital furnishings have been cleaned very recently, perhaps even today.*

Stella walked across the corridor into a similar room, one that lacked windows. She hoped Thelma had not been housed in here, for even though her friend was almost completely blind, she perceived light and had a rim of vision outside her macular loss. Thelma was happier near a window.

This windowless room had four beds like the last but had not been as well swept. Or rather, it had been swept, but the detritus was pushed into a corner. Stella shifted her handbag on its strap behind her back and bent over to examine the sweepings. These were made up of medical wrappings, crumpled tissues, a small plastic cup as for medicine, and a single turquoise sock, size large. Thelma was definitely not a size large.

In the next windowless patient room, Stella discovered more sweepings and a large mound of linens. Gingerly, she picked through them to be sure they were used linens on their way to laundry, and she discovered a bottom sheet with a bloodstain showing clearly in its middle.

This was the first bloodstain Stella had come upon in her role as an amateur sleuth, and she felt a professional satisfaction that the bloodstain, although not an indication of violence, was indeed a clue.

Indubitably.

Observe all clues; draw no conclusions. Soldier on, gumshoe Stella.

Something made a pattering noise out of her sight in the corridor. This was the first sound she'd heard but for her own footsteps as she made her way around the Bones, Muscles, and Joints ward. It could only be somebody else's footsteps, speedier and quieter than her own. A nurse's soft rubber soles? Stella was about to call out when she identified the sound as one she had heard before, at Fairmount Manor. It was a sound she heard only when she was alone, as she was now. It was not soft shoes at all, but bare feet on institutional flooring.

Stella froze inside the fourth room of the empty ward. The sound of footsteps stopped. She frowned. It would be just like Mad Cassandra Browning to tease her into a chase along an empty corridor. Mind you, she had no proof that the barefoot scurrier was Cassie. But if it was, her presence here would prove once and for all that Cassandra Browning was indeed a ghost. For there was one thing Stella knew about Mad Cassandra: she was nimble as a forty-year-old jazz dance instructor and supremely unlikely to be admitted as a patient to Bones, Muscles, and Joints.

Stella moved past several more nearly identical patient rooms towards the centre of the ward. She left behind her the big blue curtains and discovered several doors. These opened onto two small offices, a staff break room, two washrooms, four storage rooms, and in the centre of the office area an enormous curving desk that backed up against the break room. This was truly a trove of investigative possibilities. Where to begin? She'd studied the empty ward bedrooms, so now she would investigate the persons in charge of the disappeared patients.

Stella set about examining the two offices.

Inside the first she found a desk, a garbage bin, and a rickety shelving unit. Several binders, mostly dark blue, lay in stacks across two of the shelves; the other three shelves were empty. This was, to somebody of Stella's lifelong experience in institutional settings, rather suspicious. She didn't think she'd ever seen an office where binders, booklets, and the paraphernalia of professions didn't crowd every shelf, leaving almost no room for the dying succulent that graced most work areas. Stella found this room's succulent in the plastic garbage bin next to the desk. Also inside the bin she found papers and food wrappers, two pens — out of ink — and, beside the bin, a large brown cardboard box of the sort that housed items ordered for delivery over the phone, as Stella had always done, or via the internet, like the rest of the world.

There was no computer on the shiny-topped desk. But this proved nothing, as laptops were portable. It would be no surprise to learn that staff took laptops with them when accompanying patients to treatments and tests, so as to complete work while they waited. But the details of hospital workers' schedules were unknown to Stella, and furthermore, she was determined to keep an open mind.

She took her open mind into the second office. This room did not differ greatly in content from the first, although in arrangement it was less tidy. She found empty binders and loose papers strewn across the shelving therein. Moreover, the bin was on top of the desk, which was marked with sticky rings. In fact, the only dust was in the sticky substance. That was very interesting indeed, and Stella made a mental note.

To Clue 1 — *No dust in the patient rooms* — she added Clue 2: *The only dust was in the coffee rings on the desk of an obvious slob.*

Stella didn't consider the office worker's untidiness a suspicious circumstance in itself. She knew only too well that institutional slobs were often among the hardest workers and most valued colleagues. And often they were the most tolerant and cheerful. Still, old dust not cleaned up in a dustless place might well turn out to be a significant piece of the puzzle.

She decided to check out the central desk area, where one might normally find many fine professionals hard at work. Her first glance had assured her that the circular area was indeed unstaffed this afternoon, and her second now showed her that it was stocked with computer terminals: four of them. And all four showed blank screens. Stella reached out to turn on one of the computers but pulled back when she remembered that she was in a public hospital, and that patient records could be erased by an untutored hand as quickly as a teaching friend with literary aspirations had once erased 2 0 0 , 0 0 0 words of his unpublished first novel.

Stella leaned upon the desktop and cast a lynx-eyed look about the area. What to investigate now? Storage rooms? Washroom? Staff room?

As if in answer, she heard a voice whisper two words. *Staff room.* The sibilant at the start sounded snakelike in the empty space. It might have been her internal gumshoe, speaking in her head; it might have been Mad Cassandra Browning, always a most helpful undead; or indeed, it could have been some other ghost in a building where a century of deaths might result in institutional haunts.

Whichever it was, there was one way to test the suspicion growing within her sleuth's brain (open-minded though it was). She walked around the counter and pushed open the door marked *Break Room. Staff Only.* Here she found sofas, desks, plastic chairs, posters of a medical inspirational nature — *Nurses give TLC without prescriptions* — and more sweepings, but she felt no need to sift through these. Her attention was drawn to the sink and counter near the window. There were two closed cupboards over the sink and another inspirational sign that read *I didn't go to nursing school to learn to wash your dishes.* She couldn't see a kettle, but somebody, not the slob in the second office, might have tidied it away. She opened the cupboards over the sink and found not a mere clue, but actual proof that her growing suspicions were correct.

As a gumshoe detective she now had all she needed to solve the mystery of the missing staff and patients, for there was not a single box of tea, bottle of instant coffee, or packet of sugar substitute in the cupboards over the sink. All that remained to mark the passing of the nursing staff's consumables was an empty box of Wagon Wheels and a broken cup with an anatomically correct heart on it.

Her observations allowed only one conclusion: Bones, Muscles, and Joints was a closed ward. No matter what the receptionist downstairs had read on her computer, staff and patients, Thelma included, would not be returning here today, or possibly ever.

Stella left Bones, Muscles, and Joints, and returned to the outer corridor. She looked to her right, which according to Wallace's mnemonic was the path back to the elevator, and to her left, where a glass door stood closed and unlit behind the usual pasted-up health-related notifications. Evidently, this was a second abandoned department. It looked so much like the first, with its almost post-apocalyptic debris and darkness, that any further investigation was unlikely to yield anything in the way of new information. It was time to search out members of staff and interrogate them.

She turned right, left, and right, blessing Wallace all the time, to the elevator, which she had all to herself again. She pushed what she thought was the button for the ground floor. But a moment later, the door juddered open to reveal not the ground floor corridor with its painted arrows, but instead a brick archway leading into a patio garden. Curious, Stella passed under the archway and studied the garden around her. She guessed the green space would have been designed to offer a haven of leaves and vines for staff and visitors. The garden was planted around its perimeter with rhododendrons and acid-green laurel and rectangularly shadowed by the glass towers that grew like everywhere downtown. Still, a ray of sunlight had found its way to pool on the bricks at the centre of the area. Stella felt herself drawn to stand in the sunlight, the way she was drawn at Fairmount to sit under the skylight in Corridor Park. The greenery waved and whispered to her:

Stop here for a moment.

Take advantage of the unexpected.

Beauty doesn't last, you know.

Stella decided she could afford to give beauty a minute of her time before returning to her quest. She walked into the centre of the garden and rested there for one minute, and then another. Sunlight placed a warm hand on the top of her head and suggested she stay for a good long while. If she liked, she could move with the light as the sun made its way across the sky towards night.

Above her, the blue-grey city sky was reflected many times in the tower block windows all around. *It had been a good idea to place a garden here,* she thought, so that medical staff could escape from pressing duty and the needs of others. And judging by the cigarette butts devolving under the laurel bushes, they did so. But not only staff could spend time in the garden, for patients capable of walking would make their way here too. Might they not come with visitors? She imagined children playing about the garden while their parents discussed issues for their own post-operative care. Yet there would certainly be patients who came here alone, to perch on the brick walls and study the sky while they weighed their choices and their chances.

And maybe this sunlit space wasn't, after all, an encouraging place to consider one's mortality and chances for survival, because even she could feel in her bones the garden's siren call to stop, lie down, place her head on her hand, and sleep. Perhaps forever. The call to halt was sweet.

She wondered whether Thelma heard it too, wherever she was.

That thought jerked Stella out of the sunlight's spell. She hurried back under the arch to the elevator. The doors opened. She stepped inside and found the right button for the main floor.

Soldier on, she urged the elevator. It shifted ancient hips and complied.

The doors opened on the ground floor and Stella stepped out of the elevator. She murmured, "*Left*—check!—*Left*—check! And now, *left* again." She wished she had such a clever mnemonic to help her find her way around Fairmount Manor's twisting corridors. It was not beyond possibility that Theo, with his background in teaching music at the university, might help her create one.

She approached the final right turn. She had been investigating the Bones, Muscles, and Joints ward so long that she fully expected to find the corridor seating area empty, but up ahead she saw Wallace, ensconced as before in the centre of three chairs. Stella fantasized that Wallace had been set in place upon his seat by the gods of Ancient Greece, like a smiling siren, past whom all who navigated these hospital corridors must travel.

Stella waved, and Wallace's smile lit his eyes and widened his moustache. He opened his mouth in song.

"*Here she comes, Miss America.*"

Stella made the patting gesture that she had used in her career as an educator to quiet rooms of up to four hundred chatting students. It had worked with them but had no effect upon Wallace, who segued neatly into a rousing rendition of Guy Mitchell's 1953 hit, 'Look at That Girl'.

She walked up to him, feeling self-conscious in a way that reminded her of her high school years, when a boy looked at a girl passing by his lockers the way Wallace was looking at her now. She sat beside him and put a hand on his arm.

Wallace finished up, "*. . . can't believe she's mine.*"

"You're a very sweet person," she said.

"You found your friend, then?"

"No. The place was empty."

Wallace nodded thoughtfully. "Quite a few of us were wheeled or walked out of there this morning."

That was interesting. "Have you been sitting here so long? That's terrible."

"Andres brought me a sandwich. They're up to their ears today."

"Hospitals are up to their ears every day. But usually patients are in their departments, and Bones, Muscles, and Joints was like a desert island. What in this blue planet is going on?"

"Let's ask Andres. He knows everything."

Stella followed Wallace's gaze. An orderly approached, looking in his flapping white trouser legs like a friendly albatross.

He smiled at Stella and helped Wallace to his feet. Wallace adjusted his cane and offered his free arm to Stella.

"All aboard," he said to her. Then he turned to the orderly. "Andres, meet Stella. She's just been to Bones, Muscles, and Joints, looking for a friend. But the friend wasn't there. Where might she be?"

Andres nodded in the direction of reception. "That ward transferred this morning. Don't you remember? You were the last man out."

"Was I?"

"Yes, and you still haven't met with your therapist."

"My therapist Mahalia," Wallace explained to Stella. "She is tough but fair."

Andres nodded. "I'll get you in to see her once we're there."

"There?" Stella asked, a little louder than she had meant to sound. More quietly, she continued, "Andres, where are you taking Wallace?"

Andres looked at Stella with the kind but dubious expression Stella was accustomed to receive from the Nameless Dear care workers who wouldn't dream of saying she was gaga out loud.

"You know, of course, that this hospital is closing?"

Stella stared at him. She did not know. But she thought it provident to say, "Of course."

Wallace said, "It was in the papers. But they didn't notify me of any change, so I thought I'd better show up here as usual. I guess the new hospital isn't as ready as they thought."

Andres nodded. "Computer glitches, all part of the moving blues. Plus, construction always takes longer than anybody dreams. So, the new hospital isn't ready for patients yet, and you're all going to General."

"General?" Wallace said. "Goodness, now I see. You mean the general hospital across the bridge. Sorry, Stella. I thought he meant a general ward or something."

Stella felt the stone of inevitability form in her throat. What would she do now? She wished she had Icarus the Saab back, to wing her out of here and on to the next hospital. She thought of returning to the taxi stand, and what it would take out of her to direct a taxi driver. Then there would be hours of searching at General, which, at three times the size of this hospital, was bound to be overburdened and thus underorganized.

"Easy mistake to make," Andres said cheerfully. "General this, general that. Let's go, Wallace. Your transport awaits. Nice to meet you, Stella. Watch out for the movers with their trolleys, won't you? They ought to have indicators and alarms."

Wallace said, "Oh, Stella's coming with us."

Andres began, "Only caregivers and family members …"

Wallace said cheerfully, "Oh, Stella's a family member."

Stella wished he had said caregiver, as she was registered here as such and was comfortable with the designation. But she supposed that sister was not too far a reach.

Wallace said, "Stella is my fiancée."

Andres blinked. "Congratulations."

"That counts as family, right? At our age?"

"At any age."

"That's the attitude I like to see. Right, Stella?"

"Er, yes," Stella said.

"That's my girl."

She tucked her arm into Wallace's, and they followed Andres along the corridor.

At first Stella couldn't make out what tune Wallace was humming. But when she did, she thought, of course. Of course it would be the wedding march.

They made their way towards what transportation this hospital would afford them as it sank like Atlantis into the sea of age and obsolescence. The end of institution, of history, of good care and long service.

Amidst the bustle of workmen pushing equipment-laden trolleys, the receptionist directed Andres, Wallace, and Stella to the exit in Emergency, on the far side of the hospital building. When they stepped through the double swinging doors, they found in the busy parking lot a twelve-passenger van shining in the afternoon sun. The side door of the people carrier showed a half-dozen patients drooping in their seats, with room for several more. The driver's sweaty brow was creased, as if his day had been long and the traffic bad. He hooked an elbow over the back of his seat and motioned to Andres to hurry up.

Wallace said, "I'm not going in that."

Andres said, "There's plenty of room."

"But I wanted to go in an ambulance."

"This is an ambulance."

"It's not a proper ambulance, with me lying on a stretcher and Stella here holding my hand." He winked at Stella.

"Just get in and buckle up, Wallace," Andres said. "This is the best transport we can offer."

"Either way, I'm going," the driver said. "You folks are more than welcome to take the next ride."

Stella saw her safe route to Thelma at General going up in the smoke of Wallace's burning desire for romance. "I'll hold your hand," she said. "Give it here."

She took Wallace's hand in hers. It was damp — romantics' hands were always damp in her experience — but not unpleasantly so. She led him to the van, and Andres helped them both inside.

"Everybody buckled?" the driver asked. "Better check them, Andres. I feel like I've been driving cats and chickens around all day."

Andres checked while Stella gave the driver a stony glance.

She said, "If you have to compare patients to animals, I would prefer to be a horse."

There was a laugh from behind her, and an elderly woman spoke up. "I would like to be compared to a wise owl."

Wallace said, "Me, a polar bear."

The driver said, "All right, all right, and I'm a pig. I apologize. Traffic's been a bastard. I mean, it's been tough."

"How long have you been doing this?"

"Since seven this morning," the driver said.

"That is a hard day for a driver," the woman behind Stella said. "Maybe we could all sing to keep the driver's spirits up."

Wallace asked, "Does everybody know 'Look at That Girl' by Guy Mitchell?"

Stella had, in her career in the public school system, ridden with many a field-trip driver, and she knew something of their feelings towards passengers belting out songs on the journey.

She said, "I think quiet would be more pleasant. Let's all just look out the windows and enjoy the ride."

The driver said, "I think I love you, lady."

Wallace said, "Hey, buddy, she's mine."

Stella sat with her handbag on her lap and her hand in Wallace's. She gazed out the window and appreciated the quiet rumble of the van. Outside, the greater world rolled by, and inside at the back, one of the passengers fell asleep so that his stertorous breathing connected the van's riders with the engine noises and the outside traffic.

All told, it was a soothing atmosphere, and several more passengers dozed off, including Wallace. His grip on her hand loosened slightly. Stella spent the last five minutes of the ride liberating her hand in small increments of movement so as not to wake him.

She succeeded in freeing herself just as the van pulled into the large semicircular drive behind a similar vehicle, also jammed with patients. Stella folded her hands across her handbag and watched the back bumper of the van in front of them rise with the exodus of its passengers. Once empty, it drove off, and Stella's driver rolled forward to the hospital's reception doors. The driver stepped down to help his passengers out the side door. He offered a hand to Stella. She gazed at Wallace, asleep in the seat beside her.

She said, "Thank you, Wallace." But she said it very quietly.

Wallace didn't wake but lay with his head back and his mouth open, peaceful as a sleeping bridegroom.

Stella let the driver help her down from the van and thanked him. Before anybody else could alight and follow her, she hurried into the noisy, congested reception hall and lost herself in the anonymity of the crowd.

This afternoon, the city general hospital's foyer boiled with patients in chairs and visitors on phones. Stella stood uncertainly in the centre of the hubbub and wondered how best to proceed.

Soldier on, Stella. Her fatigue had eased over the course of the van journey, and she felt charged with a watchful edginess that she supposed all sleuths, amateur and professional, must experience when nearing the final stage of their pursuit. She judged it vital, now, to tighten rather than loosen the reins of investigation. To stop worrying about investigative style. Of course, style, like logic, carried its own justification. But overridingly she felt she must guard against overconfidence, for, having stolen Riley's Saab and employed various falsehoods and aliases, she had perhaps profited from rather good luck. She fully intended to play out her role as Miss Marple, but she was conscious that she was nearly as much Papillon, absconded from institution without possibility of parole, and a whisper away from recapture.

She stood tall, straightened her fleece jacket, and ran her thumb along the bulging line of the travel wallet tucked under her trouser waistband and inside her underwear. She rested her thumb on the crossbody strap of her new handbag and felt as ready as she'd ever be for what she fervently hoped was her final approach to Thelma Hu.

Caution murmured that she should minimize contact with persons of authority. Therefore, she decided this time to eschew the line-up for the receptionists and try one of several free-standing computerized map kiosks to find the Bones, Muscles, and Joints department at this latest hospital. There were short queues for every computer map console except the one nearest her. Stella soon saw why: a small boy was planted in front of the screen, feet apart and shoulders hunched. His air of immobility and reluctance to share was instantly recognizable to Stella from her four decades in the elementary school system. She looked around the crowd for his parents—another thing teachers learned was that modern parents, like adult bears in wilderness settings, never wandered very far from their offspring in public places. And the ones you couldn't see were the most dangerous.

She approached the little boy, observing his clever swipes and prods at the kiosk screen. He appeared to be about eight years old, and he was nicely togged out in a golf shirt and coordinating shorts.

Stella cleared her throat.

The boy didn't look up.

She said, "How interesting that there are video games here for visiting children to play. I call that very thoughtful."

The boy shrugged and swiped at the screen.

"My grandson Derek tells me updates are very important. Do they update these games to the latest releases?"

He shot her a disbelieving glance. "It's not a game."

"My goodness, but you seem very good at it. An expert, as far as I can tell."

"It's just a map."

"A map?"

"Yes. It's stupid, but there's nothing else around here to play on." He scowled at the screen.

"What's the best thing about playing with it?"

"Nothing." He held a thumb on one of the coloured sections of the map, and after a moment it began to blink.

"Is it broken?" she asked.

"I didn't break it. Blinking is all it does."

"May I please have a turn?"

He looked her up and down and grimaced. "What do you want?"

"Well, just to try it."

"I mean, what do you *want?*"

"Oh, I see. Well, I'm looking for a friend named Thelma Hu. Can you find her for me on the screen?"

"Nope." He turned back to his swiping. "It's a map. They don't put people on a map."

"What about finding the ward for bones, muscles, and joints?" He prodded at the screen. "No such place."

This seemed to Stella impossible, given Andres's testimony about the movement of patients from the Bones, Muscles, and Joints ward in the downtown hospital to this one. She was about to ask the boy to look again when two adults approached the console. She cursed untimely parental proximity and moved two steps backward. In an effort to fit in with the crowd, she glanced up at the clock above the doors and then fished in her handbag as if looking for her car keys or her phone. However, it was obvious from the way both golf-shirted parents were staring at her that her stratagem had failed. She decided that if they spoke fiercely to her regarding her interaction with their son, she would reply in French, which she had taught at the elementary level and in which she'd grown in proficiency over the course of several summer holidays spent near Carcassonne.

But French was not required. Both parents pinned her with scowls and dragged their son away from the map kiosk.

Stella heard the mother ask, "What's the rule?"

Stella knew the rule, and she was certain the boy did too. But he didn't recite the rule.

Instead, he looked back at Stella over his shoulder and called out, "I found it. It's called Complex Joints at this hospital, not Bones and Muscles."

The family group moved off towards the outside door. The boy had left the computerized map blinking and unreadable, but he'd gifted her with a solid clue. She looked around for signage for Complex Joints, wondering why on earth the powers that be would call the department here Complex Joints when it was named Bones, Muscles, and Joints at the prior hospital.

One would think the same knees and hips in the same people in the same city would have the same name. And one would expect that there would be enormous, easy-to-read signboards to offer directions in case computer map screens were blinking and unreadable. By now, Stella would even have welcomed some blue arrows to point the way.

A woman about her own age walked up to her. She wore a green cap lettered with white that read *Community Aid*. "Can I help you find what you're looking for?"

Stella was about to ask her where the Complex Joints unit might be found, but she recalled her vow of caution. Hers was a simple enough inquiry, but she reminded herself to keep her cover intact while she made it. *Don't get cocky*, she told herself. A voice deep inside her answered, *But what if I like being cocky? It's got me this far, hasn't it?*

She straightened her back and hooked her thumb onto her handbag strap. "I'm a carer for a patient recently transferred to Complex Joints from the downtown hospital."

"I see. Would you like me to help you find your client?"

"Do you have time? All these people …" She looked about her for a queue of people waiting for help from the woman in the green hat, but nobody was looking at either of them.

"I have time."

Their eyes met, and Stella understood. You could put an official green cap upon an elderly woman, but you couldn't make a busy world ask her for help.

"Please do show me where Complex Joints may be found," Stella said. "Thank you."

The woman's cheeks flooded with colour, and her eyes lit up.

"Follow me, dear," she said. "I'm Cynthia, by the way."

"Call me Tanis Marie Seton," Stella said. She twitched her warm-up jacket straight and followed Cynthia down several corridors and up two separate elevators towards Complex Joints. Along the way they left behind them the human scents of sweat, cologne, and deodorant for the odours of hospital suppers, heavy on the broccoli. The shift in smells created for Stella a compelling connection between these corridors and those of Fairmount Manor, and it significantly raised her hope that she would soon return to Fairmount with Thelma Hu safely in tow.

Cynthia was a whiz at inquiry, easily the equal of one of Sherlock Holmes's Baker Street Irregulars. One intense minute of questioning staff at the nurses' station in Complex Joints brought Cynthia results.

"Follow me," Cynthia said.

Stella followed.

The room was apparently meant to hold four beds, but in a pinch it could, and today did, take six. Stella scanned the recumbent patients for Thelma and spotted her in the bed nearest the window. She made her way among the beds and scattered visitors standing about bedsides. There was no place for visitors to sit, for the usual chairs were stacked and relegated to the corridor to make room for the extra beds. But the fates had left Stella a boon: a visitor's chair overlooked and turned sideways between the window and bedside in Thelma's corner. Stella wiggled herself into it and gazed down at Thelma's sleeping face.

Afternoon sunlight through the window lit the white threads among the black in Thelma's hair. Stella's friend lay on her back, and her small figure raised the coverlet only slightly.

Thelma's skinny, knobby fingers lay folded across her breast in the attitude Stella always associated with a composed and self-determined death — as so often, she referenced Tennyson's 'Lady of Shalott'.

Her heart pounded and then gentled when she made out the slight but certain rise and fall of Thelma's breast beneath the cotton blanket.

Stella let out a long breath. With it went the fear, unspoken even to herself, that she was too late: that Thelma had taken a lonely and permanent departure from hospital, that she had released her grip on life the way she'd let slip away the ship that could have returned her to China and her family.

Thelma was still here. Alive. She hadn't left the world without Stella.

With care not to wake her friend, Stella manoeuvred her legs up to rest on the bed. She leaned her head against the window and set her elbows on her armrest, hands clasped around the strap of her travel handbag, and fell into a light doze. When she awoke, the light in the room read late afternoon. Thelma was staring up at her from her pillow.

"Is that you, Stella Ryman, or is that your ghost?"

"I was dead tired, but that is exactly how far I intend to go in that direction." Despite a heavy neckache and one foot asleep on the bed beside Thelma, Stella felt a surge of energy. "Wait a minute. Let me get my foot working."

She wiggled her foot around and put both feet on the floor in the tiny space beside Thelma's bed. There she got a charley horse and stretched that out, groaned, and sat down. Thelma chuckled.

The man in the bed across from Thelma's looked up from his phone and applauded. He said, "I got that on video. Do you mind if I post it?"

Stella knew she had looked ridiculous and said so.

Thelma said, "You didn't look ridiculous."

How would Thelma know? But there was no polite way to ask that question of a woman with macular degeneration and only a fingernail's worth of peripheral vision.

Stella shrugged. "I guess it doesn't matter what I look like."

The man with the phone said, "Come and see. She's right, you don't look ridiculous."

Thelma said, "That's because you have to be ridiculous to look ridiculous."

Stella frowned. "Everybody's ridiculous sometimes."

"Everybody *feels* ridiculous. That's quite a different matter."

The man nodded. "Just watch the film. Even if I put in clown music, you look resilient and even rather dignified. But funny. I think I've got a winner here, if you say okay to post."

Stella was about to say no, thanks for asking, though, when Thelma said, "At our age, we should never miss a chance to be discovered by Hollywood."

"Oh, go ahead," Stella said.

"I just filmed your agreement." The man grinned and zoned back in on his device.

Stella turned to Thelma. "Are you all right?"

"Huh. What exactly do you mean by all right?"

"Have you seen a doctor? When's the operation? Can I come in with you?"

"You're a little late, Stella Ryman. They put a pin in my hip around lunchtime."

"Good heavens. You mean you're all done?"

"Yep," Thelma said.

Stella didn't miss the note of victory in her tone, as if she hadn't avoided all help for her hip for weeks.

"I'm all done. They've already had me exercising it in bed. They call me …"

A nurse crossed the room and stopped at the foot of the bed. "We call her Xena, Warrior Princess. Fastest walker over ninety we've ever had."

Stella said, "She's only eighty-eight."

"Don't spoil it," Thelma said.

Stella said, "Not for the world."

Thelma looked out the window. "I want to go home right now."

The nurse crossed her arms. "You're going nowhere tonight, young lady. There's such a thing as postoperative blood clots."

Thelma said, "There's such a thing as hunger strikes too."

Stella pulled the nurse aside, out of range of Thelma's hearing and the phone man's as well. "I'm Thelma's carer, Tanis Marie Seton."

A snort from Thelma's bed told Stella she hadn't moved far enough after all.

Soldier on. "Because of her age, I'd like to get her home as soon as possible."

"I understand your worry, Mrs Seton …"

"Ms," Stella corrected her.

"Ms Seton, but we will certainly not release her tonight."

"Exactly how likely are blood clots?"

"Not likely. But we watch for them all the same."

"But the very elderly are at risk for hospital infections."

"We'll send her home as soon as possible. However, she'll have to pass a couple of simple tests."

"What kind of tests?"

"We have a little set of stairs, and most importantly she'll need to get to the washroom on her own steam."

"Let's go," Thelma said.

"Physio will conduct the tests," the nurse said. "And Physio has gone home for the day."

The nurse hurried out. Thelma thumped her head on the pillow and growled at the ceiling.

Stella touched her arm, and Thelma shook her off.

The phone man said, "This will cheer you gals up. I've gotten likes already. I'm going to edit you to music."

Nobody had edited Stella to music in her whole life, not even parents who videotaped their children's school winter concerts.

She said, "Can I see it?"

He said "Betcher bottom. I'm Jase."

"I'm Stell—" Stella started, and then remembered she was using her mother's name as an alias. "I mean, I'm Tanis Marie Seton."

"I like Stell," Jase said. "Okay to use it?"

At the speed this fellow worked the internet, she guessed that she was Stell out there already. It was her own fault for having misspoken her own alias, so she said, "That's fine."

Thelma shook her head. "I'm so glad you're here, Tanis Marie Seton, even if we both leave this hospital feet first from the fun of it all."

Jase looked up from his phone. "Feet first? Stell, what's going on?"

"Nothing that isn't always going on," Stella said. "Thelma is just making light of death."

"You both look in the pink, but now you've got me feeling guilty. I should have asked. Is there any reason this film will come back to bite you in the ass?"

Stella imagined the Warden viewing Jase's video of her at the hospital. But saying so would only make Jase feel sorry, and to what good?

"You know, at my age and Thelma's, the film would have to move pretty quickly to reach us in time to bite us where you mentioned."

Jase tilted his head, and Stella saw the penny drop. "Can I film you saying that?"

Stella looked from Thelma, who was listening to their banter with lively interest, to Jase and his phone.

"Does that phone actually phone?" she asked him.

Jase blinked. "Can I film you asking that?"

"Just listen for a second, Jase. I need you to call somebody. Or somewhere. But I don't have the number."

"Sure. Who?"

"Who second, where first."

"Ready." Jase held up his phone.

Before Stella could instruct him further, Thelma threw her bedclothes aside and sat up on the edge of the bed.

"I'm ready too."

Stella said, "I'm sure it must be too soon for you to move around, Thelma."

"That's not what the nurse said. I'm supposed to do everything I can to move around on this pin in my hip. Better to get my joints moving too soon than too late. Film this, Face."

"Jase," he corrected her. He held up his phone. "I might be onto something here. I'm not sure anybody else is doing this kind of video."

Thelma slipped down to the floor and felt her way barefoot along the side of the bed. Stella looked around her for Thelma's red silk slippers but couldn't see them. The woman in the next bed huffled in her sleep and rolled over, and Jase filmed away with a steady hand. He said, "There's never been a better time to be a filmmaker."

"Where's the toilet?" Thelma demanded. "I want to do the toilet test."

Stella stood, ready to search out the facilities, but the nurse returned first.

The nurse said, "Blood clots."

Thelma said, "Toilet."

"You're not going home tonight, but the toilet is straight ahead. Go on and walk." The nurse helped Thelma into the corridor and set her up with a walker. "I'm right behind you."

"Not too close," Thelma said. "And while I'm in there, you go find those little stairs I have to climb."

"You're not going home tonight, Mrs Hu."

"It's Ms."

Thelma and the nurse clattered out of sight.

Stella returned to Jase's bedside. "How are you feeling?"

"Not as good as Thelma," he said. "She got a simple pin, and I got a whole new hip. I'll have to climb the stairs too, I guess. Do you still want to make that phone call?"

Stella told him who to call. It took Jase about ten seconds to tap in his requests, and then he handed the phone to Stella.

"Fairmount Manor, front office."

Stella didn't recognize the female voice on the other end, which was just as well. Even so, she disguised her voice with a smoker's rasp. "This is Tanis Marie Seton phoning from the

General. I'm in Thelma Hu's ward, and I need to speak to Riley right away."

"How is Ms Hu?" the voice asked.

"Thank you, she's recovering well. May I please speak to Riley?"

"He's working …"

"We're all working, dear," Stella said. "I really must speak to him in regard to some paperwork for another patient, Stella Ryman."

"My goodness, is Mrs Ryman all right?"

"Yes. May I please …?"

"I'll get him."

A long moment passed while Stella gazed out the window at the lowering light of evening and wondered just how much more she could accomplish in a single day. Since this morning, she had solved two cases of theft, impersonated a sixty-nine-year-old, stolen a car, taken a bus downtown, become a fiancée, and found Thelma at last. She ought to be as tired as an old shoe, but to her surprise she didn't feel drained of all energy, but rather ready for anything, if only she could take a short nap first.

Riley's voice sounded over the line. "Who is this?"

Stella said, "I'm so happy the police let you go, Riley."

"Not so loud, Mrs Ryman." Riley lowered his voice. "And do you mind very much telling me exactly where you put my car?"

"All in good time." Stella told him precisely what to do.

His initial fury would only make his eventual quiescence more satisfying and help in some small way to create a better balance of fairness in this youth-heavy world.

Sometime in the middle of the night, in that overpacked hospital room, Stella discovered that even with her feet up on Thelma's bed, she was so far from feeling comfortable that she could hardly remember what the word meant. In an attempt to placate her outraged back and neck, she reminded herself of incidences of worse physical torment.

1. There was labour, of course — eight stunning hours of it when Junie was born.
2. She was unlikely to forget the mid-seventies flight to London in which she had been seated between two strangers with pointy shoulders. The plane had stopped twice on the fourteen-hour journey.
3. And she well remembered one night in her extreme youth when she had slept *al fresco* on a sloped clearing with nothing but a homemade sleeping bag between her and a lot of roots and stones.

Sadly, these memories were not much comfort. Stella stared across Thelma's room at the fluorescent-lit corridor, and the glowing green walls united with her discomfort to make her feel like she had been tied up and was waiting for mobsters to put her to sleep with the fishes.

She returned her gaze to Thelma. This was a woman so tiny that she made the single white bed look big enough for two.

Without further mental discussion, Stella crawled onto the bed and curled up next to Thelma. There she slept soundly until the nurse shook them awake. Stella started and wiggled off the bed.

When Thelma didn't open her eyes, the nurse patted the

older woman's thin shoulder. Stella peered up at the nurse's face, trying to read there what she hoped to see — and not what she feared had come to pass.

The nurse shook Thelma's arm a little harder.

Thelma made a gentle sound, and then another, a little like a cough.

The nurse looked at Stella. "What did she say?"

"She didn't say anything." The sun through the window felt warm on her shoulders, almost as good as a friend's embrace. "She's laughing."

Thelma struggled up from the pillow onto her elbows. "You nurses are complete pessimists."

The nurse put her hands on her hips. "I love the funny patients. Especially the ones who pretend to be dead. They get my blood moving in the morning."

But she helped Thelma to sit up, set her into her walker, and led her along the narrow crowded way among the beds to the corridor.

"I'll be back," Thelma said. "Just let me show that little set of test stairs what's what."

"You're the boss," the nurse said.

"I don't want to be the boss," Thelma retorted. "I want to go home."

Stella had appreciated Thelma's pretence at dying, because she felt rather like death herself. She longed for her Room 34 at Fairmount Manor, and for the dining room with its cups of weak tea, cold toast, and the dubious company of the Greek Chorus.

She was grateful that the staff had let her sleep undisturbed next to Thelma all through the night, but she felt it would be stretching her welcome to ask for breakfast.

She fumbled on the floor for her travel handbag and slung

it on. She said good morning to Jase and the other patients and stepped outside the ward, walking slowly at first until her joints loosened.

An old fellow in a green *Community Aid* hat directed her to a coffee stand near the reception area. She brought one for herself and one for Jase, who invited her to sit on the side of his bed. Here she awaited Thelma's return, watching the videos directed and produced by Jase on his little phone screen.

The coffee went down easily, which was fortunate, because when Riley stormed into the ward and called Stella by name, the cup she dropped was empty.

By ten that morning, Thelma, like the grumpy trooper she was, had climbed every step with a cane, mastered her walker, and independently visited all the washrooms in the ward. Jase had filmed much of it, although when she went to the washroom, the nurse made him erase every second of the footage.

All the while, Riley leaned against the wall with one foot crossed over the other and drank cup after cup of coffee through pursed lips.

At last, with Thelma's walker folded in the trunk of Riley's Saab, all three of the Fairmount Manor party rode silently towards home. Up front, Riley rested one forearm across the steering wheel, riding the clutch and clomping down on the brake. In the back seat, Thelma dozed. Stella was secretly delighted to be reunited with Icarus the Saab. She passed the journey wide awake and deeply engaged in plotting their smooth return to the care home. Despite going what the Director might term 'absent without leave', there was little danger she'd be tossed out of Fairmount, which, like a country, was obliged to take back from abroad even its most wayward citizens.

However, Stella had no wish to reveal to Mrs Perdita Warren her actions of the day before. She was certain they'd be added to the slate of delinquencies the Warden of Fairmount Manor kept on her.

It was not only Stella's pride that was at risk, but also her scope for activism: every time Stella made a well-founded complaint and petition on her own behalf and that of the other residents, that slate was the Warden's best weapon against Stella's demands.

Stella took stock of the cases that would soon need defending: the return of justice and peace of mind for the beleaguered Rose Corridor women, as well as generosity in dealing with Dotty's mystery cat, who must inevitably be discovered. And *that* would be a can and a half of worms.

Riley turned right with a jerk of the wheel. His jaw was set so hard she was worried he'd hurt himself. Stella decided to break the silence.

"I see you successfully retrieved your car, Riley."

He shot her a look that said *mistress of the bloody obvious.* "You noticed that, did you?"

"I was worried about your licence after the police incident."

She saw his fists tighten on the wheel, and he gave the brakes an unnecessary snub. "Yeah, I have to appear in court. Thanks for that."

"Don't blame me. I suggested you drive off for a sandwich, not a series of beers. What did Mrs Warren have to say about it?"

For a rejoinder, Riley swerved right onto a side street, where the Saab came to a halt behind a garbage truck. Riley swore, reversed into a driveway, and retraced the Saab's path. It was answer enough. She knew he wouldn't tell the Warden.

Stella covered her laugh with a cough. She didn't like Riley, but she had much to thank him for. Primarily she was grateful for his help in returning Thelma to her side and driving them safely homewards—well, fairly safely, considering Riley's reckless ways at the wheel.

But she had by no means forgotten that he was responsible for certain wrongs at the care home. She considered what she ought to do about it.

She had no doubt that Riley's arrest for drinking while in charge of driving one of Fairmount's residents was a career-buster. And, for an underdog rebel for residents' rights, this kind of power over a care worker only loosely fitted with a conscience was as good as money in the bank. Out of respect to her own hard-driven but operational conscience, she promised herself not to overdraw on his cooperation.

She covered another smile by gazing out the window at a corner mall. "I know this area well. I used to buy wine at that shop." Too late, she realized she'd put her foot in it.

"Rub it in, why don't you?" Riley asked. "Please, if you have any more alcohol jokes, do trot them out."

"Riley, I promise I wasn't referencing your arrest for drunk driving. I only meant we must be about five minutes away from Fairmount."

"Maybe," Riley answered. "Or maybe eight. Or nine."

Stella allowed him his grump without comment. Like Churchill, she believed that no victory should be entirely one-sided.

Laurel hedges and cherry trees flicked past the Saab's window. These had formed part of the area's well-established flora throughout Stella's life. The cherries, past blooming in this season, fluttered new leaves against the late spring sky. She wondered whether she'd live to see them return to full flower, parading down the side streets like pretty prom-goers; but she'd asked herself the same question the year before, and the year before that. *No bathos required here, Stella Ryman.*

Stella had nearly forgotten the feeling of returning home from travel. She recalled coming back from afar on school holidays and how buzzy her brain always felt fresh off a flight—a very different sort from her flight from Fairmount the previous day. In those earlier times, when she still owned her house, the taxi would take her home via these same streets, shaded by these same cherry trees and lined with the same laurels. When the taxi neared her address, she would pass paper money to the driver and would haul her own suitcases through her front gate. The yard always overgrew its bounds while she was away, and the blowsy, uncontrolled boughs and blossoms would lean out to touch her as she passed, their manners most personably welcoming. Now her house was gone, sold with everything else when she came to Fairmount Manor; but strangely, just now she experienced the same good feeling: that she was coming home. How amazing that she could embrace such a deep-seated, joyful expectation at the thought of setting her feet on Fairmount's familiar soil, or rather its grubby tile flooring.

But she mustn't forget that her return today was different in ways that the sensation of coming home couldn't disguise.

1. She didn't own Fairmount as she'd owned her own beloved house. She didn't even own Room 34 in

Daffodil Corridor.

2.   She had no solid plans to take future voyages. (Although she did have her new travel handbag, with those travel gadgets still in their dollar store boxes.)

3.   Most importantly, this was the first time she had returned home with a friend she'd not left with.

She squeezed Thelma's arm and leaned forward to speak to Riley at the wheel. "Thank you for driving us. What a treat to take another ride in your good old Saab."

Riley's icy silence melted at the compliment to his car. "The Saab's definitely a cooler ride than any ambulance. More like a hero's return, right?"

He patted the dashboard. Stella remembered doing the same to Icarus the Saab the day before. She also remembered feeling stylish at the wheel. The next time she stole a car, she would have to remember to wear sunglasses.

She peered ahead through the windshield and made out Fairmount Manor's boxy shape amongst the trees and shrubs ahead of them. As the car drew nearer, she saw that a grey-haired fellow was standing out front. For a breathless moment, Stella felt certain the man was Theo, somehow made aware of their return and poised to welcome them home. But proximity revealed a younger man than Theo. He was, in fact, a member of the care home's board, one of those who had visited at breakfast-time the day before. She couldn't remember his name, but surely he was one of the two real estate agents on the board.

When Stella had first laid eyes on this fellow, he'd been measuring Fairmount's road frontage with a long tape on a roller. Now, he stood with his hands on his hips, and she followed his gaze up to Fairmount's black tarred roof. It was mossy on the ridges and somewhat ragged, as Stella well knew because the leaky skylight cut into it over her chair in Corridor Park. This member of Fairmount's Board of Directors was doing no harm standing and staring like that, but she couldn't imagine he was up to any good either.

Riley drove past the board member, pulled on the brake, climbed out of the Saab, and stretched. He strolled around to the trunk, where he'd put Thelma's folded-up walker.

Stella shook Thelma awake. "We're back. So those who leave Fairmount *do* sometimes return."

"Stella Ryman, let me be. These car seats are more comfortable than any piece of furniture in Fairmount Manor, including my bed."

"You can't live in a Saab, Thelma. We're home, just like you wanted."

"It's always something, isn't it?" Thelma stirred herself to sit up. "Well, I guess I'd better say thanks for coming to get me when I was alone."

"I was the one who was alone," Stella said.

Thelma scowled. "I forgot to ask you. Did you get me anything?"

"Oh. Well, I got you home."

"Ha. But I'd be ashamed to visit somebody in hospital and not bring them at least a box of almond cookies."

Behind them, Riley banged the Saab's trunk closed, and the walker clattered onto the driveway.

Stella brought her handbag around to her lap and opened it. "I did bring you something. Here." She handed Thelma the second money belt.

Thelma held up the belt to one side of her face, where Stella knew she had a scrap of vision. She ran thin fingers over the belt's zipper. "What am I going to do with a money belt? You never found my money, did you?"

"Not yet," Stella admitted. "But I do have some money for you. I can't show it to you right now, though."

"Don't let that Riley see. He'll take it quick as you can bite. Did you get me anything else?"

Stella glanced out the car window at Riley, who was crouched over the walker's wheels. Over on the grass by the roadside, the real estate fellow with his offensively possessive posture was making his way towards the far corner of Fairmount.

"I did get you another gift. But Riley might see it too if I take it out of my bag right now."

"Don't show me, then. Just tell."

Stella knew Thelma would hear the smile in her voice at the thought of the third, most precious of the travel gadgets in the Krownkind Security Triple Pack she'd purchased at the Dollars4More store. "I brought home travel door locks. One for each of us. We can lock ourselves in anywhere, whenever we want."

"Lock ourselves in the bathroom?"

"Could be."

"But we don't want the locks to be confiscated. We'll have to be careful."

"Discretion is certainly the better part of privacy."

Thelma frowned out the window at Riley. "Can we lock other people up?"

"Sadly, I think not."

"Well, we can lock them out, anyway. If we're tricky about it."

"My friend," Stella told Thelma, "I believe that's

our specialty."

Riley opened the Saab door. "You've arrived at your destination, ladies. Thelma — I mean Ms Hu — your walker awaits you."

Riley fiddled with the walker's bar, and Stella seized the opportunity for a quiet word with him.

"I trust, Riley, that you'll make sure the Director doesn't find out about my travels yesterday. Nor about your … little trouble with the police?"

Riley frowned. "Perdita Warren can't see farther than her nose. I'd do a better job running this place. In fact, you'd do a better job running this place. Why are you in a care home, anyway?"

"I'm old. That's why."

"You're not that old. Why are you here?"

Stella came as close as nothing to responding with the truth, viz. *because the excellent life I designed for myself turned on me, towered up, and chased me four blocks over into Fairmount Manor.*

Instead, she said, "Let's get Thelma to her walker, shall we?"

Thelma, aided by her cane, stood upright and glared at nothing.

Riley said, "If you're tired, Ms Hu, sit in the walker seat. It makes a little wheelchair, see?"

"Don't say *see* to a blind woman."

"You told me you're not blind. You have macular degeneration."

"I think I know whether I'm blind or not."

"Sorry. Here, let me help you into your walker."

"Did you test it?"

"I set it up."

"You set it up, so you sit in it first."

Riley huffed a breath, shook his head, and sat down. The

walker buckled underneath him, he ripped his pants pocket on the Saab's back fender, and hit the ground. Stella imagined how Jase would have enjoyed filming the scene; to hide her smile she left Riley to his axle-and-lever articulations and walked towards Fairmount Manor's front door.

Through the glass she saw that the foyer was occupied. Two people stood within, and as she neared the doorway, she recognized Dr Terry and Reliza, engaged in furious, nose-to-nose discussion. What a crying shame that nothing had changed for these two part-time lovers.

She reached the door and was about to rap on the glass when she saw Reliza raise a hand and touch Dr Terry's cheek. They turned to see her, and Stella's relief and pleasure at Reliza's gesture of peace must have shown on her face, because their faces lit up too.

Dr Terry held the door open and waved Stella inside. "Are you all right, Mrs Ryman?"

"I'm fine," Stella said. "Thanks for asking."

Dr Terry nodded. "Good to see you looking fit. Does Riley have your hospital paperwork?"

Stella said vaguely, "It sounds likely. Reliza, how are you?"

"The better for seeing you back at Fairmount. And how is Thelma?"

"A very good nurse said she'll need physiotherapy."

"I know an excellent physio," Reliza and Dr Terry said in unison.

Stella smiled. Things in this quarter of the world of romance were looking up. She wondered what had tipped the scale. It might have been their shared worry over Thelma and Stella herself, but more likely that their reunion could be traced back through the simple rhythms of romance: the ups and downs, draws and resistances, riffs and fugues that make young love such an enduring pursuit.

Stella said, "I must ask you two for something, and Riley can't know I told you."

The doctor and care worker exchanged a look. Dr Terry said, "I might tell that guy the time of day, but that's about it."

Reliza nodded. "What do you need?"

Stella looked over her shoulder. Riley was engaged in wheedling Thelma into her walker. He couldn't possibly overhear. "It's about Rose Corridor. Don't let Riley dispense their meds anymore. He's been withholding meds when he doesn't like cleaning up accidents. So, it might not be enough just to give him the cold shoulder. I'm afraid he'll bear watching."

Dr Terry frowned out the window at Riley, who was helping Thelma into the walker's seat. "I'll see if I can have him fired."

Stella wanted to say better the devil you know and can keep an eye on, especially when Riley would doubtless go to another care home where they didn't know his little ways. But she could see it for the poor argument it was, so she only said, "You'll have a hard time proving grounds for his dismissal to the Warden on *my* say-so, but good luck to you. What about the diaper situation in Rose? Any more threats from the board to send the incontinent ones to other homes?"

Reliza shook her head. "Rose Corridor as a group is wearing pull-ons so that none of them is singled out to leave Fairmount for long-term facilities."

Heroes. They were everywhere, weren't they? Stella tipped a salute in what she hoped was the direction of Rose Corridor. She supposed there might come a day when that particular band of sisters would break up, but today was not that day.

Theo appeared at the entry to the foyer. He tugged his yellow cardigan straight around his middle, and a smile crossed his dear face. In fact, he looked happier than Stella had seen him for months. An urge to show him her new travel handbag and relate to him yesterday's adventures overwhelmed her, and she stepped up beside him and slipped her arm through his. They exchanged smiles of easy friendship, for she and he were unified still by the shared architecture of this institution, by similar, quiet senses of humour, and by the bone-deep patience of career educators — hers in the elementary school system, his at the university level.

Together they watched Thelma make her way up the little shrub-lined path to the front door. She did so on her own terms, pushing the walker before her rather than riding in it, while her cane teetered on the walker's seat. Riley hurried around her to open the foyer door.

Above the rattle and roll of Thelma's walker wheels, Stella heard the click of the front door as it shut the lot of them inside Fairmount's foyer. It was the sound of closure, and with it her pleasure at returning home vanished. Now she felt that she had lost something vital and irreplaceable: her citizenship of the outside world. Yesterday, she had belonged out there — a senior citizen, but a citizen. With the click of the door, that entitlement was gone as if she had never left Fairmount at all. As if her final connection to a normal life was severed.

Tears pricked her eyes. *Soldier on.*

Outside the window, Icarus the Saab's door opened on its own. Maybe that simply meant that Riley should take more care than to leave doors imperfectly closed. But a second later she recognized the message of the Saab, which was that she'd got her situation all wrong. She had not left the outside world, for she was still connected to it through this very Saab and their shared adventures. From there, the Saab was connected to the road, which was connected to the city, wherein lived people she knew, however short- or long-term these friendships had been, because they were social networks unbound by proximity or even chronology. Along with a lifetime of connections she'd made in school and out of it, she now knew the young couple expecting the baby, the Voltaire-reading shop clerk, the bus-riding woman with her perfectly tied scarf, Wallace and Andres (she felt badly about abandoning Wallace, but that guilt was a connection too), Jase and his phone, the nurses and the Community Aid volunteers in their green hats.

All these persons were connected to one another as of yesterday, and, if you investigated that network, the source of these connections was none other than Stella, right here in Fairmount Manor. She stood up straight, gripped Theo's arm tighter, and hooked her other thumb through the strap of her travel handbag. Nothing and nobody could take away her pleasure in her adventures over the past day. Nor could anything diminish her success in finding Thelma and returning with her, rather as if Stella's friend were a sort of elderly Golden Fleece.

The staccato patter of good-quality high-heeled shoes approaching at speed heralded the arrival in their midst of Mrs Perdita Warren, Director of Fairmount Manor. Her arms were full of flowers, as they'd been the day before when she was adorning the bulletin boards in anticipation of the Board's visit. But these blossoms were not cut out of paper.

These were the real deal: a grand bouquet of orange and red gerberas, drooping lilacs, and spiky pink carnations, all tied up with straw ribbons.

"How pretty," Stella said.

The Warden clacked to a stop. She looked from Thelma to Theo to Stella. "These are for you."

She pushed the overwhelming mass of flowers at Stella, who let go of Theo's elbow to take hold of them.

"Who sent me flowers?"

The Warden dug in her suit jacket pocket, pulled out a small envelope of the sort that florists attach to deliveries, and held it out to Stella. Stella passed the flowers to Theo in order to examine the note. She observed that the envelope had been opened, no doubt by the Warden herself. She imagined the curiosity and condescension with which the Warden would have read Stella's personal correspondence and burned with displeasure.

She pulled out the card; had Vaughn sent her a bouquet to follow the gift of money he'd given her the previous morning? In her day, when boys sent flowers and a gift within a twenty-four-hour period, the girls called it *rushing*. Moreover, girls were wary of rushers.

Stella opened the card and found that somebody had hand-written the words *Thanks, Stell!* and what was certainly not a V for Vaughn but a J for Jase.

The Warden said, "Another grandson, perhaps?"

"Just a friend. Thank you."

One might have thought that Mrs Warren's manners, if not her ruddy job description, might have prompted her to welcome Stella and Thelma back from hospital. At the very least, she ought to congratulate Thelma on her rapid recovery from surgery. Instead, the Warden turned on her expensive heels and paced swiftly away. Stella exchanged a look with Riley, who winked at her, jingled his car keys, and walked out the door towards his Saab.

Reliza took the flowers from Theo; Jase had certainly gone overboard with the bouquet, which was so colossal that it hid the young care worker's upper body from view. She offered to find Stella a vase of an appropriate size.

"And then, I'll put them on the bureau in your room."

Stella thanked her. "Let's have them in the dining room instead. And keep my name out of it, if you don't mind."

Reliza smiled and walked in that direction. A few blossoms fell from her arms as she walked. Dr Terry followed and retrieved the fallen flowers, like a hair-gelled Ruth gleaning the field where a pretty Boaz passed.

Stella's heart lifted. She took Theo's hand, gave it a squeeze, and let it go; but he took her hand back in his. His gesture reminded Stella that despite inequities, aches, and pains, these later years of life weren't always tragic.

Nor were they the second childhood the world promised for your old age. That particular promise always sounded to Stella more like a threat, as if in her old age the world would give her something to cry about. She smiled to herself and then spread the smile around to Thelma, who couldn't see it, and Theo, who returned it.

Stella helped Thelma turn her walker into position to take on Fairmount's circuitous corridors. She and Theo stood on either side.

"Are you sure you're up to this?" Stella asked. "I don't want you to fall down and end up with a second pin in your hip."

"Stella Ryman, you heard that good nurse tell me to walk. I told her about you" — she jerked her head towards Theo — "walking everywhere around and around Fairmount.

She said you'd probably live forever."

Theo thanked her in his quiet tones, and Thelma grunted. Stella appreciated the value of being one of three friends. Two friends together had fun, the way a bicycle with its two wheels was a delight to ride. But three was a solid number of chums, like a tripod or one of those three-legged stools common to homes from prehistoric to Swedish Modern times. Three standing together could endure any strain.

They strolled—Stella and Theo—and rolled—Thelma—their winding way towards Corridor Park. When they rounded the corner, they found that all the bright paper flowers the Warden had lately stapled to the bulletin boards had been unstapled and strewn about the floor. Above this scissored garden, the Greek Chorus sat in a prim row against the wall of Corridor Park. Iolanthe and Lucille looked up from their crewel work at the three new arrivals, and Sally lowered her golden snips.

Iolanthe said, "My goodness, how lucky. We were hoping that you weren't dead."

Lucille said, "Of course, nobody's irreplaceable. I learned that at work."

"But nobody's interchangeable either," Iolanthe added. Sally nodded.

Stella took a second look at the paper flowers lying on the floor and deduced the reason for them.

"All this for us?" Stella gestured at the display and clarified for Thelma, who would see only scraps of colour at the periphery of her dying vision. "They've spread flowers in our path, Thelma."

"I don't believe it," Thelma said.

"Unless it was you, Theo?"

Theo shook his head.

"Thank you," Stella said to the Greek Chorus. They exchanged looks.

"Well, it's more or less a sop," Lucille said.

"An indication of our appreciation," Iolanthe said, although she was in general one of the least appreciative persons on earth. "And we rather hope that you'll take on a case for us."

"A case?" Stella felt her ears prick up.

"An investigation. Have you seen that real estate fellow with his measuring tape? There's nasty business happening here."

"I smell money." Lucille, with her long career as a loans officer for a major bank behind her, narrowed her eyes.

"Everything always leads to money," Thelma said.

"And where there's money, don't think you won't find a rat." Iolanthe pointed her needle at Stella. "We've been watching, and we have several motives and suspects."

"We're not the sleuths, though," Lucille said. "We are the sniffers of smoke."

"There's smoke, all right," Thelma said. "I still want to know where all those mahogany tables got to when they exchanged them for the aluminium cheapies we've got now. Those tables were worth a little bundle in the furnishings trade."

"It's all connected, that's what we think," Iolanthe said.

Stella inclined her head. "And there are missing funds budgeted for food. I saw some of the numbers when I stole the Warden's papers not too long ago."

"Do you still have them?" Iolanthe demanded.

"I do." She had hidden them in her bureau under her least favourite floral knit shirt, the one with all the purple on it.

"Well, why haven't you brought these people to

justice already?"

Lucille said, "Stella's too busy gadding about the city. Look at her with her new cross-body handbag."

Thelma rolled her walker back and forth with one red silk-shod toe. "If it's a really big fraud, it's going to be outside as well as in."

Funny business with prime real estate property—property dedicated for the use of one of society's most vulnerable populations—would indeed be a serious matter. A very significant concern indeed. Stella smiled.

Theo helped Thelma into her chair with her cane and pushed the walker against the wall. Stella sat down on her own chair at Thelma's side. Now that a new mystery loomed, she felt happier to be back under her skylight—what she sometimes thought of as the last stop on the bus route of life—than she could have imagined possible before her voyages outside.

The adventures of the preceding two days had proven that, even here at Fairmount Manor, life was not over until you actually died. And what a comfortable thought that was. It was an understanding that managed to include all of humanity and at the same time be unique to her in her situation here at Fairmount, to be enjoyed with Thelma at her side and Theo nearby.

Theo raised his hand in adieu before leaving to walk Fairmount's corridors.

"There he goes again," Iolanthe sighed. "Off on his own."

"And rumour has it, to live forever."

The four of them smiled at the in-joke. Even though Fairmount residents had little control over their surroundings and were bound by the strictures and structures of institution, they and all Fairmount residents comprised a society unto themselves.

The world outside, getting and spending, wasn't interested in their dull days in here, or in the lives they'd led in service to their communities and greater mankind. But the residents themselves knew what lives they'd led. Some had lived adventures beyond the imaginings of following generations, and some had lived microcosms of small, sweet love stories and family drama. Theirs were tales like old books with thick pages that most people these days would never read.

If Stella looked at it from that angle, it was clear that she, Theo, Thelma, and the rest of Fairmount's residents could boast the great treasures of privacy and social independence, accorded by society to only the most boring of folk. And the beauty was that, with untold rich lives behind them, they didn't have to be boring if they didn't want to. However, they could be as restfully and obnoxiously dull as they liked, and no care worker or visitor would blink an eye or weigh in with a remonstration. As long as a resident could toilet herself and present a bland facial expression to the Warden, she could operate beneath the radar of administration.

Stella was still not allowed to go outside, but in a way, she was freer now than she'd ever been in the course of her busy life. She was also closer to death than she'd ever been, but perhaps it was a good moment to question the linearity of a lifespan. Arguably, she'd been nearer to dying when she was twelve and the safety strap on a fair ride snapped; at thirty-eight, the time the car ahead of her had been T-boned; not to mention the repeated and nearly infinite fatal possibilities that had never terrified her, for the hammer of death had fallen and missed her, without her ever knowing.

Stella smiled. Theories of mortality were welcome to wheel

about in her mind, even though conclusions often eluded her. She longed to ask Sartre whether, existentially speaking, and given the dangers of modern traffic, all human beings were not equidistant to their demises. She also desired to interview Descartes, not regarding *'I think therefore I am'*——she had ceased to credit this credo since arriving at Fairmount——but to talk over his mathematic proposal, that life was geometrically a ray rather than a finite line segment. She wondered whether Descartes might not agree that everybody's lifetime was made up of an infinite number of points.

This mathematical thinking pleased her, because in math, the number of points on a line was infinite, and so nobody's life should ever quite reach its end. Furthermore, although Descartes had not weighed in on this extrapolation so far as Stella knew, she believed there were as many unsolved mysteries in the world as points on a ray.

She said, "The next game's afoot, Thelma. Let's take a minute to rest our bones, and then we'll have at this new mystery."

"I'm with you, Stella Ryman. But let's take as many minutes as we have bones," Thelma suggested.

Stella tilted her head back, gazed up at the blue sky above her skylight, and counted her bones and her blessings.

Acknowledgements

My deep thanks to JM Landels, Susan Pieters, Amanda Bidnall, Sierra Louie, Ellen Spacey, Carol McCauley, and Mark Halden, who generously read manuscripts and made each one better because of their own talents, methods, intelligence, humour, and grace.

My gratitude also to all the readers who review my stories to say how much they like Stella Ryman, as this keeps me conniving at more mysteries and typing away.

Mel Anastasiou, September 2025
Bowen Island, BC, Canada

Stella Ryman walked into my life one April afternoon as I was hanging about in a care home corridor, waiting to help move an enormous television into an elderly acquaintance's new bedroom. I liked the staff and the elderly women who sat in the corridor, chatting just as if it were a park. Corridor Park. I asked myself, What if I lived here? What on earth would I do with myself? How do you wake up every morning, knowing that people are responsible for you but that you are responsible for nothing but agreeable behaviour? (There seemed to be some possibilities for rebellion here.) We all need a good reason to get out of bed in the morning. What would that be? Television? Hell no. Complaining about the food? Possibly. But Stella Ryman would have a better idea. And so she becomes … (tag line approaching) … an amateur sleuth, trapped in a down-at-heel care home.

You'd be cranky too.

The Seven Swans

Book 1

One

Spring sunlight listed at a five o'clock angle across the London rooftops and in through the window by my battered desk in the tutors' room. And, on this day of all days, wherein everything I had known, loved, or endured for forty years teetered atop a precipice, I sat with the sun's glow on my cheek and told myself stories. Beginnings of stories, at least; lately I'd been feeling too worried, restless, and impecunious to imagine happy endings, or even what sort of hero I would like to be. But I love a mystery, and when I star in one, I try to rescue a heroine in it if I possibly can. On the day my imaginary worlds collided with real life, I had last seen my real-life heroine forty years before, if you didn't count her picture hidden in my wallet behind the National Health card you are issued when you move permanently from Canada to the UK.

As for my wife Angelica's photo, I kept that in plain view on my desk out of affection and appreciation for her good looks. At our desks where we interviewed our students, all we tutors at the Cheapside College of English as a Second Language displayed caringly framed photos of our spouses. It gave the young girls in their flippy little skirts something to look at while they tried to raise their grades by wishing out loud. My wife's picture was an excellent one. In it, Angelica, in linen top and trousers, sat posed upon a beach ball outside Wordsworth's cottage at Grasmere, holding a cup of coffee in the rain. She glowed. Our old friend Byron—Angelica's ex-husband—had taken that photo. He'd captured her high-beam smile and shining dark curls. My desk picture of Angelica was an object of envy for most of my fellow tutors. I must add that it was just about the only thing they envied me; that and my desk by the window, attained not through promotion but by outlasting all previous occupants of the room.

In fairness, Angelica at sixty could not be expected to compete with the twenty-year-old Holly, whose photo I had carried with me for forty years.

I heard cheering and looked up from my imaginings and Holly's picture. Two desks over, my colleague Albie was grading his papers by tossing them towards the stairwell door to see which travelled farthest. But the cheering stopped when a delivery man unfamiliar with young Albie's evaluation process walked in holding a large tape-wrapped carton, slipped on the papers, and thudded to the floor. The box landed among the compositions beside him, wrong way up.

The delivery man was a fellow of about my own age. I ran over and helped him to his feet, while my colleague Glory rescued the carton and set it right side up.

"You came down pretty hard," I said.

One hand on the small of his back, the delivery man said,

"I'll outlive the lot of you."

"I know about bad backs," I said. "Shouldn't you get something for yours?"

He screwed up his face. "Maybe. Once I get the rest of these bloody boxes lugged up those effing stairs."

"I'll help you out. And my fellow tutors will give us a hand."

They did: Albie led our colleagues in an ironic round of applause.

"Ah, the old jokes are the best," I said tolerantly.

"You should know, Spencer," Glory joked back. Five o'clock struck, and most of the other tutors rose to get their tea, but Albie and Glory stayed behind, and together we followed the delivery man down the plunging stairwell to the street. There, from a battered van, we took identically sized but differently weighted cartons and made two trips up and down the stairs before the youngsters' wind gave out and they joined their fellows in the lounge. Then we two oldies finished the job.

When about a dozen boxes were stacked on the prep room floor to the right of my desk, the delivery man and I stood at my open window, breathing hard and trying not to show it.

"I could murder a pint." The delivery man gazed with obvious interest at Angelica's picture on my desk. "Lovely woman, your wife."

"Thanks. I can get you a still water from the staff lounge."

"Cold water after a climb like that. At our age? You're simply begging for a heart attack. Sign this." He proffered a little electronic box and stylus.

Stylus poised, I said, "There's no name on the boxes. Who are they for, anyway?"

"All the client said was, for the oldest person in the room."

"Oh." Sarey was the second oldest in our tutoring staff, but she was elsewhere with a student. I took a deep breath. "Who asked you to deliver these boxes to me?"

He jerked his thumb at my wife Angelica's picture. "She did."

I swallowed hard.

He said, "Sorry, mate."

"Not your fault," I managed.

He squeezed my arm and wished me luck before heading back to the stairs.

I stood alone in the staff room. Through habit, I opened my wallet again. Holly's photo was so very different from my wife's. Angelica's photo was taken against grey clouds and white drizzle, while behind Holly's golden head the long-ago Mediterranean sky shone a pale, hot blue.

I closed my wallet again as the tutors filed back into the prep room and gathered around the boxes. Young Albie pushed at one with his toe, and it rattled brokenly.

Two

What is the opposite of *architecture?* Because I want to tell this story correctly, and I nearly wrote that the architect of my marital dissolution entered the prep room. But architects build structures or at least design them so that they may be erected. They do not bulldoze or demolish. So, I will write instead that at this poignant moment, with the afternoon sun striking white light off the shiny foreheads and noses of my colleagues and gleaming on the packing tape securing the piled-up cartons containing all my earthly goods, the wrecking ball of my twenty-year marriage to pretty Angelica entered the room.

Or did not quite enter the prep room. For Byron Standard-Clarke stood in the shadows just outside the prep room door and gazed in at us. From this high point — because Byron was a tall thin glass of Pimm's — he could stand with all eyes upon him, while he ignored everybody around him.

Everybody except me.

My fellow tutors swivelled their chairs to study him. Admittedly Byron was always worth watching. Especially today, in what I could only call his ascendency.

His eyebrow arched. I rose to my feet, schooling my features to give nothing of my thoughts away.

Byron said, "Wotcher, Spence."

I answered, "How's it hanging, then, Byron?"

"Much as it has been for months, I'm afraid." He inclined his head and tactfully did not refer more pointedly to his affair with my wife these past six months. "But then we're both at the mercy of Angelica's sense of timing, aren't we?"

I replied, "Apparently so."

Byron set his large, slender hand atop one of the stacked cartons. His hair gleamed in the sunny room, the exact yellow of his cashmere V-neck. "How awkwardly Angelica-esque all this is, Spence. I'm so sorry."

"I'm sure," I said drily.

"*Be* sure," Byron urged me. "And anyway, admit it — who's the poor devil stuck with Angelica now?"

"True," I said, conscious of the twenty eyes upon me. "Still, I'll have to work hard to feel sorry for you."

"You're just the fellow for the work."

The other tutors watched us like Wimbledon. Byron slapped the top box, and we could all hear the tinkling sound from within. "Gosh, were those your Hummel figurines?"

"Angelica's Hummels."

"She says they're yours."

"Her parents gave one to us every year, with a cheque wrapped round it. The Hummels were addressed to both."

"But the cheque made out to her? So, in fairness, with the breakup of the home, you receive the Hummels. Anyway, she told me she was tired of them, so she's getting rid of them."

I knew just how the Hummels felt.

"Well, never mind, Spence. Imagine when she gets tired of me, like she did twenty years back," Byron said with a sympathetic lift of his eyebrow. "Maybe she'll box me up again and send me off too."

"Leave old Spence here alone, why don't you?" young Albie burst out.

"Yeah. What's your deal, anyway?" Glory demanded.

"Thanks, but Byron and my wife are—"

Byron interrupted, addressing all those present. "Old Spence here will have painted me the Scarlet Woman in this lover's triangle. But have a heart, who would ever have thought that Angelica would fall for a skinny, toffee-nosed old git like myself?"

Glory said with spirit, "He didn't say a word about it. But I think you're a sod to steal Spence's wife." There was a rattle in the carrels, a little like the sound of swords drawn at the ready. I had heard that clatter before, and so I stepped back out of the way as a hail of erasers, paper clips, and correcting pencils flew towards Byron, and he covered his head with his hands.

"That's nice of you," I said, touched by their loyalty. "But to be fair, Angelica's got a tendency towards Byron. He was married to her twenty years ago."

"Boo," my co-workers cried. "Yar sucks!"

"Any more missiles?" Byron said. "No? Thank you. And I agree, poor cuckolded Spence! But don't lose hope, everybody, because Angelica's papa and maman have an offer for him."

Glory said, "It had better be a good one. I've seen Spence's credit card bills."

A rumble of agreement followed from my colleagues.

"Your colleagues burst with loyalty and integrity, Spence, but the time has come to talk without the cheers from the benches." Byron drew a thick white envelope out of his trouser pocket. It was clearly labelled *Expenses*. He opened the envelope, pulled out a fistful of ten-pound notes, and held them up for all to see. "Three of these for the first to put on his or her coat and take leave of us. Two for the second. And the rest of you wankers get one if you're gone within a minute."

Thirty seconds later, the prep room stood empty. Tucking the slightly depleted envelope away in the back pocket of his trousers, Byron shrugged.

"Alone at last," he said.

But I was thinking furiously about that envelope. And the handwriting of the word *Expenses*, so clearly a product of French Lycée instruction. "They sent you, didn't they?"

"Who?"

"Angelica's parents. They gave you that money to get quit of me."

Byron cleared his throat. "Of course. Just as they gave you an envelope of expense money twenty years ago to get rid of *me*, if you recall."

I did remember. "And it worked. But here you are again, the third husband, second time round."

"Repetition, employed for word power! Superb writing craft! I hope they've made you the head of the department."

"No."

"Then you're still broke. Perfect. Papa and Maman did ask me to use what I needed for an incentive to make a healthy break."

"It's not as fat an envelope as the one I gave you back then," I pointed out.

"Denominations, perhaps?" He inclined his head. "Smaller bills, larger packet. This might hold a thousand-pound note for all you know."

"There's no such thing."

"There could be stock certificates worth …"

I held up a hand. "Don't even bother. I know how Papa and Maman operate."

"Of course you do." Byron nodded. "But you don't know how I operate."

"I remember that twenty years ago you took their money and left town. I never will."

"If you'll look closely, you will see in my eyes the enduring respect I have for you, half hidden by my natural restraint."

I said, "If I give *you* twenty pounds out of that envelope, will you leave and return it to Papa and Maman?"

He sat down in my chair, and with thumb and forefinger flicked at the paper clips and marking pens scattered across my desk, sending them through the open doorway to clatter onto the steps. "I told them there was a sporting chance you wouldn't accept the money."

"You know me too well," I said coldly.

"Gosh, Spence, we've been friends for forty years. And everybody in the world of our acquaintance knows about your circumstances—the recklessly extended credit, the wracking debt."

"All incurred for Angelica." I rolled Glory's chair over to my desk and sat on it. "You know as well as I do that's how she operates. You were nearly broke when she divorced you."

"Vacations in Florida," Byron said gloomily.

"Parties in Majorca."

"Queen Anne replica settees. Replica! You really stepped in it there, you old pauper."

I threw an eraser at his head. "Byron, how much of that envelope did you spend on the yellow cashmere you're wearing?"

"Spence, I knew I could count on your generous spirit of long friendship to help me out as I begin a new life."

"And long enmity. Aside from sartorial elegance, what did you spend Papa and Maman's money on?"

"I spent most of the money in the envelope for you, Spence."

"Really? On what?"

"Well, the delivery company," he said, indicating the boxes stacked on the prep room floor. "And wining and dining Papa and Maman."

"With their own money!"

"On your behalf," Byron said sturdily. "Also, I paid my last three months' strata fees and council taxes. I had to, to sell my flat to move in with Angelica. That took a fair bit out. So, this has been fantastic, really." Byron patted his back pocket.

"First rate," I said coldly.

"First rate for you. Because now we come to the real offer that Angelica's parents have asked me to make. Spence, how do you like your newly landed status as the owner of that bright jewel on the shores of the Grand Union Canal, Hertfordshire, the Seven Swans pub and eatery?"

Three

I shaded my eyes from the nearly direct sunlight through the prep room window and scowled at Byron. "There are at least two reasons why I, who have never run such a business—"

"Or indeed any commercial enterprise at all—"

"—shouldn't do it. My famous inability to add a string of three four-digit numbers together, for one thing."

"And you can never calculate a tip, much less keep a ledger. I did mention that to Angelica's parents. Also, there's the concern about …"

I interrupted. "Exactly. I do not drink."

Byron narrowed his eyes and nodded. "As long as that really is still true, you ought to take their offer."

The biggest reason not to waste a moment of time on thinking about running a derelict Hertfordshire pub was that the suggestion came from Angelica and her parents. And Byron. Above all the rest, write in yellow cashmere letters the name 'Byron'.

Furthermore, it is never a good idea to take financial advice from a competitor, particularly not if he has been sleeping with your wife for the past six months.

I said, "Look, Byron, what makes you believe that I would want a rundown pub in Hertfordshire?"

"Because it's located on a canal. A peaceful waterway, glittering in sunshine, overhung with willow trees and graced with hawthorn."

Compared to this grubby college prep room, it did sound beautiful. I could picture the timbered walls, blue sky above the red-tiled roof, and the gentle trickle of cold black Guinness into a pint glass—

Hmm. A pub did involve drink. Which I must resist, along with this offer of a canal-side beauty spot. If I was not very careful, Byron and my wife's parents would have me in their pockets as sure as Holly's photo was in mine.

I walked out. Byron followed. I suppose I knew he would.

I stumped down the stairs, his clever tapping brogues close behind. I led the way out the door and around the corner onto Lower Tower Bridge Road. A moment later, his arm slipped through mine, and he drew me down a snicket into a timbered Victorian pub called Wooster's World. It was jam-packed with garrulous City people and there wasn't an empty seat in the place. Because I didn't touch alcohol, I had steered clear of pubs for the last twenty years, since Angelica and I had married. If she hadn't sent my possessions to the office that day, I would have spun on my heel, slipped out through the door, and made a run for Tower Hill Station. Instead, I found a spot against the wall and leaned there, hands in my pockets.

Over the chattering denizens, I said, "You know, Byron, you may have made one good point."

He leaned towards me. "What did you say?"

"Looking at this place, I can see that a well-run pub could at least make a profit."

Byron's eyebrows shot up; he knew me as well as I knew him. He said, "And I know how badly you need money. Or your creditors do, at least."

"Bless their helpful hearts," I said. "But that just goes to show what a poor financial manager I am. So, I'll tell you what. If it's such a gold mine, you take it, Byron. Buy me out with some of your recent inheritance from that uncle of yours. When was that? About six months ago?"

"The inheritance is down for the count, I fear. You know Angelica," he said. "Her excellent taste in home furnishings and discriminating buying practices."

"Well, borrow from your next inheritance, then. And cut me in on half the profits of the pub. Start with a down payment tonight from Papa and Maman's envelope so that I can rent myself and my cardboard cartons a new place to live. I'm thinking of Islington, near the canal, because you've described canals with such evocative power."

"Cheeky," Byron observed.

"Not at all. It honours the letter of Papa and Maman's request and benefits us both."

Byron gazed at me from beneath hooded, rather intelligent blue eyes. "I'm getting us a drink."

He pushed away from the wall and off through the crowd. "I don't drink, remember?" I called after him, but my words were swallowed by the drinkers with their goblets of ruby and pints of golden clear. I frowned, asking myself exactly how much of the contents of that envelope I could wiggle away from Byron. Contents meant for me. My existing credit would scarcely cover a single night in a central London hotel.

I was just imagining that with cash in hand and access to my computer at the college, I might find an immediate roommate in a dodgy corner of the City, when a hand gripped my arm. Glory from work shoved half a lager against my open palm and closed my fingers around it. "Compliments of your fellow work slaves, on your maiden trip here to Wooster's World."

"No, thanks very much, though."

She hid her hands behind her back. "You're with that golden-haired dickhead, so you'll need at least one."

"It's very kind, but …" I frowned at the half. Carling, or Becks, I guessed. I'd never told the staff about my old problem with alcohol.

She grinned. "Take two big slugs, toss the rest in his face, and come join your happy colleagues around the corner on the smoking patio. It's Albie's round."

With a wink she left me, my back to the wall, staring down at a half pint cool as a January day. I was thirsty, and there wasn't a person in sight who would know or care whether I drank this glass of lager or not.

Four

You don't expect to see fists come towards you in a City pub like Wooster's World. Indeed, up to this moment, standing beneath the decorator shelves of fruit and drink that embellished the pub walls, the only fists that had come near me were those of peaceful businesspeople, fingers wrapped around halves of IPA or glasses of white wine and soda, or else their opposite fists, the ones they'd used to wave their cigarettes around with directive emphasis. But since the ban on smoking in pubs they'd jammed their hands inside suit pockets, saving their lungs and spoiling sartorial lines. Thus, despite all that I knew about Byron and his boxing days at Cambridge, his unpredictability after forty years was so damned predictable that I was not expecting his pale, narrow fist to spring out from among the three-season-suited onlookers to land itself on my face.

So unexpected was the blow that at first, I thought that the shelf of Pimm's and bottled fruit above my head had toppled. Then, I realized that he had slugged me. And in that fateful, brief second between the blow and what-comes-of-it, two thoughts flashed through my mind. The first was, *The benefit of his Cambridge education is that he remembered to keep his fist straight when he hit me.* The second, stronger thought was, *Don't spill my beer!*

But it was too late; as his punch hit, the beer glass flew from my hand and cleared a space behind Byron. Forty years ago, Byron himself had taught me to swivel my torso, clench my fist, and deliver an answering blow. So, I pulled back a little farther and straightened my wrist to deliver the volley. I knew that when I landed it, a battle would begin in earnest, even in the midst of all these staring City types, because Byron, when he started a pub fight, always shouted, *Take sides, you bastards*, and then people did take sides, even if only for or against taking sides, or for or against allowing toffs to call them bastards. But it didn't, because before I could connect with his narrow, beckoning chin, my back went into spasm.

Until now, I'd fancied myself as the silent hero of the scene, in calm receipt of the slender villain's attack. Now, I let out a yelp a large dog would have been ashamed of, twisted, and fell to the floor. I lay there, unmoving, my legs straight out in front of me, my eyes on the shelves of Pimm's above, and my shoes in the puddle of lager and broken glass. A sudden, closing-time silence fell over the pub. Everybody in the place stood as vertically unmoving as I was horizontally so. Then, with a shift of brogues and tasselled loafers, of Clark's strapped pumps and John Lewis boots, the crowd moved closer round Byron and me.

"Steady," I heard somebody say.

The bartender barked from the far-off bar, "Do us a favour and take it outside. The law's on its way."

"Sorry," Byron said, not to me, but in the barman's direction. "It was an accident."

Laughter sounded, the relieved sort that arises from the understanding that one's after-work drink is not to be seriously interfered with. Glory pushed her way out of the crowd and knelt at my side. I looked up at her. At that moment, I was lying in an A-shaped design of limbs and torso. So long as nobody touched me, I was not in too much agony. I hissed, "I'm all right."

Glory looked from the mess of lager and glass on the floor up to Byron. "What did you hit Spence for?"

Byron said, "I didn't hit him." He turned to the business-suited men and women around us, all of them chatting as if nothing had happened. He asked, "Did any of you possible witnesses in an assault case to be tried during banking hours see me hit him?"

"Not a thing, sorry …"

"I was in the loo …"

"At the bar, as it happens …"

Only Glory stood up and faced Byron down. I stared up at her. I had thought myself alone in an uncaring universe, but here was somebody who was at least asking the question: "Why?"

"Why what?" Byron asked her.

"Why. Did. You. Punch. Spencer."

"If he was a gentleman, he would have punched himself."

"I'd like to punch you, then," Glory said.

"Spence knows I did it for his own good." Byron poked my middle with a shining shoe-tip.

From my spot on the floor, I said, "I wasn't going to drink that beer. I never would. Not in a million years."

"You looked like you were. Well then, you pass the test after all, and you can be a sot and still run the Seven Swans pub."

Glory's eyes widened. "Spence, are you an alcoholic? No wonder you never drink with us. Sari wins the betting pot, then. *I* thought you were henpecked and your wife wouldn't let you come to the pub with the rest of us. Albie thought you were off chasing one of the students. He saw a picture of one of the girls in your wallet."

"I'm not interested in girls, or even young women," I protested. And it was true, except for Holly and her young face and figure in the photo I'd thought I had hidden so well in my wallet. And Holly wasn't a young woman, anyway. She was sixty-two by now, just like me.

"Tell that to Albie," Glory said drily. "He thinks you're a letch."

I grunted, but through my grunt I heard the whine of a distant siren.

Byron said to Wooster's World at large, "Help me get Spence to his feet before the cops get here."

I bit my tongue and managed not to moan as Byron, with the help of a couple of nearby IPA drinkers, lifted me onto my feet. Byron thanked them and said to Glory, "There is a point, like the still point of a tornado, where Spence can stand quite still and not feel his back pain. I think we've found that point."

I tottered and bit my tongue. Byron said, "Just help me get the poor old fellow to a cab, won't you?"

The two of them wrestled me, a rigid, silent stick figure, outside and under the awning on the road, where the police on their way in stepped aside to let us pass. Byron thanked them and raised his hand to hail a cab.

Byron with cabs is like some people with dogs—no sooner did he whistle than one lurched up to the curb. Byron and

Glory got me sitting, white-knuckled, against the far passenger door. Glory said farewell and disappeared back inside the pub as more police arrived. Byron murmured something into the cab driver's ear and climbed in behind him. We pulled swiftly out into traffic.

I said, "My back pills must be in one of those boxes at the college. Or I can get some at the pharmacy on Old Street."

"Closed, old boy. Are you sure you weren't going to drink that lager?"

I glared at him.

"Swear? Good."

"Just get me medical help," I said.

Byron, who hit me, and Byron, who slept with Angelica, said, "Of course," and patted my shoulder, gently and with sympathy in his hooded eyes.

My left hand gripped the cab door. My right clutched the back of the seat. I squeezed my eyes shut, so that I could visualize holding my spine in the particular line that brought the fewest, least bitter slices of agony. Forget over-the-counter remedies. This kind of pain was going to take proper prescription drugs, and maybe painkillers of the sort that nurses inject, the kind of drug that just to think about it brings a smile to the face of certain excitable weekend users I'd known in my youth, travelling Europe on my outstretched thumb. Demerol. Morphine. At any rate, painkillers plastered with warnings, the ones that feel like cool streams running down the surface of one's mountain slope of pain.

"Are we there yet?" I croaked. "Are we at Old Street? Have we reached the hospital?"

Byron nodded, "Not yet, poor old fellow."

"How much farther, then?"

"Do you know, I hear that they're bringing back hospital matrons. That'll shake up the hypochondriacs."

"How many more turns until we get to the hospital?"

"With the one-ways, only fourteen," the cabbie said over his shoulder. We eased over a speed bump, and I strangled my groan.

Byron said, "Spence, I have long held that it's only since the hospital matrons were disbanded that the economy went to hell. Cleaner wards bring a stronger pound, don't you think?"

"I love the National Health Service," I said. "You, on the other hand, had better watch out when I get my mobility back. If you hadn't slugged me …"

I broke off the threat as the cab sped up, squealed round a corner, and jerked to a halt.

"Here we are," Byron said. "Don't worry, I won't tip the driver."

"Tip him," I mumbled. "Wife and children."

I rolled an inch to one side in anticipation of wiggling out of the back seat with Byron's help. After that, I'd be amongst the warm hands and cool drugs of the orderlies and nurses who would band together to come to my aid at Old Street Hospital Emergency.

"My poor sainted invalid," Byron murmured.

"Everybody stay calm. I'm sure I'll be back on my feet in no time …"

Just then a door banged, and a new voice spoke. Not the cab driver. Not a nurse. A woman, and one whose voice I knew well.

"You've got him all right. Well done, Byron."

My eyes snapped open. My wife, dark curls shining, was gazing down at me where I lay across the back seat of the cab.

Angelica wore an expression of friendly, even wifely, concern. "Can you walk, Spence?"

"Certainly," I assured her. "With a big man on either side of me to hold my spine straight. Thanks for coming, Angelica."

She turned to Byron. "Pay the man, you brainless, handsome thing. And you there—"

The cab driver started.

"Wait. I want your help."

Byron fished the notes for the fare out of Angelica's parents' white envelope. I looked past Angelica for the hospital entrance sign. Instead, I made out the familiar Regency doorway with its call buzzer; above, the sitting room window; above that, our bedroom window. I was home. In Bloomsbury. Was Angelica taking me back? I felt an odd dizzy happiness followed by a mysterious feeling of sorrow that I attributed to my back pain. I felt the onset of tears, for no matter our troubles, in my hour of need Angelica had made Byron bring me home.

The cab driver lit a cigarette, sat himself on the bonnet of Angelica's blue Twingo, and openly savoured his smoke. I myself was savouring the knowledge, gained by experience, that the one thing better than hospitals and concerned medical help was twenty-four to forty-eight hours of lying on my own carpet, with my legs up on my own coffee table, with my own wife who knew the drill, bringing me back pills and tea until agony departed and normal service resumed.

But, at a gesture from Angelica, the cab driver stamped out his cigarette in the gutter by the Twingo's back tire. He and Byron hauled me out of the back seat of the cab, onto the sidewalk, past the front door of our house and over to Angelica's blue Twingo. She pulled the passenger seat back and they wrestled me, stunned and silent, into the smaller back seat of Angelica's car. The car doors slammed shut.

I peered between the seats to see that Angelica was bent over the wheel of the Twingo, while Byron sat beside her in the passenger seat. He met my look and asked whether I was all right.

"Yes, thanks," I lied. I would not be a moaner in front of Angelica. "I'm fine, don't worry. Leave it all to the doctors. Thank you both so very much for driving me to the hospital."

Byron took Angelica's hand off the stick shift and kissed it. I witnessed the fond and forgiving look she gave him in return, the exact same look she'd bestowed upon me at regular intervals before and during our twenty years of marriage, right up until six months or so ago when Byron stepped back up to the batting plate and hit her home.

I shifted my legs so that my feet were braced against the driver's seat. And then, at last, my shoulders twisted, my legs crossed, my spine quivering in some kind of demi-spiral that averted the worst of the pain and permitted rational thought.

Rational thought told me that, as Angelica had allowed Byron to kiss her hand in front of me, she did not want me back.

On the other hand, she was driving me to the hospital, so she did still care at least a few figs for me. And although honour would not let me tell her that Byron had hit me, she would eventually find it out, as she eventually found everything out. And might not that knowledge someday turn the tide back to me?

I gazed up at the shining black curls that I had for nearly twenty years taken for granted, and thought of all the other things about Angelica and me that I realized made up our married life together: the differing political views, the shared pots of tea, the cosy bickering over the washing-up, our underwear mingled in the common warm waters of the washing machine. *Let us face facts,* I thought. *I have taken my wife for granted, and naturally, she has returned to her other, secondary port in a storm — her ex-husband Byron.*

She took a corner at top speed and sent a spear of pain up my spine. I pushed myself to sitting through it and rested the back of my head against the window. I couldn't see ahead of us, because from my position I couldn't see past Byron and Angelica. However, I could look out the side window nearest my feet. The Twingo was putting along Islington High Street, heading west towards Camden.

Is it not possible …? I asked myself. A bump shook me, and I gave a cow-like moan.

Was it not possible that within our marital context the fault lay not alone with Angelica, but with the fact that I had made more and greater mistakes than I had ever acknowledged, even to myself? And mistakes could be corrected.

And if mistakes were corrected, wouldn't she really rather have me than Byron?

Well … I found myself answering my own question with another question. *That depends, doesn't it?*

On what?

On just where these two are taking me.

For Angelica swept into and through a roundabout, and the Twingo headed north through Chalk Farm on the road out of London.

FIVE

After what seemed an hour or maybe a year, the Twingo left the paved road, rumbled along some sort of unlit rutted way, and rolled to a stop. With gentle hands, Byron and Angelica slid me out of the car and arranged me flat on my back with night-damp grass underneath me.

I blinked up at Angelica. Her downward gaze appeared evaluative. This was hardly the moment for negotiation, but I found myself promising to change.

"Give me another chance, Angelica," I said. "We do very well together on the whole."

"Have you still got that woman's picture in your wallet?"

I blinked. "I ripped it up."

Before I could even reach for my wallet to try to turn the lie into truth, Angelica vanished inside the Twingo, and I heard the car door slam shut.

Byron stood over me now. Angelica switched on the parking lights, and his yellow-cashmere-draped midsection glowed like a soft and slender moon against the dark sky. He cast a stealthy look towards the Twingo. "Sorry, old friend," he said. "But you know what she's like."

All I could do was clench my fists. "Twenty years ago, I didn't slug you and dump you in a park at night."

"Be fair, old man. You didn't have to. I holstered my guns and strode manfully into the sunset, by which I mean I flew to Ibiza and brightened six months of parties with my presence. You're much more likely to fight back or resort to begging."

"And you think this treatment's going to stop me?"

"You tell me." Byron wore his usual look of detached benevolence.

"I'm not so easy." But when I glanced at the Twingo, I felt just at this moment no great love for my wife.

"Spence, I admit this is extreme." The Twingo's engine started up with a rattle and the taillights cast a red glow across Byron's intelligent, friendly face.

"Help me up, then." Ignoring the warning spasm of pain, I raised my head. "Put me back into the car. Drive me to your apartment. Get me my back pills."

"See? You're begging." When Byron raised his arms as if to say *aha*, I saw that he held, in one hand, a small brown bag. Letting his arms fall back to his sides, he added, "Anyway, what Angelica wants she generally gets. We both know that."

I couldn't argue there.

He frowned at the Twingo. "Tell me if you know, old sport. Why do we love her, anyway?"

"She's very pretty," I said.

"She's one of a kind," he agreed. "Still, fish in the sea, *et cetera*."

"Right. Well then, I don't know why we love her. We just do."

He looked down his slender nose at me. "Here," he said. He centred the paper bag upon my chest.

Byron folded his long body into the passenger seat of the Twingo and slammed the door. Taillights brightened, springs jounced, headlights dimmed and disappeared. I lay alone on my grassy bit of land. I gazed up at the sky and rested my hands upon the bag Byron had left me. There was a patch of sky not blanketed with clouds and I could see stars to wish upon. I made several wishes before the stars disappeared and darkness took over completely.

SIX

If I had to be lying on uneven, damp terrain, I wished at least that there were no small prickly plants needling me through my summer-weight shirt and trousers. If I had to be lying alone in the night, I wished at least that there were clear skies to cheer me on and show me what was in the bag Byron had left me. I waited to see whether the changeable English skies would alter the mood of the darkness. And the weather did change. A spot of rain smacked down on my forehead. A second landed just below my ear and ran down inside my collar.

"Really?" I asked the sky.

The sky didn't answer, not even with a third raindrop.

But other sounds made themselves known. Somewhere close by, the sound of water told me I was not far from a river or canal. Tree branches brushed against each other. I heard the flutters of the breeze that had moved them. And there, at last, raindrops aplenty, travelling along the waterway towards me.

I thought back forty years to a rain shower that I had shared with Holly, the young woman whose picture I kept in my wallet. We had stood upon the crumbled ruin of the Roman wall in Umbria. I was holding a brown paper bag, something like the one Byron had left me this evening, but it had contained a prosciutto sandwich, and I slipped the bag into the front pocket of my jacket because I wanted both hands free for what I intended to be our first kiss. But the skies had opened, and her face was limned with streaming, starlit rain. Holly had laughed at the look on my face and pushed me off the wall into a puddle. *You're not made of sugar. You won't melt.* I stepped back up beside her and we stood silent while thunder cracked. We didn't kiss. Not then, anyway.

I tipped out the paper bag's contents onto my shirt, and my fingers explored four nubbly sheets of plastic. I let out a long groan of relief. Byron had left me my back pills, plasticized and entire. A fortnight's supply! I wrestled four pills out of their wrapping and swallowed them dry.

Prone on my bit of rough grass, hoping to regain the power of movement and listening to the approaching rain, I sensed that I wasn't alone. My skin prickled as it had that long-ago evening with Holly under thunderous skies. The hair stood on my thighs and forearms. A stillness off to my right contrasted with a feeling of open space on my left. I smelled stale charcoal, as from a long-dead fire.

In that moment, the rain moved off the way it had come, and the stars broke out overhead. In their light, I saw what stood to my right — a slope-roofed, black-windowed building. A couple of yards away from the building a river shone, silver and black.

And there the weather's cooperation stopped, but I knew what building I must be looking at. The Seven Swans public house, on the banks of the Grand Union Canal, the derelict pub Angelica's parents were pressing me to take in lieu of financial settlement upon our marital dissolution. The clouds rushed back, obscuring the building, and brought the rain with them. As drops ticked and splattered on and around me, I took a deep breath. The pills had not yet begun to work any sort of magic, but I rolled onto my stomach and began to wriggle towards shelter.

SEVEN

I had lived in the rainy UK for many years now, but here under the black torrential sky, it occurred to me I had never before been rained on while slithering across an open field. The experience was novel, but not because of the dampness of the grass or the sopping feel of my cotton shirt against my shoulder blades. It was the way the rain hit the back of my head and ran down the little valley just behind my ears, around the hinge of my chin, down into the hollows at my neck and shoulders, the valley of my spine, under my belt, and away southward.

I moved my left arm and left leg and then rested. I dug the heel of my right shoe into the grass, lost purchase, found it again, and pushed another inch or two towards the empty, black-eyed pub. Then, I considered whether I should lie there forever, die and be buried under the springtime and then summer grasses, or be rolled companionably along the grass and into the water by some passing hiker, becoming fodder for the fish and then, for the fisherman, supper on the table. This seemed to me an excellent way to go out of life, quiet death and useful in its way. Then I remembered that I had taken four of the back pills that Byron had left me, and although they hadn't worked yet, hope impelled me onward.

A hero soldiers on, goddamn it. I moved my left arm and my leg slid forward at least three inches this time. And another four …

I rested my cheek on the patchy grass and soft mud. I closed my eyes and let the water run over me. What a pitiful creature I was, my only good fortune being that there was nobody to see me.

Or was there?

Byron had stolen my wife, driven me far from civilization, and left me out in the rain like a basket of neglected washing, but he was more than capable of a kind act, such as returning, unbeknownst to Angelica, to help me out. I lifted my head and shoulders in the manner of a bull seal on an outcrop of rock and barked, "Byron?"

He didn't answer.

I gazed from the black and silver riverbank to the darker angles of the derelict pub. Perhaps it was a little closer than before. As I let my head drop, preparatory to wriggling onward, I caught sight out of the corner of my eye of a moving slip of white beyond the pub. I stared at the shape as it grew, nearing me. It paused for an instant, long enough for me to make out in the gloom and rain that a young woman was staring down at me from a few yards away. Drenched and muddy in her long white dress — a nightdress? — she hesitated, and then approached, in the manner of Alice's deer, neither friendly nor hostile. I could see that she was young, and therefore pretty. She looked oddly familiar.

I said, "Can you please give me a hand?"

She approached and bent over me. Her wet white sleeves slapped at my neck. She shook me by the shoulder, and it was like being struck by lightning.

She said, "Help me."

Help her? With her long pale hair and big eyes, she looked so much like Holly that she might have been a near relation. "How about you help me up, and then we can deal with your problems, all right?"

She didn't answer. She rose to her feet, turned away from me, and gazed towards the Seven Swans. As she turned, I was able to see the back of her. Against the white dress I made out the slender feathered shaft of an arrow that had pierced her back.

The warmish night turned cold.

The young woman, who reminded me of Holly, turned and ran. I left off gaping and found myself on hands and knees, crawling after her into the black shadow of the Seven Swans pub.

Eight

The rain slowed and stopped just as I reached the pub. Above the Seven Swans, clouds parted, and I saw that the moon had come up and hung low, lighting the river and the woods beyond. I laid my cheek on the cold, wet lintel stone at the doorway.

I peered sideways into the building. Moonlight found its way inside through the windows and lit up tumbled shapes that might have been stacked cartons or furniture and creature-like shapes that were more probably rubble and rubbish. I couldn't see the arrow-shot woman anywhere, although you'd think that long white dress would be visible.

I said into the darkness, "We need to get you to Emergency."

No answer.

"I don't have a car, though. But we'll figure something out." I pictured myself crawling at her feet like a pet dachshund all the way to a Hertfordshire hospital. My back spasmed again, but after the four pills I'd taken, maybe not so hellishly as before. I listened for her breathing, but there was only silence from within, and from without, the sound of the river and of branches moving and the splash of a waterbird landing.

I had seen drawings and plans for the pub long ago when Angelica's parents were considering selling it. I remembered that the male and female toilets were outside in a little outbuilding of their own. Somewhere beyond the black line, amongst the filth and rubble, must be a bar, and then a storage room. And I thought that in the way of these early pubs, there would certainly be a second barroom off to the right, with a separate entrance. The woman who looked like Holly might have wandered through, then, and would be on her way to find help on her own. With a patter that sounded like a thousand bird wings, the rain started up again. At the same time, the interior of the building grew darker, but I didn't care about that or the filth and rubble that I lay in.

I took stock and found that I felt a good deal better. I pulled myself to hands and knees and then dared to use the door frame to pull myself upright and then slid back down to sit on the floor. From this vantage I saw the woman in white fall inside the low open window on the wall closest to the river to land on the pub floor. She was silent, except for a breathy rasp.

"Dear God," I said, attempting to get my feet under me. "You might have landed on the arrow's shaft."

She didn't answer or even look at me. We were both working hard to stand up, she with the help of the ledge of the open window, and I by pulling myself up inside the door frame. As soon as I was upright, I staggered around the upended chairs and boxes, keeping my footing with difficulty on the jagged bits of rubble and sticks. And something underfoot that felt like thickly wadded tissues. "Hang on, I'm almost there."

She stood swaying by the window, but when I reached out to steady her, she pulled away. Outside, a dog barked, and we both turned to look at the door. I heard a man's sharp whistle, followed by the clatter of claws. The doorway darkened and I smelled wet dog and sweating human, leather and blood. The moon came out again.

"Look, guy, this woman is injured."

The man stepped inside, glanced at her, and took a swipe at me with his arm. He was neither tall nor heavy, but the blow he dealt me was sturdy and practised. I fell back to the floor, too worried about the woman now even to curse. I tried to stand up again, but the dog ran by me. White birds dangled from a string, jouncing across the man's back.

I said, "Whatever you do, don't pull out the arrow."

He walked by me as if he, the noisy dog, and the young woman were the only souls in the pub.

I added, "And I didn't shoot her. Have you got a car?"

He didn't answer. He reached the woman and she looked up at him. Neither welcome nor fear showed on her pale face when he reached behind her shoulder and grasped the arrow's shaft.

I shouted over the barking dog, "Don't pull it out! It might kill her."

He turned and looked down at me. Something large fell from his shoulder. A bow.

I asked, "Was it you? Did you shoot her?"

He made a noise of disgust. He leaned over us, the dead swans swaying on his back. The dog watched, quieter now and breathing heavily, as the fellow put his hand on the shaft again. The woman shivered as he touched the place where the arrow had pierced her. He smoothed the soft cloth of her dress around the arrow, and I could see that it had lodged near her right shoulder blade. I struggled to my feet at last.

I was too late. He pulled hard on the arrow, and it came away in his hand. I saw a bloom of black across the back of her dress.

She spoke then. She said my name. *Spencer.*

"Yes," I answered.

At the same moment, the other fellow said, "Yes, it's me. It's Spencer. I'm here, Heloise."

I crawled across the pub floor to reach the other Spencer. I pushed him away—it was like pushing a tree trunk—and fumbled the woman Heloise into my arms. I pressed the flat of my palm against her wound to stop the blood. "Give me your shirt. We'll make a bandage and staunch her bleeding …"

I was so confounded by rain, the arrow-shot victim, and darkness that I hardly felt the blow as he lashed out with his fist to the side of my head. Heloise tumbled out of my grip, and I toppled full-length on the floor.

When I think back to that moment, I am certain that by the time I dropped young Heloise and fell to the floor at her side, it must have been close to midnight. And midnight is the traditional time for dreamers and storytellers like me to see ghosts or maidens in jeopardy. And it is the hour for drunks, even dry drunks, to see six impossible things before falling flat and unwanted by the world into a grubby corner somewhere. And here I was, lying on the floor, but at least I wasn't drunk. So, Heloise and her arrow wound, along with this thug who wore my name, had to be real.

I remember saying, "You idiot, Spencer. Get her help."

And I will never forget the sound of her voice whispering my name.

Spencer.

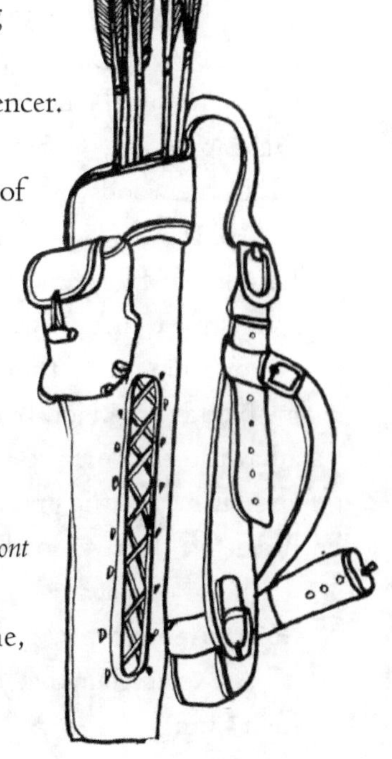

Nine

Spencer. *I was myself.*

I was not myself.

The Seven Swans pub's grimy, dilapidated front room was all around me.

No, the pub building was gone, supplanted along with the canal by thickets of hawthorn and beds of watercress beside the river. Day replaced night, and the sun stood at mid-morning height.

But whoever, wherever, and whenever I was, Heloise, with the arrow in her back, still lay curled up on the ground, and my dog Bruno barked to wake the dead.

I looped my bow over my shoulder, and without a care for the bowstring or the birds I'd shot, I crouched beside Heloise. Bruno bent his heavy head to watch.

I pushed him away. "Let Heloise breathe."

Bruno barked again, and Heloise opened her lovely eyes, bright as day's eye flowers. "Spencer, did you do this?"

At the accusation, I stood up straight. "You think I shot you?"

"You have a bow. And arrows."

"So does half the world," I pointed out. And did not add, *Besides, I've always loved you.* I peered at her shoulder; the shaft must have hit the bone, or wouldn't she be dead? "Where did this happen to you, Heloise?"

"In the woods," she said. "Just this side of the abbey gate."

"What were you doing at the abbey gate, I'd like to know?" I did know. His name was Gervase.

Heloise didn't answer me.

For a moment I thought the arrow had done its work, and my blood turned icy. But when I saw her reach up to hold onto a hawthorn branch to help her gain her feet, I picked her up and sat her on the grass, my right arm about her for support. Beside us, the river made a laughing sound.

She swayed against my arm. "Thank you."

"You're welcome."

"Are you certain that you did not shoot me? Took me, perhaps, for a swan?"

I scowled and held her tight. I'd known Heloise all my life and was too wise to argue with her. "We'll go into town. Let your mother look at this."

"And worry her when she's ill? Not likely."

"She'd be more than worried if that arrow poisoned your blood."

She looked up at me, startled. "I'll live through this. At least, long enough to — oh, never mind." She pulled free, turned, and took a couple of uneven steps away from me back in the direction from which she'd come. I didn't need to see her face to know that she was furious. And I didn't need to ask her to know that she was not angry with me. I almost wished she were, but it had been a long time since Heloise had felt anything for me, good or bad. I was tempted to let her go, the way I always did, and trust the world to bring somebody better, richer, loftier than me to help her. Somebody like Gervase.

I would have let her go, but I could see that she was barely keeping on her feet. "Why are you returning to the abbey?" I called after her. "Do you want another arrow like the one you've got already?"

"I want to know who killed me."

I swallowed. "You're not dead."

"The one who killed me might not know that."

"But what will you do when you find him?"

She stopped short at the question. Then she turned, a white pillar like Lot's wife. She waited until I caught up with her. Then she touched my bow. "You can give the arrow back from me to him. Come."

I knew I shouldn't. I should take her to her father and let him deal with the abbey, because the abbot was no friend of my family. I ought to hand her over to her mother to know what leaves to put on the wound when it was gone — or a spider web, maybe?

But at the abbey was a brother who was a remarkable healer, better than any mother, if not as kind.

And there I might find out who had shot Heloise and make the fellow sorry.

Equally to be reckoned with was the fact that I had not had my arms around Heloise for several years, since we were sixteen and she sent me on my way, saying *What promise did I make you, Spencer?*

So, I picked her up. Bruno at my heels, I carried her across damp fields and around thickets in the direction of the abbey. She weighed not much more than a small deer.

She said nothing for a long time. Maybe the arrow wound was paining her, or maybe she was asleep. But I had to keep going and so I did, over the hill and through the woods until she tugged on my shirt and begged me to stop for a moment. It was here, she murmured, that she had been shot in the back. She assured me again that she hadn't seen the archer who had done it. I stood holding her on the thinly treed slope and gazed across at least fifty arrow-lengths from this spot to the abbey wall.

The abbot kept a pair of brothers on the wall, armed, posted there since the first news of plague had reached us. From there, he could administer to his flock without coming anywhere near us. He could say a prayer from atop this wall over us people of the fields and towns before he hastened back out of sight. Nobody had entered the abbey since the last postulant, a day or two before the plague had reached us, and the abbey gates were barred behind him. The name of this last postulant was Gervase, and when he gave up the world to take orders, he had kissed his true love goodbye—the same true love I now held in my arms.

Gervase was one of two monks guarding the walls.

"Who's that?" he asked.

At the sound of her lover's voice, Heloise stirred in my arms, but I whispered to be still, and for a miracle she was.

"You can see me here, Gervase," I answered. "It's Spencer standing below your gates. I have Heloise in my arms, pierced by some man's arrow."

Gervase cried, "Not Heloise! You lie, hunter."

"I don't lie, and neither do I shoot women who come to the abbey in search of help."

"There's no help here for anyone, unless you want a prayer," Gervase said. But he had come to the edge of the wall and was peering down. The second, taller brother, a man called Barnabas, had appeared on the wall and was peering down as well.

He said, "Is it bad news?"

"When has it lately been good news?" Gervase leaned out farther. "It's not Heloise. I don't believe you."

"It is. And shot by an arrow sent from the wall where you're standing. Who shot her?"

The second man turned to Gervase, both their shaved pates shining in the sunlight. Gervase said, "I swear …"

Barnabas said, "I'm going for the abbot." He left the wall, vanishing down the steps I knew to be set into the back of the wall.

I looked down at Heloise. It was unlike her to let me do the talking.

"Be silent a while longer," I said. Heloise didn't answer, nor did she move in my arms. But she was warm, and her heart beat against my chest. With care, I set her down on the rough grass at my feet.

I scowled up at the postulant monk on the wall. *Pustulent would be a better word for this one.* I said, "Gervase, can you imagine any of the brothers raising a bow against this young woman?"

"By all that is good, no. Who would?" Gervase demanded.

I spoke before I thought. "The abbot, to keep peace?"

"You're a fool. He—"

Several of his brothers mounted the wall behind him.

Gervase shut his mouth with a snap. I said what he could not, with a dozen monks gathered around him. "Yes. The abbot is old, and it would take a stronger arm than his to pull back the bowstring."

Still more monks joined Gervase. They stood in their brown robes with their elbows on the wall, leaning over to look at Heloise and me. It was midday by now, and sunny. The monks dabbed at their shiny scalps with their sleeves. I counted twenty-nine of the full thirty before the abbot joined them at last. Aldus, Elric, Piers, Ermo, Hann, Gregory. I looked for Ralf, a bent old fellow, but didn't see him.

A very tall monk, hooded, followed the abbot onto the wall and stood at his side. Thirty holy men looked down at Heloise as she lay in the grass in her bloodstained gown. The abbot asked, "Is she dead?"

"Not dead," I told him. "Somebody shot her, but she lives."

"Whom does she accuse?" the abbot asked. "Some hunter?" He eyed me with dislike.

This abbot had long ago cheated my uncle on the price of a sow and none of my family liked him either.

I said, "I know it wasn't you."

The stranger said, "You know better than to address the abbot without proper respect."

The abbot grunted, either of agreement or displeasure. It amounted to the same thing with him.

Gervase said, "Father, this fellow Spencer believes that one of us shot the girl."

"Woman. And you know her name," I interjected. "Heloise."

When I spoke her name, she stirred but didn't open her eyes.

I said, "The abbot gives the orders. He might have ordered her to be shot."

"You think you only vilify me, but that is not true." The abbot pulled himself up to full height and turned to leave the wall. "Since God willed me this office, you slander Him as well. I'll leave you to His judgment."

Before he could vanish, I warned him, "Abbot, if you take your leave now, I will go and alert the townspeople to the situation."

He turned slowly and returned to the wall. "I gave all you townspeople blessings."

"And we took them. And they worked, for look! I am free of plague. As is Heloise." I frowned at him.

"Exactly my point," the abbot snapped.

Bruno barked at him, and I put a hand on his back. Heloise turned and lay full length on the grass. The sun shone on her yellow hair, pale cheeks, and rosy lips. I tidied her skirts about her feet, while the monks craned to look at her, beautiful and unconscious.

I said, "Where is your healer? Where is Ralf? Send him out to her."

The abbot said, "He is sick."

This was bad news, and not just for me and Heloise. "How sick?"

"Not the plague," the abbot said firmly. "Just a fever."

"Thank God," all the brothers said nearly at once.

With the healer sick, I couldn't think what to do. Return Heloise to her mother, who was ill as well? I looked at the holy men crowded about the abbey wall, shifting and sweating in their wool habits. One of them was responsible. I would find out who or eat my own bow for dinner. "Heloise came here to the abbey earlier today. For what reason?"

"How would I possibly know?" the abbot asked tiredly.

I bit back my reply and looked up at Gervase. "Do you know why she was here?"

Gervase glanced at the abbot. "What are you asking, Spencer?"

"Did she call at the gate for you?"

Silence. The abbot looked at the brothers gathered about him. The stranger watched me. I wondered what he thought I'd do.

I asked again, "Did Heloise ask Gervase to come outside to her?"

Gervase said, "I'm not allowed outside."

"But Heloise has a mind of her own and makes her own rules," I said. "You and I know that better than anyone."

Gervase jerked his head in acknowledgement.

"And she won't be turned." I pressed.

The abbot interrupted. "What was this woman's aim?"

I answered, "Ask her lover."

The abbot and the monks looked at Gervase.

"Not since I took orders!" He covered his face with his hands.

"Enough of this foolishness," the abbot said. "I won't listen to scandal and rumour about my monks."

I reprised my warning to him. "If you take your leave now, I will go and alert the townsfolk to the fact that you are once again not acting in the town's interests."

"I find it difficult to believe that I ever thought you worthy of my blessings," the abbot said.

"Or I, that I took them," I acknowledged. "Heloise was meant to be Gervase's wife. And when the news of the plague approached and her betrothed abandoned her for the safety of the church walls …"

Gervase protested, "You'd have done the same if you'd thought of it."

"I'm not so easily turned from my life. And Heloise is not easily turned from her aim." I looked down at her and thought I saw the ghost of a smile on that pale face. "It took an arrow to stop her."

"Stop her from what, exactly?" the abbot asked.

The guard, the stranger, and the abbot turned to Gervase, who scowled. "I have no idea what this hunter means …"

This obvious lie was too much, at least for Barnabas, Gervase's fellow guard, and he blurted, "You said you were afraid that she was so pretty she could lure you outside, kiss you, and give you the plague."

"I didn't mean it," Gervase said. "Since I heard the plague was coming this way, no townswoman is pretty in my eyes. I see purple boluses in my sleep."

The other monks looked thoughtful.

I nodded. "That's the problem, isn't it?" I asked. "Heloise is beautiful, but that's not enough to tempt you at a time like this. None of you."

"I should hope not ever, plague or no plague," the abbot said stiffly.

The tall stranger shifted uncomfortably and raised his empty hand to wipe his face. His robe moved, and I saw what he held in his other hand.

"Is that a bow?" I asked.

The abbot looked back. "What of it? Gervase and Barnabas are guards today and they have bows too."

"More as a deterrent, I guess, than a threat." I looked from Gervase and Barnabas, each of them clumsily grasping their cheaply made bows.

I addressed the man in the hood. "That's a yew bow you're holding, isn't it?"

"It is." The stranger stepped forward. "I see you have one also."

"My arrows are fletched with russet, while the arrow that pierced Heloise was white," I said. "Can I see your arrows? Are they fletched with white?"

"You may not see my arrows," the stranger said. "But only because I spent every one in practice earlier on. As it happens, all the abbey arrows are fletched with white. As are half the towns-people's. Swan feathers are found everywhere along the river."

"So you say."

Gervase shot the stranger a quick look.

"What if," I said, rolling back my right sleeve, "you show me your arm? You see what an archer's arm is like." I held mine up, flexed to show the muscle; Heloise had once told me it was among her favourite of my various body parts. That was before Gervase.

He said, "No."

I said, "Ah."

The abbot said, "Show him your arm. You tell the truth, so it will do no harm, and I do not want him running off to rouse the rabble in the town."

"The plague-ridden rabble," I said calmly. "All of them with purple boluses." I hadn't seen any myself, but the plague would be here soon. Give it another week, and I wouldn't be speaking exaggerations. "They will all want to know why they've tithed you all these years and now that they need you, you shut these abbey gates."

The monks on the wall shifted and murmured.

I said, "The knights we serve are meant to protect us. Where are they? They've run off to their castles and shut their doors with a clang."

More murmurs.

"I always thought the knights were craven bullies, so no surprise there. They have their own world, and leave them to it," I pushed on. "But the clergy we support are meant to save us all. Why are the abbey gates closed against your people?"

The abbot scowled. "How are we meant to save those who survive the plague if we all die of it?"

I laughed aloud.

In an angry gesture, the tall stranger raised his bow. "None of us shot her," he said. "It's well known that plague sends men mad. Most likely a townsman shot her."

I said, "Show me your arm."

"I will not."

"Do it, Lionel," the abbot said.

The name rang a bell in me, but I couldn't think what.

His hood still shading his face from view, the stranger rolled up the heavy sleeve of his robe. He held out his right arm. It was not so well developed as mine, but it was not a soft arm either, like Gervase's or the other monks'.

"You're a beginner," I said.

"I was. Not very good either, but I brought my bow from home. I was to use it to defend the abbey."

"Against what enemy?" I asked.

"You know what enemy," he answered. "It's your enemy too."

"The plague has only just arrived," I said. "And even so, you can't shoot the plague."

"You can shoot the carrier and kill the plague."

"You can try. Who sent you to defend the abbey?"

"My father." The stranger rolled down his sleeve. "He sent me here when news of the plague reached us, to become a brother so that I would be safe behind the abbey gates. And he made sure that I brought my bow to defend them in return. I was to be trained …" He stopped.

"Well?" I asked. I glanced in the direction of the town.

The second guard said, "He was being trained by another brother who fell sick."

"Another brother sick? Like Ralf?"

"It's not the plague. Our abbot swears it. Don't you, Father?"

"I do." But there was something about the abbot's stillness that made me think he was lying.

At last, upon the grass at my feet, Heloise stirred and murmured. I couldn't hear what she said, but I crouched at her side and told her, "Don't worry. You're going to be all right."

She opened her eyes then.

She looked past me towards the wall and said, "Gervase."

I asked her, "Did Gervase shoot you? Was he trying to keep you out, in case you had the plague?"

She said, "No."

Gervase almost danced atop the wall as Heloise declared him innocent.

"Who, then?"

The abbot and his friars stood perfectly still. Heloise said no again.

I looked from the wound in her back to the woods where she'd been pierced. It was a long shot, all right. A lucky one, if he meant to hit her. Or perhaps an unlucky one, if he only meant to warn her.

Heloise stirred again and looked up at the wall. The monks looked at her as well, and all looked very sorry for her, except for the hooded stranger, whose features I couldn't see.

"You," I said. "The archer. Put off your hood. I want this woman to see your face."

"I don't put my hood down for a hunter," the stranger said sturdily.

"Put it down," the abbot said. "I am tired beyond measure of standing here in the blazing sun and I want to lie down. Put your hood down, I say."

The stranger put down his hood. I didn't know him and said so. He swept the hood back up, just as Heloise called out. "Lionel!"

When I heard her say it, I knew the name. "Heloise, you have a cousin called Lionel."

Up on the wall, Lionel seemed to shrink inside his robes.

The others turned to him.

Gervase burst out, "Lionel must have shot her. He shot her to keep her from entering."

I said, "But she was shot in the back, running away. She was not trying to get in."

"I thought she wanted to see Gervase," the abbot said.

"Did either of them open the door to you, Heloise?" I looked up at Gervase and Lionel the archer and added, "I'll think much more highly of them if they did."

"I was going to," Gervase said, but looking at the abbot, he added, "but then I remembered my duty."

"And the plague," I added. "Let's think this through. The abbot could not shoot her because he is too old and soft to pull a bow. And you, Barnabas, you are holding that bow like a roast leg of chicken."

The second guard looked down at his bow. Bruno tensed at my side.

"Gervase is just as clumsy, and also I have come to believe him entirely too cowardly to open the door to Heloise. So that leaves Lionel. With his little bit of training. Do you hate your cousin Heloise so much that you shot her? To keep her outside with the plague, not inside the abbey and safe with you?"

"I love my cousin like a sister," Lionel said fiercely. "Tell him, Heloise."

Heloise opened her eyes. "He does." She shut them again.

"Then did you shoot her to save her?"

"Save her?" The abbot looked from Lionel to Heloise.

"From the plague inside the abbey."

The abbot fell silent, while magpies shrieked in a tree nearby. At last, he said, "The plague is outside."

"It's inside too," I said. "The brother who is teaching you archery. He is sick. And Ralf. It's the plague."

"It's not," the abbot said, while the other three looked over their shoulders into the abbey. "There is no plague here."

I said, "I don't need you to admit it, sir. Soon enough, the plague will speak for itself."

Bruno rose to all fours. I picked up Heloise. She made a soft noise of protest.

I said, "There is nobody here who can help you now, Heloise. The healers can't heal themselves." I took a last look at the men on the wall. "Lionel, I am sorry for you. You spoke the truth—you do love your cousin Heloise. Thank you for trying to scare her away."

Lionel raised his bow, and I saw that his hand trembled. "I just meant to warn her. Heloise never listens to anybody! I didn't mean to hit her."

"An unlucky hit. But your lot in remaining in your abbey is less lucky still. Farewell to all."

The abbot stood silent, looking down inside the abbey behind him. Brother Barnabas raised his bow. "God go with you," he said.

I made Heloise comfortable in my arms. Bruno gave a warning bark at the wall and then followed us closely. I strode out towards the abbey woodlands. Heloise seemed heavier than ever.

"Heloise, I will find a quiet place near the river, where nobody lives, and I will make you broth to strengthen you and clean your shoulder well. Is that all right? I know you don't love me anymore, but is that all right?"

She sighed. "I went to see Gervase to tell him he was a fool."

Pleasure washed over me along with the midday sun. I said, "And what about me?"

"I think you know," she said. "You always did know. But it may make no difference. We may both die, after all."

"We may," I said. I still had those birds I'd shot hanging on my back, so that would be our supper.

At that moment, nothing mattered but the sun, the dog at my heels, and the woman in my arms.

Ten

Should you ever be kidnapped and dumped near a canal in the mud liquor of a rainy night, and should you then desire to find your way back to London, just look up at the trees rising above the banks of the canal. Train tracks were laid parallel to canals. The trains roar by at teeth-rattling speeds.

Swans rush you on the side of the canal, but worse things than swans happen in the world—plague and arrows, for example, literal and metaphorical, then and now. And one thing seemed like it might be true: live through an arrow wound, live through the plague, and you may end up with your own true love in your arms.

The thought filled me with a bright energy, as did the morning sun dancing off the water by the Seven Swans. I turned my back to the pub and settled into my stride at the canal side. My movements felt easier with every step. Nonetheless prudence suggested a couple more pills to be sure that agony, like the plague, the archer, and Heloise, stayed in the past where it belonged. I put two on my tongue and wished I had some clean, non-canal water to drink.

As if by magic, my wish came true. It started to rain again.

An hour later I was on the train. All of me was dry by then except for my feet and my wallet.

The older woman in the seat across from me wrinkled her forehead. "I must say, I'm gobsmacked that they let you on as you are, filthy as a gym shoe. What have you been doing, following rabbits down holes?"

"I've been taking stock of my life."

"Good for you."

"Thank you. For the first time ever, I'm going to start taking my work seriously."

"How old are you?" she asked.

"Sixty-two. They keep offering me head of the department and I'm going to take it."

"I really think you should," she said.

"And I'm going to win back my wife Angelica."

"Good on you. Better wash up first."

"I will," I said. "But listen, I've got a problem."

"Only one?" Her sudden grin showed me the girl inside her.

Out of my back pocket I tugged the sodden lump of leather that had been my wallet. "It's just, do you know anything about drying paper?"

"Cheer up, money's tough stuff."

"It's not money, though. I've got a photograph inside and it's one of a kind. I've had it for forty years, and I can never get a copy. I don't know whether I should pull it out while it's wet or let it dry undisturbed." I was already trying to remember Holly's features and failing.

"Let me see." She leaned forward and prodded my wallet with her forefinger. "Oh, dear."

"Well, what do you think I should do?"

"About your photo or all the rest of it?" she asked.

"I have a plan for the rest," I assured her. "I'm getting a promotion and a raise and my wife back."

"That's a good plan." The train was pulling into Bushey, and she got to her feet. "But as to your photograph, it seems to me that when something is as ruined as that, you don't need advice, you need a miracle."

I thanked her. I looked from her upright back, as she passed out of sight along the platform, to my wallet, lumpen in my palm. I replaced it in my trouser pocket and pulled out a couple more of my back pills. I took them as the train neared London, where I put aside my discomfort of the night before along with my ongoing resentment of everything Byron and Angelica had devised and carried out for my downfall. After all, their actions, along with the vision of the can-do archer soldiering on in the midst of the plague, were inspiring me to restructure my life.

I phoned the college from the station, pleading a broken tooth, which excuse was gracefully accepted by the head's secretary, so that was all right. I had gone ahead and made an appointment to speak with the head himself at five this afternoon. That gave me two hours to bathe, shave, and change my clothes before teaching my afternoon class and then having the promised heart-to-heart about my solid future with my boss.

Fifteen minutes later I was hammering on Byron's flat door. He opened it and looked me up and down.

"I want clothes," I said.

"We all want something, my dear boy," Byron said. "Come on in."

Eleven

Byron's Savile Row and German Street splendour carried me brilliantly through my afternoon classes. I was teaching a course called Postwar Canadian Literary Short Fiction to a class of mostly eighteen-year-old girls, and I couldn't help noticing the sharp interest in their gazes as I taught like nobody's business, while they eyed my Eton tie and the superb line of my lapel. During the next hour I had to brush off several of the honours-grade-chasing girls to reach the College Head's office only two minutes late. I found him at his desk, eyeing the clock.

I apologized. "Some of the older girls were asking me questions, and I didn't like to leave them without a proper response."

"Mmmmm." Through the window behind him I could see the golden crown of London City's Monument to the Great Fire of 1 6 6 6. *London rose from its ashes,* I told myself, *and I can too.*

The college head was a red-faced man in a blue suit. He was staring at my neck, where Byron's school tie hung. "Why are you wearing an Eton tie?"

I remembered too late that the head had attended Eton, as I had not. There is no worse sin to an Old Etonian than wearing an unearned tie. I thought like lightning. "Gosh, I forgot I had this on. An old friend and I exchanged ties. Like football shirts," I explained. "But without the football."

He said, "You must give it back."

"Quite right." I tugged it off and put it in my pocket.

He leaned forward, red-knuckled fingers woven into a double fist. "Look, Spencer, I'm sorry to drag you in here at such short notice."

"You're the boss," I said. "And anyway, you generally wave me in from the hallway when you offer me promotions, and very kindly too since I kept turning you down."

"Man is a creature of habit." He sucked his lip.

Except for the business with the tie, it all felt much the same as the times I'd turned down his proffered promotions. The view of the Monument outside the window, the smell of beef gravy left over from his lunch. His frown.

But this time it would be different. This time I would accept his offer.

I was about to tell him so, when he burst out, "There have been complaints."

"Complaints?" I stared. "How can there be complaints about postwar Canadian literary short fiction? Pure as the Saskatchewan snow."

"Not the course. You."

I sat back in my chair. "What on earth?"

"You and your students. The girls, I mean."

"*Young women*," I corrected him. "But that's ridiculous. I keep my distance. I'm as blameless as …"

"Postwar Canadian literary short fiction?" he asked drily.

I let out a long breath. "If you're joking about literature, then I'm all right. Look, these kinds of charges come and go — they're part of teaching senior students. Nobody's immune, so what do we do about them? Really, with respect, it's down to you to handle the thing. If not, it could damage my career."

"It is down to me," he said. "And I'm afraid that I'm going to have to let you go."

I leapt out of my chair. "On unfounded charges? You really must be joking now, sir."

"Lower your voice." He sucked his upper lip and waited. I sat back down. "These charges are not unfounded. I've had several reports of girls behaving flirtatiously with you in the prep room and talking about their marks …"

I interrupted. "That's them, not me! Nobody ever saw me touch a one of them. Not one! Because it never happened." But I remembered that Albie had told Glory that I had a picture of a young woman in my wallet. How to explain, when the head was telling me how difficult it was to believe my protestations?

He continued, "I'm told it's common knowledge that you've been seeing one of our older students out of college hours. It's been reported that you carry a picture of her in your wallet."

I pulled out my wallet. "Here it is, but it was taken when I was as young as she was, and I've been carrying it since I was nineteen."

He took my wallet and narrowed his eyes at the ruined photo. "Did you destroy it?"

"No," I said. "No, I got caught all night in a rainstorm ..."

"It's unrecognizable." He sighed. "We don't have a student complaint, so we won't pursue charges. You leave today without another word. And, as is traditional in these cases, you'll receive a severance package."

With my debts, and without a salary, how else would I live? But if I accepted the severance, it was an admission of guilt. "I'm going to fight this, sir."

"Will you?" My boss looked at me kindly for the first time in the interview. "No, you won't."

I did not slam the door behind me. It's the only thing of merit I achieved that afternoon.

TWELVE

The note was taped to Byron's flat's cream-gloss front door.

Spence,

I may have forgotten to tell you that I'm moving out of my dear old place today. Don't knock, as it wouldn't be kind to disturb the new owners and their Rottweilers. But don't worry as your once and my future wife has put everything you need here.

Beneath his florid signature Byron had drawn a swooping arrow that pointed to the Fortnum & Mason's bag at my feet.

I squatted down and emptied the bag onto the corridor carpet. Apparently, *everything I needed* was:

- a twenty-pound note
- my shaving things and my sponge bag
- an envelope with my name written on it in Angelica's round hand
- an unopened packet of Marks & Spencer Y-fronts, navy with white piping, in my size

The Y-fronts were from our last Christmas together a few months back, unopened because I don't wear Y-fronts and never have. The toiletries were welcome, as was the twenty-pound note. I nearly smiled as I looked at it, because the sum had obviously been well thought out, as was everything Angelica did; twenty pounds was enough to buy bread, milk, tea, and bacon, but not enough to stay in a London hotel for the night. I tucked the twenty into my jacket pocket with the severance cheque from the college and picked up the envelope.

I knew what must be inside. I unfolded the document. Legalese-embellished, it said that I had the right to occupy and make a living from—but never sell—the buildings and the land belonging to the Seven Swans public house, including canal-front moorage and a small gravel parking lot. As I folded it back up, two items fell out of the folds of the deed paper. One was a square of white paper with a few words written on it in Angelica's hand. The other was a railway ticket. The rail ticket was a single, dated today, for the same Hertfordshire station I'd journeyed from this morning.

I heard the unmistakable sound of dog claws on the other side of Byron's front door and remembered the Rottweilers that had moved into his flat. Swiftly, I jumbled the items into the

Fortnum's bag, except for the Y-fronts, which I tossed outside the door for the dogs to savage at their leisure. As a final act, I tore the note from the door. It took off the paint in a crackly scab, but it would have, anyway. And this way the Rottweiler owners would not know that it had been Byron who was responsible for the tape that scarred their brand-new door. It was a minor act of kindness, but it was absolutely all I could manage for him that particular late afternoon in April.

Of course, at six o'clock on a Friday evening you'll never get a seat to yourself on the train, but I found a place to crouch among the coffee cups near the toilets to read Angelica's note. Except it wasn't exactly a note. She had scrawled a few words on one side of the paper: *I bloody well was good enough for you, Spencer. At least Byron knows what he's got.* And the other side — she must have found it in my wallet and had it duplicated for some bitter wifely reason — was Holly's photograph.

I gazed at Holly, golden, smiling, and twenty, all the way to Hertfordshire.

Adventures and mysteries in time — and at present — lie ahead for reluctant sexagenarian lover and adventurer Spencer Stevens in the seven Hertfordshire Pub Mysteries that make up the Seven Swans stories by Mel Anastasiou. Look for these, for Stella Ryman and the Fairmount Manor Mysteries, and for the Monument Studios Mysteries starring the Extra, Frankie Ray.

Mel Anastasiou loves her writing life in BC and the UK, devising mysteries for Stella to solve. She can be found every day writing and drawing, walking for miles to look at inspired Victorian architecture, and eating scones with clotted cream and jam—hence the walking.

In non-fiction, Mel has published two illustrated writing guides and workbooks with Pulp Literature Press: *The Writer's Boon Companion: Thirty Days Towards an Extraordinary Volume* and *The Writer's Friend and Confidante*. For news on new novels by Mel Anastasiou—including her serialized novels *Pretty Lies: A Ghost Story* and *Take My Hand: A Ghost Story*, and for updates on box sets of the Fairmount Manor Mysteries, the Hertfordshire Pub Mysteries, and the Monument Studios Mysteries, you're invited to follow pulpliterature.com.

Also by Mel Anastasiou

THE EXTRA: A MONUMENT STUDIOS MYSTERY

Vancouver schoolmarm Frankie Ray runs away to Silver Screen Hollywood to test her conviction that an actress who lacks glamour but has talent and an enterprising attitude can make it in the movies. But when a dissolute, womanizing matinee idol turns up dead on her sofa, Frankie's career hopes shatter. She'll need all her acting chops to sleuth out the murderer and clear her name.

STELLA RYMAN AND THE FAIRMOUNT MANOR MYSTERIES

On this particular sun-and-shade April morning at Fairmount Manor, Stella Ryman no more entertained the idea of becoming an amateur sleuth than she did of entering next spring's Boston Marathon. For not only was Stella eighty-two years old, but she had lately sold her home and a lifetime of gathered possessions and washed up at Fairmount Manor Care Home in such a state that she would have bet her remaining seven pairs of socks that she'd be dead in half a year.

THE LABOURS OF MRS STELLA RYMAN:
FURTHER FAIRMOUNT MANOR MYSTERIES

When the machineries of institution fail to protect Fairmount Manor, octogenarian amateur sleuth Mrs Stella Ryman rolls up her fleece jacket sleeves to protect Fairmount from a thief, investigate a gun-toting resident, set right a mishandled investigation of a man's death, pursue spectres and footpads walking at midnight, and discover Thelma Hu's long-lost fortune. No good deed goes unpunished, though, and Stella will face struggles, mysteries, and sacrifices that hit her where she lives.

PULPLITERATURE.COM

9 781988 865799